Reasons to divorce my husband:	Reasons to stay together:
• He thinks tofu is a major food group (Hello? French fries!)	• Fabulous sex
• He reads the paper neatly section by section and hates when I leave it lying about	• He's thinking about giving me the house
• 5 a.m. is not a reasonable time to be awake (it's still dark out!)	• And our dog
• He runs five miles a day. I only run when Micky D's is closing	• He looks terrific in a Zorro mask (don't ask)
• No one walks out on Zada Clark.	• He always gives me what I need
	• He's still the only man I love.

more . . .

Praise for Candy Halliday's Previous Novels

Mr. Destiny

"Funny, cute, and charming . . . This story is a light . . . romantic comedy with an enjoyable, uncomplicated plot. In other words: brain candy!"

—ContemporaryRomanceWriters.com

"A delight . . . A great story with some truly good surprises inside."

—RomanceReviewsMag.com

"Sparkling . . . engaging tale . . . [with a] sweetly sensual romance."

—*Publishers Weekly*

"A fun, modern-day cross-boroughs romance."

—TheBestReviews.com

Dream Guy

"A fun romp."

—*Publishers Weekly*

"Fun story, good reading, and plenty of hot sex thrown in . . . cute, funny."

—RomanceReviewsMag.com

"A lighthearted, contemporary war of the sexes using technology to further the skirmishes . . . Fans will enjoy this fun tale that is one click away from providing the *Dream Guy*."

—Midwest Book Review

Your Bed or Mine?

ALSO BY CANDY HALLIDAY

Mr. Destiny

Dream Guy

Your Bed or Mine?

Candy Halliday

WARNER
FOREVER

NEW YORK   BOSTON

Cover design by Diane Luger
Book design by Stratford Publishing Services

Warner Books
Hachette Book Group USA
1271 Avenue of the Americas
New York, NY 10020

Printed in the United States of America

First Printing: August 2006

10 9 8 7 6 5 4 3 2 1

DEDICATED TO THE MOST AMAZING
DOMESTIC DIVAS I KNOW:

Shelli Cottingham

Kimmie Clark

Judy Miller

Kim Poe

Pam Mathews

Marian Farrell

Tracey Simmons

Amy Patrick

Annie Klick

Lisa Thomas

Erin Sutton

Lynnette Schwiegeraht

Trish Link

Beth Burt

Jo Hughes

Thanks always to my fabulous agent, Jenny Bent.

Special thanks to my editor, Karen Kosztolnyik, for coming up with the Housewives' Fantasy Club idea, and for believing I could handle the challenge.

Thanks to my brainstorming partner, Emilie Rose, for keeping me sane through every book. And for insisting that this book needed a blind dog. Simon thanks you for giving him life on paper, Em.

Thanks to Angie Narron for her expert legal advice.

And thanks from the bottom of my heart to my family for their love and support. Blue, Shelli, Tracy, Quint, and Caroline—I love you all more than words can say.

Chapter 1

———🍎———

Zada Thornton Clark didn't miss the frown on her divorce attorney's face as she hurried up the courthouse steps. The disapproving frown should have intimidated Zada.

It didn't.

The fact that the revered Angie Naylon was known around Chicago for her killer instinct in the courtroom, didn't mean squat to Zada, either. There was just something about having personally held your college roommate's head over the toilet more than once that served as a pretty good equalizer.

Zada reached the top of the courthouse steps.

Angie's frown only deepened.

"Are you kidding me, Zada?" Angie looked her up and down. "This is your idea of a mousy-looking outfit for the judge's benefit?"

"No," Zada said stubbornly. "This is my idea of an eat-your-heart-out outfit for *Rick's* benefit. I want Rick Clark to get his last good look at what he lost when he walked out on me."

"And how shallow is that?" Angie said with disgust.

"Today," said Zada, "shallow suits me just fine."

"Obviously," Angie snipped when two suits and ties walked past, craning their necks around for a second look at Zada's curvaceous nothing-skinny-about-her figure.

Angie looked back at Zada and said, "Your all-about-me dress certainly leaves nothing to the imagination. And here's another news flash for you. Red is *not* listed on the *mousy* side of the color chart."

"But red *is* listed on a brunette's side of the color chart," Zada argued, tossing her long, dark hair. "Ask any brunette. It's our signature color."

"It's the *judge's* signature you need to be worried about." Angie frowned again. "I warned you this judge was old school, Zada. He doesn't take divorce lightly. That dress blows any chance we had of him believing you're a meek and mousy heartbroken housewife, only asking to keep your home and your poor blind dog."

Angie wheeled around and stomped into the courthouse.

Zada hurried after her.

"Oh, come on, Angie," Zada pleaded when she finally caught up. "I'm about as mousy as a wolverine, and you know it. You could dress me in a nun's habit, and I'd still look militant."

"We don't have time to argue," Angie snapped, glaring at her again. "Your case is the first one on the docket after the lunch break. That dress is enough to sway the property settlement in Rick's favor. The last thing we need is to be late for your hearing."

Angie forged ahead, her briefcase in a death grip.

Zada picked up speed, trying to keep up.

"But we still have the poor blind dog hook," Zada pointed out, trying to make amends. "*I'm* the one who's taken care of Simon since Rick walked out on us."

Angie sent her another mean look.

"How many times do we have to go over this, Zada? Simon is *Rick's* dog."

"The dog Rick left with *me*," Zada said.

"And the dog who saved Rick's life," Angie reminded her. "Rick's attorney will make a big production over Rick and Simon being injured recovering that explosive device at O'Hare. Separating a man from his heroic life-saving dog is *not* going to be an easy task."

"That's when you bring up the fact that I didn't even know Rick when he and Simon were injured," Zada said, "but that I was so touched when I heard Simon was blinded in that explosion, *I* visited Simon at the vet's hospital every day and even wrote a children's book about him."

"And Rick's attorney will remind the judge that Rick is one of the top trainers of explosive-detection dogs in the nation," Angie said. "Rick trains dogs professionally every day of the week."

"Yes, Rick does train dogs professionally every day of the week," Zada said. "Twelve to fourteen hours every day of the week. But *I'm* Simon's stay-at-home mom. The mom who *didn't* walk out and leave Simon behind."

"It doesn't matter," Angie insisted. "Rick's attorney will say the only reason Rick left Simon behind, is because *Rick* had your house specifically equipped so poor, blind Simon *could* function as a normal dog again."

"Wrong again," Zada said. "Simon could have learned to function like a normal dog without all that high-tech equipment Rick had installed in the house. Any owner of a blind dog will confirm that. Rick never gave Simon a chance to learn to manage on his own. Rick's a techno-geek. Plain and simple."

Angie stopped walking and turned around to face her.

"And *you* were supposed to be a plain and simple housewife," Angie reminded her. "But now that you've blown that strategy to hell and back, you tell me, Zada. Who do *you* think the judge is going to say deserves Simon and house?"

"Me," Zada insisted.

Angie groaned and walked off again.

"Angie!" Zada called after her. "*I'm* the one who's practically made Simon a household name with my *Simon Sees* children's series." When she caught back up, Zada said, "Be sure and point that out. *Publishers Weekly* and the *New York Times* have both hailed *Simon Sees* as an inspiration for children with disabilities everywhere. Simon and I already have a national tour of children's hospitals scheduled around Christmas this year."

"How convenient," Angie quipped, "since red *is* your signature color." Her eyes cut sideways for a second. "Take my advice this time, Zada. Wear a different dress for the children's tour."

Angie turned down a corridor.

Zada clipped along behind her in four-inch heels.

At least Angie hadn't said anything about the shoes. Her sling-back red pumps were as sexy as the dress. Or maybe Angie just never got past the dress.

When they finally reached the designated courtroom, Angie pulled Zada aside and pointed a finger under her nose.

"Keep your militant mouth *shut*," Angie said. "I mean it, Zada. I don't want even so much as a peep out of you in that courtroom."

Zada made the zipped-lip motion with her fingers.

Angie said, "You walk in there and sit down as quickly as possible before the judge notices the lower half of your dress is missing. And it wouldn't hurt to slump a little. Judge Parkins is in his seventies. The way that dress clings to every inch of your body, the old fart could have a heart attack and croak right there on the bench."

"Sit and slump," Zada said. "Got it."

She tried smiling brightly at Angie.

Angie *didn't* smile back.

She tossed her auburn hair back from her forehead.

She adjusted the jacket of her gray business suit.

And she marched into the courtroom.

Fine. Be that way, Zada decided.

Maybe short and clingy wasn't the best choice.

And maybe red wasn't the best color.

But Zada quickly changed her mind when she saw the look on Rick's face when she walked into the courtroom.

He was already seated at one of the tables at the front of the room with his attorney. And now with an eyes-popped-out expression on his dropped-jaw face.

Zada smiled inwardly.

Screw slumping!

She threw her shoulders back.

She thrust her breasts forward.

She held her head high.

And walked right past her soon-to-be *ex*-husband.

Rick was already nervous, but there was no doubt in his mind about why his mouth suddenly went dry. Zada always had that effect on him. Long, shimmering dark brown hair. Sultry, dark brown eyes. Voluptuous curves that had the power to bring any man to his knees.

Except Rick was done.

No more on his knees, begging Zada to reconsider.

A man's pride could only take so much.

Yes, they'd had one hell of a fight. Yes, they'd both said horrible things to each other. And no, he shouldn't have walked out. Especially when he knew exactly how Zada felt about the "walking out" issue.

Zada's father had walked out on her mother when Zada had only been six, and her younger sister had just turned four. They'd been in their teens when her mother took her father back—something Zada had never fully forgiven her for doing.

Unfortunately, younger sister Sally served as proof that history does have a way of repeating itself. Sally had allowed her own husband to come and go at will, begging Zada to understand that she had two young sons to consider; another huge sore spot with Zada.

In Zada's mind, walking out was the ultimate taboo.

Rick had known that.

And he'd cursed himself every day since he walked out; for allowing his pride to get in the way when Zada gave him that damned you-walk-out-now-and-it's-over-between-us-for-good ultimatum.

Except Zada knew ultimatums were his pet peeve, which was the exact reason she'd hit him with an ultimatum.

Rick sighed inwardly.

Some days you were the dog.

Some days, the hydrant.

He'd expected her to be angry, sure. Only angry didn't cover Zada's reaction. *Furious* was more like it.

Zada had changed the locks on the house the same day and filed for separation papers two weeks later.

Any chance for a reconciliation had walked right out the door with him. Zada had told him so—in those exact words—during the one and only verbal conversation he'd had with her since the day he left.

After that conversation, she'd refused to speak to him at all. Their only direct communication over the last six months—except through their attorneys—had been via brief one-line e-mails. Him confirming every Wednesday he would stop by to see Simon. Zada confirming she would make arrangements to be gone for the hour he would be at the house.

They'd lived apart for the required six months now.

The legal separation period before a divorce.

Zada had no intention of backing down.

He had no intention of backing down.

They were two strong-willed, hard-headed people— each determined to bend the other to their own way of thinking.

And where had their stubbornness gotten them?

Straight to divorce court.

Now, Rick found himself sitting in a courtroom, ready to face a judge who would put an end to their marriage. Yet, all he could think about was how great Zada looked in that red dress, and what a damn fool he'd be if he let her go through with the divorce.

Rick was still looking at her, Zada could feel it.

It should have given her immense satisfaction knowing she'd definitely gotten his attention. But as good as she knew she looked in her new red dress, Rick looked ten times better.

I never should have glanced in his direction.

His cream-colored summer sports coat really showed off his tan. And his a-little-longer-than-fashionable Matthew McConaughey-style hair was still damp and sexy-looking from the shower he'd obviously taken before he left the dog training center to appear in court.

If she dared look directly at him, Zada knew his eyes would be a deep, brooding blue. Rick's eyes always turned darker when he was angry or under pressure.

Funny, but she'd never been attracted to blond men before she met Rick. Funny also that the second she did meet him, her tall, dark, and handsome preference switched to tall, *blond,* and handsome in about two seconds flat.

His ex-marine fine-honed body hadn't deterred her from switching to the blond side of gotta-have-him, either. If any man had a fine-honed body, it was Rick.

Supposedly thanks to his stupid health food.

Zada's lips pursed in a pouty frown.

Proper nutrition was an obsession with Rick.

Her idea of a balanced diet was a cookie in each hand.

She hoped Rick felt stupid when he died of nothing.

That's all health was anyway—the slowest possible rate at which a person died.

As for her, she wanted to slide through the Pearly Gates—a doughnut in one hand, a chocolate éclair in the other—yelling, "Show me the bakery!"

She'd often wondered what she'd been thinking going from a whirlwind romance straight into a marriage. Other than the fact that Rick excited her like no man ever had, or ever would again. Unfortunately, if any two people had ever been total opposites, it was definitely the two of them.

Opposites attract, sure. But that didn't mean they could live together. She and Rick had sure proved that point, in more ways than one.

Rick liked the house kept military-standard neat and tidy. Her idea of daily cleaning was a sweeping glance around the room.

Health-food-nut Rick prayed to the tofu gods who kept him in tip-top physical shape. She was on a first name basis with Ronald McDonald.

Early-to-bed-early-to-rise Rick ran five miles before breakfast every morning. Burning the midnight writing oil meant she rarely got up for breakfast—and *her* idea of exercise was jogging over to the fridge for another Dove ice-cream bar.

Living together had been a total disaster.

The fact that they were both type A personalities with limited skills when it came to the art of compromise, didn't help matters, either. Zada was surprised their marriage had lasted even a year. In fact, it was a miracle they hadn't killed each other that first week after the honeymoon. If the sex hadn't been so fabulous, they probably *would* have killed each other.

Fabulous sex.

Zada quickly dismissed that thought.

Reinforcements zoomed forward to take over.

Mind-boggling sex tapped her on the shoulder.

The twins—*hot and sweaty sex*—whispered in her ear.

Pleasure ran an enticing finger up and down her spine.

Ecstasy did a lively little tap dance just below her belly button.

Zada squirmed uncomfortably in her seat.

She reached for the water pitcher sitting on the table in front of her, poured a glass of water, and took a cool, calming drink. Only then did she chance her first real look directly at Rick.

Dammit!

He was staring right at her.

She still loved him, truly she did. But there was more to marriage than just great sex.

Damn you, Rick Clark!

Why did you have to walk out on me like that?

"All rise," the bailiff announced.

Angie grabbed Zada's arm, pulling her to her feet.

Zada didn't dare look at Rick again.

But when a sinking feeling hit the pit of her stomach like a wrecking ball, Zada decided slumping wasn't going to be any problem for her at all.

Rick was only half listening as his attorney, Bob Thompson, argued back and forth with Zada's attorney over the property settlement. Bob had already assured him there was no way the judge would rule in Zada's favor. Especially with Rick's generous offer to purchase a condo or any other residence of Zada's choice—gratis, of course.

Against Bob's advice, he'd insisted on making the offer to purchase Zada another residence himself. He still loved her. Hell, he'd always love her. They just couldn't live together. The least he could do was make sure Zada was settled and happy on her own.

What he wouldn't do—and the reason he'd held firm on his desire to keep the house—was uproot Simon again.

He owed the dog his life. Simon had learned to maneuver freely with the aid of the high frequency sensors he'd had installed in the house he'd bought shortly after he and Zada were married. Simon could maneuver so well in his new environment, in fact, no one would even suspect the dog was blind.

The state-of-the-art equipment had cost a fortune and was well worth every penny as far as Rick was concerned. But going through that expense again, only because Zada was trying to punish him by keeping the house, was ridiculous.

Almost as ridiculous as her expecting to keep Simon.

Which wasn't going to happen.

Not without a fight.

Simon was his dog.

He'd never prevent Zada from seeing Simon.

But dammit, Simon was *his* dog!

His dog, dammit!

Rick glanced back at the judge again.

Judge Parkins was the epitome of what a judge should look like. Somewhere in his mid-to-late seventies. Gray hair, slightly thinning on top. Regal-looking in his black robe. A wise expression on his slightly wrinkled face.

When Parkins ruled in his favor this afternoon, he'd be able to take immediate possession of Simon and the house in Woodberry Park—all thanks to the stipulation Bob had been smart enough to include in the property settlement. Zada had been given full notice she would be expected to vacate the premises immediately should he be awarded the house. That meant by the end of the weekend, he'd be completely settled and moved back into his own home.

And not a moment too soon, Rick thought.

Living in the furnished apartment he'd rented month-to-month for the last six months had been nothing short of a nightmare. He'd endured the type of agony all apartment dwellers endure, from less-than-desirable neighbors to no privacy whatsoever.

Had Bob not been so confident the judge would rule in his favor, he might have considered going ahead and buying another house. Possibly even having the house equipped to accommodate Simon.

But Bob had assured him the victory would be his.

He'd held out and dealt with the inconvenience.

Handing over the apartment keys to the complex manager earlier that morning, however, had been the equivalent of being let out of prison.

Now, he was only minutes away from being a free man.

Free to go back to the suburbs.

Back to his neighborhood buddies in Woodberry Park.

Back to Saturday night poker games with the guys.

Back to Sundays on Woodberry Park's private golf course, the eighteenth hole of which could be seen from his own back deck.

Back to an empty house without Zada in it.

Rick frowned at that thought.

Don't go there.

Enough is enough.

Not once during their separation period had Zada given him any indication she'd regretted filing for the divorce. Once the judge ruled in his favor, if Zada did have any regrets, she'd just have to . . .

Voices raised suddenly.

Rick's head jerked to the right.

A face-off.

The debate was growing hotter by the minute.

Rick glanced back at the judge.

Judge Parkins looked anything but pleased.

"Order in the court!" Parkins declared. He banged his gavel twice.

Rick flinched both times.

"We are in an esteemed court of law, counselors, not some backyard brawl!"

Parkins boomed this from the bench as he glared from one attorney to the other. Both attorneys, Rick noticed, stood up a little straighter.

"A *busy* court of law," Parkins added. "Too busy to waste time going over a property dispute that should have been settled before you ever walked into my courtroom."

Rick glanced at Bob.

His usual cool-and-confident attorney, the all-American linebacker from Notre Dame who had known no fear on the football field, seemed to wilt under the judge's cold stare.

"Your honor," Bob said, "if it pleases the court . . ."

Parkins cut him off. "For the record, Mr. Thompson, *nothing* about this case pleases the court."

The judge looked over at Zada for a second.

Rick sat up straighter when Parkins looked back at him.

Parkins said, "Both parties have agreed to a no-fault divorce. Is that correct?"

Both attorneys nodded in agreement.

"So you would assume if the parties could agree on a no-fault divorce like two mature adults, they could also agree on a property settlement like two mature adults. Is that also correct?"

Neither attorney nodded in agreement with that statement.

"Yet, what we have here," Judge Parkins said, his frown deepening with every word, "are two self-absorbed people, childishly trying to outdo each other, while they waste the court's precious time and the taxpayers' money on an argument over a dog, and what appears to be the *dog's* eight-hundred-thousand-dollar doghouse!"

Several people snickered.

A loud gasp followed.

Rick didn't even turn his head.

He knew the gasp came from Zada.

"Don't shush me, Angie!" Zada said loud enough for him and everyone else in the courtroom to hear. "*I* happen to be one of those taxpayers! A taxpayer who came here to get a divorce. *Not* to be insulted!"

Typical in-your-face Zada, Rick thought.

He leaned back far enough to peer around Bob.

As expected, Zada had one of her just-who-do-you-think-you're-talking-to looks on her face. Her embarrassed attorney was doing her best to keep Zada in her seat.

The wrath of Zada personified.

Rick smiled.

Parkins will rule in my favor now out of pity for me.

Rick didn't appreciate the judge's insult, either. But being at the mercy of the court called for a certain amount of diplomacy.

He glanced back at Zada again, trying to imagine his feisty soon-to-be ex-wife being diplomatic in any given situation. The thought was so absurd, Rick almost burst out laughing.

"Do you find this situation funny, Mr. Clark?"

Bob punched him.

"No, sir!" Rick said emphatically.

"Then wipe that silly smirk off your face," Parkins warned, his ears now flushed a deep red.

What?

Zada's the one yelling.

Why are you reprimanding me?

Rick looked over at Bob for an answer.

He could have sworn Bob was trembling.

Judge Parkins pointed to Zada's attorney. "Allow the petitioner to stand, Miss Naylon."

He looked back at Bob. "Have the respondent stand as well, Mr. Thompson."

Me?

You've got to be kidding.

I'm just an innocent bystander here!

"Stand up!" Bob whispered from the corner of his mouth.

Reluctantly, Rick pushed his chair back and stood up.

But he knew better than to look at Zada again.

Guilt by association.

Damn.

Dead man standing.

Suddenly, Zada didn't feel so brave.

Her quick temper often got the better of her. But how were you supposed to react to being called an immature twit in front of an entire courtroom of people?

Keep your militant mouth shut.

Good advice, Zada realized, but sadly too late.

She gulped when Judge Parkins glared at her again.

"*I'm* the one who has been insulted this morning," he said. "I'm insulted every time a couple shows up in my courtroom to make a mockery out of the institution of marriage."

Save it, Grandpa.

I didn't make a mockery out of marriage.

Marriage made a mockery out of me.

Judge Parkins's gaze turned toward Rick. "We've all heard how devoted you are to providing homeland security for the country you so dearly love, Mr. Clark," he said.

He looked back at Zada. "And we've heard how devoted you are to helping disabled children everywhere with your uplifting and motivational children's books."

Parkins templed his fingers in front of him. "We've also heard in great detail how important it is to both of you, that the blind dog you both love so dearly, stays in the house that was specifically designed so the dog could function at a normal level."

He shook his head disgustedly.

"What I find insulting," he said, "is that both of you have more passion for your careers and your blind dog, than you do for the very person you promised to love, honor, and cherish until death do you part."

Ouch!

Those words hit home faster than a speeding bullet.

Zada winced as the words pierced her heart.

"Has it crossed either of your minds," Parkins asked, looking at her, then back at Rick, "that if you'd given your marriage the same level of commitment you've given to your dog and your careers, you wouldn't be appearing before me in divorce court now?"

Double ouch!

Slumping any lower simply wasn't possible.

"Instant gratification," Parkins said and smiled. "That's at the top of everyone's list today."

His overtly smug smile didn't cheer Zada.

"People expect instant gratification from their employers, or they throw in the towel and get another job. People expect instant gratification in their marriages, or they throw in the towel and get another spouse. And rather than take time out of their busy schedules to work out their problems themselves, people have even come to expect instant gratification in a court of law."

The smile disappeared.

"But in my courtroom," Parkins said, "the only person entitled to instant gratification is *me.*"

He looked at Zada, then back at Rick again.

"Let me assure you," he said, "nothing will gratify me more than the decision I'm making in this case today."

Crap! Here it comes.

Zada held her breath.

Judge Parkins closed the file in front of him and looked around the courtroom with authority.

"Let the record reflect that the petitioner and the respondent have ninety days to settle the property dispute between them."

He looked over the bench at both attorneys. "Don't show up in my courtroom again without this matter being settled."

Down came the gavel.

Once.

Twice.

Three times.

Only ninety days?

To reach a compromise?

Try ninety freaking years!

Except, even ninety years, Zada feared, was laughable.

Chapter 2

"But, but," Zada stuttered, looking over at Angie. "A judge can't delay a divorce just to prove a point! Can he?"

"He just did," Angie said.

Zada said, "But Rick and I will never be able to reach a compromise, Angie. Not in ninety days. Not ever. What happens when we don't reach a compromise at the end of ninety days? Can Judge Parkins throw us in jail for contempt of court?"

"Technically, no," Angie said. "But that doesn't mean Parkins can't come up with some other charge that could land you in jail. Don't chance it, Zada. Do what the man says, or you'll be trading in your all-about-me dress for a not-so-flattering prison jumpsuit."

Angie grabbed her briefcase and left the courtroom.

Zada hurried after her.

"But we can appeal," Zada said. "Right?"

Angie didn't answer.

She grabbed Zada by the arm and led her down the corridor. When they were a safe distance away from the courtroom, Angie pulled her aside, out of the busy stream of human traffic coming and going in the hallway.

"You can appeal all you want, Zada," Angie said. "But get yourself a new attorney. There's no way I'm going to piss Judge Parkins off further by filing an appeal."

Zada gasped. "You're firing me as your client?"

"No, I'm advising you as your attorney to take Judge Parkins's ruling seriously. Stop playing first grade, Zada. Accept Rick's offer. I told you when Rick made the offer to buy you a place of your own, he was being more than generous. Even if you forced him into selling the house, the equity you've built up over the last eighteen months is minimal. Take Rick's offer. It's your only choice."

"No way!" Zada shook her head stubbornly. "Rick is the one who didn't have the guts to stick it out and make our marriage work. Not me. Why should *I* be punished when *he* was the one who walked out?"

Angie looked at her thoughtfully for a second.

"You still love him, don't you?"

"Love doesn't have anything to do with this," Zada vowed. "I want my divorce!"

"Then act like it," Angie said. "Break your silly vow of silence and have that long overdue talk with Rick. Tell him what you just told me. That you don't think it's fair for you to be punished by giving up your home and Simon, when he was the one who walked out of your marriage."

Zada rolled her eyes.

"Telling Rick how you feel isn't a sign of weakness, Zada," Angie said, reading her mind. "You certainly had no trouble telling Judge Parkins how you felt a few minutes ago. If you'd kept your mouth shut like I told you to do, he might have signed your divorce decree today."

"Oh, please," Zada scoffed. "The old poop already had his nuts in a knot before I said the first word."

"You think Judge Parkins had his nuts in a knot a few minutes ago?" Angie laughed. "Then try not reaching a compromise in the ninety days he's given you to settle your property dispute with Rick. Trust me, Zada. You don't want to go there."

Zada tossed her long, dark hair defiantly. "Nor do I intend to go anywhere else to live. Except in *my* house. With *my* dog."

Angie shrugged. "Fine. But I've done all I can do for you. It's going to be up to you to reach a compromise with Rick."

Speak of the devil.

Rick had just walked out of the courtroom.

His back was to Zada, but it was evident he was in a heated discussion with his attorney.

Angie followed Zada's gaze.

She looked back at Zada and smiled.

"Let's stick around for a few minutes," Angie said. "If I know Bob Thompson, his nuts are in a knot, too. The smug bastard thought he had this case nailed down tight. Now he'll have to come up with a plan B."

Something in the way Angie said "smug bastard" made Zada ask, "And just how well do you know Bob Thompson?"

"Bob Thompson can eat poison and die for all I care," Angie said, lifting her obviously woman-scorned chin.

"And how shallow is that?" Zada teased.

Angie mumbled something about where Zada could go.

The destination *wasn't* back home to her eight-hundred-thousand-dollar doghouse in the suburbs.

*   *   *

"Thanks a hell of a lot, Bob. For nothing," Rick said disgustedly. "I believed you when you said the judge would rule in my favor. What am I supposed to do now? You even encouraged me to give up my apartment this morning!"

Bob ran a hand through his short, dark hair. "I swear, Rick," he said, "I'm as shocked as you are. I've never appeared before Judge Parkins when he didn't rule in my favor."

Rick exploded. "And that's supposed to make me feel better? That I'm your first lost case in Parkins's courtroom?"

"Not a loss," Bob corrected. "More of a tie, if you want to be technical about it."

"Bullshit," Rick said. "We lost, Bob. Reaching a compromise with Zada in ninety days, is as likely as achieving peace in the Middle East in ninety days. It isn't going to happen."

Bob frowned. "What are you saying, Rick? That you're willing to give up? That you're going to let Zada keep the house and Simon? Jesus. That's not the Rick Clark I know."

"Spare me your Fighting Irish speech," Rick groaned. "We're not on the football field."

"You're right. We're not on the football field," Bob said. "We're standing in the hallway of the courthouse while I'm trying to keep you from losing your ass."

Rick didn't comment.

"Come on, Rick," Bob urged. "Can't you think of anything that might make Zada change her mind and give you the house?"

Rick laughed. "Short of me moving back in? No."

Bob looked at him for a second.

The wide grin that followed said he had an idea.

"Oh, no you don't," Rick said. "I've seen that grin before. It always means trouble."

Bob said, "Do you really think Zada would move out if you moved back in?"

"Don't even think in that direction," Rick warned. "There's no way I'm putting myself or Zada through the nightmare of trying to live together again."

Bob said, "Not even if it means keeping Simon and the house?"

When Rick hesitated, Bob said, "It can't hurt to at least threaten to move back in. Who knows? Maybe that's all it will take to make Zada reconsider and move out."

"Don't kid yourself," Rick said, shaking his head. "You saw Zada's performance in the courtroom. Zada never backs down from anything."

"Zada's performance in the courtroom is the reason you're standing in the hallway now with no place to live," Bob reminded him. "If it weren't for her, you'd be heading out the door to start your *new* life in your *old* house."

Rick sighed. "Maybe. But I doubt Zada was totally responsible for the ruling. Parkins was already upset that we hadn't reached a property settlement."

"Zada's outburst still didn't help matters," Bob insisted. "And I wouldn't be a good attorney if I didn't use her outburst completely to our advantage."

Bob looked down the corridor and grinned again.

Rick turned around.

Zada.

Standing farther down the hallway with her attorney.

And staring right at him.

"I'll go break the news that you're moving back in," Bob said. "Give me a few minutes, then you show up to back up my threat. And really play it up, Rick. Make Zada cringe at the thought of you moving back into the house with her."

"Dammit, Bob, wait!" Rick called out.

Too late.

Linebacker Bob was already charging down the hallway in *touchdown* mode, straight in Zada's direction.

"Here comes plan B," Angie said and nodded at Rick's attorney who was hulking down the hallway toward them. "Just don't let Bob intimidate you with his super-jock attitude," Angie added. "He forgets sometimes that his college football days are over."

Zada looked Rick's attorney over with cold regard.

Bob Thompson might as well have been chanting *Win! Fight! Win!* as he charged down the hallway toward them.

"And don't expect a miracle," Angie said as he got closer. "Bob wouldn't give in that easily. He's probably going to increase the amount Rick is willing to spend on buying you a new house or condo. His way of enticing you to give up the house in Woodberry Park."

"Then he's wasting his breath," Zada said, crossing her arms stubbornly across her chest. "I don't give in that easily, either."

But that was before Rick walked up behind his attorney.

Before Rick was standing only a few feet away.

Before brooding blue eyes drew her in like a magnet.

No! No! No!

She was not going to give in to that mind-boggling power Rick had over her. That unexplainable can't-live-without-him feeling. That desperate feeling had been her biggest downfall—one she didn't intend to succumb to again.

The power Rick had over her was the main reason she'd refused to see or talk to him during their entire six-month separation period. She just couldn't trust herself in Rick's presence. Her heart overruled her head every time.

If she couldn't win the game, she simply wouldn't play.

First grade?

Yes.

But Angie's earlier accusation about her playing first grade was really rather ironic, when Zada thought about it.

She'd just started first grade when her father walked out and put a quick end to her happy childhood. Had her mother not fallen into a deep depression, blaming herself because her father had left them for another woman, Zada might not have been so devastated herself. But having to take care of herself and her baby sister while her mother stayed in bed for days on end, had taught Zada a very valuable lesson at the ripe old age of six: The only person you can truly depend on in this life, is yourself.

A hard lesson for any six-year-old to learn, true. But a useful lesson, nonetheless.

She had always been able to take care of herself. Just as she could buy her own damn house or condo.

And I don't need Rick Clark to buy one for me!

Bob Thompson stopped in front of them, his six-foot-four frame towering over even Zada, who was five inches taller than petite five-foot-two Angie. He looked at Angie and smiled. But Zada didn't miss the blood in his eye.

"I'm afraid your client's outburst in the courtroom is going to cost you, Miss Naylon," Bob told Angie.

Angie shrugged nonchalantly. "And your point is?"

"My point is," Bob said, "that your client's rude behavior has left my client in an extremely unfortunate predicament. He gave up his apartment this morning."

Intimidated, Angie wasn't.

She took a brave step in the big bully's direction.

"That's *your* problem, Mr. Thompson," Angie said, and flashed him a sweet little screw-you smile. "Your client's unfortunate predicament is of no importance whatsoever to my client."

"Oh, but that's where you're wrong," Bob said, flashing exceptionally white teeth right back at her. "Since the judge didn't rule in anyone's favor today, that means the house is still joint property. And since the house is still joint property, my client is going to exercise his right to move back into the house this very afternoon."

Zada heard the gasp.

It took a second to realize the gasp came from her.

Bob looked over at her and grinned even wider.

"Of course," he said, twisting the knife a little further, "whether your client decides to stay or leave when my client moves back in, is strictly up to her. But rest assured, my client *is* moving back into the house as soon as he leaves this courthouse."

Angie threw her head back and laughed.

But there was no laughter in her voice when she looked back at Bob and said, "And you can rest assured, if your client is foolish enough to step *one* foot on the property he willingly left when he abandoned my client, *he'll* be arrested for trespassing."

Arrested?

I'd never have Rick arrested.

Arresting him wasn't an option.

But neither was Rick moving back in with her.

Absolutely not!

I'd never survive Rick moving back in.

Zada was ready to pull Angie aside to ask about other options. There had to be some law Angie could use to keep Rick from moving back into the house. Anything other than having Rick arrested.

She was quickly approaching a panic attack, until Rick's voice snapped her back to unflappable.

"Zada can't risk me moving back in. Can you, Zada?"

Rick's question caught her off guard.

He was looking directly at her now, with a cocky grin that made Zada's blood boil.

Chomp!

Zada grabbed the bait before she could stop herself.

"And that's supposed to mean?"

He had the nerve to laugh.

"Do you really think I'm that dense?" Rick taunted. "Do you think I don't know exactly why you've refused to see me during the entire six months we've been separated?"

"Let's see," Zada said, putting a finger mockingly to her chin. "Could you possibly be referring to the fact that you became dead to me the minute you walked out the front door?"

"That's your version," Rick said. "Care to hear mine?"

"No," Zada said. "I'm not interested in anything you

have to say, Rick. I thought I'd made myself perfectly clear about that."

Rick told her anyway.

"Sex," he said. "That's why you can't risk me moving back in. We've always found each other irresistible, Zada. Give us five minutes alone together and we'd end up in bed, and you know it."

Zada's signature color flashed before her eyes.

Why, you arrogant ass!

How! Dare! You!

Zada was so angry, she was seething, but she managed a deadly get-over-yourself smile.

"Poor, delusional Rick," Zada mocked. "I hate to break this to you, but I was over you by the time you backed down the driveway."

"Prove it," Rick challenged.

Zada's heart almost stopped.

When will I ever learn to keep my militant mouth shut?

He said, "You know we'll never be able to reach a compromise when it comes to Simon and the house. If you're really over me, let's turn this situation into something we *can* settle between us."

Run! the little voice inside her head screamed.

Slip off your sexy red pumps.

Turn your badass, red-dress self around.

And run like hell!

"I'm advising you not to listen to him, Zada," Angie spoke up. "These guys are double-teaming you. Don't let them push you into a situation you can't win."

Zada looked back at Rick.

His expression was smug now.

Infuriating!

Show no fear, dammit!
Call his stupid bluff.

"What do you have in mind?" Zada heard herself say.

"A real-life game of *Survivor,*" Rick said. "Your favorite reality show. Winner takes all."

"You hate reality shows," Zada reminded him.

Rick said, "Because there's nothing real about the shows on television, Zada. But this *is* reality. Your reality, and mine. You want Simon and the house. I want Simon and the house. The first one to outwit, outplay, and outlast, wins the whole enchilada."

"Zada, don't do this," Angie warned.

"Keep talking," Zada said.

"We've already proved we can't live together," Rick said. "That's why me moving back in will be a challenge worthy of settling our property dispute. If I move out first, you win. If you move out first, I win."

"Not so fast," Angie said. She looked at Zada. "Don't risk violating your separation agreement by letting him move back in. You let Rick move back in, and you'll have to start your separation period all over again."

"Not so," Bob said, calling Angie on her erroneous statement. "Law dictates that two parties can still live separate and apart in the same house while they're going through a divorce. The parties just can't share the same food or the same bed."

Rick said, "And sharing the same food certainly won't be a problem for us, will it, Zada?"

There was that smirk again.

Zada felt like smacking it off his face!

"Sharing the same bed won't be a problem, either," Zada said, staring Rick down. "In fact, I'd actually gag on one of your rancid tofu burgers before I'd let *you* back in my bed again."

There!

Mr. Irresistible can take his smirk and stick it . . .

"Well," Bob said, rubbing his hands together. "Do we all agree, then? Have we finally figured out a way to settle the property dispute, people?"

Angie held her hand up. "Again, not so fast. What happens at the end of ninety days if neither party has moved out of the house?"

"I guess we'll renegotiate," Bob said.

"There won't be any need to renegotiate," Rick said with confidence.

His smirk faded.

A challenging smile replaced it.

"My thoughts exactly," Zada said with just as much confidence. "I'm sure walking out the second time will be even easier for you than it was the first time you walked out on me, Rick."

Rick lost the smile.

Zada found it.

This time Angie motioned to Zada.

They walked down the hall, away from Rick and Bob.

"Can't you see he's playing you?" Angie said the second they were out of hearing range. "Rick knows your weakness, Zada. He knows you're not the type of person to back down from any challenge."

You've got it all wrong, sweetie.

Rick is my weakness.

Resisting him is going to be my challenge.

"Don't do this, Zada," Angie pleaded. "Tell Rick to

forget it. If he tries to move back in, we'll have him arrested, just like I said we would."

Zada shook her head. "No. I'd never have Rick arrested and put a blemish on his record. He could lose his government contracts if I did that."

"And you could lose Simon and the house if you go along with his stupid *Survivor* game idea," Angie reminded her.

"I am *not* going to lose Simon and the house." Zada even believed it herself. "I give Rick two weeks, tops. Believe me, he'll run screaming from the house after living all neat and tidy by himself for the last six months."

Angie let out a deep sigh. "I still think you're making a big mistake."

Zada said, "Maybe. But like you pointed out earlier, unless I plan on trading in my all-about-me dress for a prison jumpsuit in ninety days, I really don't see what other choice I have."

"Good point," Angie said. "Plus, you'd have to change your signature color to orange."

"Very funny," Zada said.

"It would be funny, if this were a laughing matter," Angie said. "But this isn't a laughing matter, Zada. If you're really going through with this, you'll have to stay ahead of the game. Rick could decide to play dirty to get what he wants."

"Meaning?"

"Rick knows you inside and out. What's the one thing Rick could do that would make you walk out the door and never look back?"

Zada blinked.

Several times.

Another woman.

Walking out was bad enough.

But bring another woman into my house and I'd walk out and never look back.

Even the thought made Zada want to throw up.

"Remember the stakes," Angie warned again. "Winner takes all."

Chapter 3

———— 🍎 ————

"Hot damn!" Bob said, slapping Rick on the back. "Now that's the Rick Clark *I* know."

Bob's enthusiasm was wasted on Rick.

Rick was still in shock over the dumb stunt he'd just pulled. *And* mortified that he'd let Bob suck him into a potential no-win situation.

Bob said, "Man, your *Survivor* challenge was pure genius, buddy. All you have to do is move back in, be your usual obnoxious self, and Zada will never be able to hold out the full ninety days."

Usual obnoxious self?

Rick frowned.

"You think I'm obnoxious?"

"Hell no," Bob said, "I don't think you're obnoxious. I *know* you're obnoxious." He punched Rick playfully on the arm. "You're a good friend, Rick, but you carry that boot-camp mentality of yours too far sometimes. Like that fishing trip we went on with the guys a few months back. No one wants a drill sergeant barking out orders about keeping the camp in tip-top shape while you're trying to have a good time."

Rick frowned again.

Is that how the guys really see me?

A drill sergeant barking out orders?

Well, screw them!

He was an army brat, dammit. An army brat whose *real* drill sergeant dad had naturally run his household military style. Besides, what was wrong with maintaining order and keeping everything in tip-top shape? Control was the key in any situation.

Control achieved power.

Power achieved victory.

He'd eaten those words for breakfast right along with his preservative-free granola every morning of his life since he'd been old enough to chew!

Victory.

That was his goal: keeping Simon and the house. The main reason he'd offered Zada the challenge.

Pure genius?

Or total insanity?

Rick wasn't sure.

He'd decided to play along with Bob when he saw the expression on Zada's face after Bob announced Rick was moving back in. *Not* the expression Rick had been expecting. He'd expected Zada's chin to come up, ready for battle. That panic-stricken look on her face, however, told Rick something he hadn't realized until that exact moment.

Zada didn't detest him at all. Quite the contrary.

Zada was still attracted to him. That's why she'd been avoiding him the last six months!

In a split second, Rick decided to make his move.

By forcing the issue, he'd truly hoped Zada would finally put an end to the madness, accept his offer to buy her a place of her own, and hand over Simon and the keys to the house.

They both needed to get on with their lives; ending their marriage was the only solution. Zada knew it. He knew it. Simply put, they drove each other bat-shit crazy.

Yet, Rick still couldn't stop thinking about the stern lecture Judge Parkins had given both of them back in the courtroom.

A mockery of the institution of marriage.

That's what Parkins had called it.

Would they have ended up in divorce court if they'd given the same commitment to their marriage that they'd given to Simon and their careers? Could they have gotten past their differences and salvaged their marriage if they'd been more tolerant of each other's little idiosyncrasies, instead of expecting instant gratification in their married life?

Valid questions.

Questions that would never be answered now.

Zada had taken control away from him the second she filed for the separation papers, leaving him with no choice in the matter whatsoever.

Now, the tables had turned.

Now, he had a chance to get that control back.

Only a damn fool wouldn't take it.

Rick kept watching her.

She was standing farther down the hallway, talking innocently to her attorney, yet arousing every nerve ending in his body at the same time.

Drop-dead gorgeous.

No doubt about it.

Everything about her body turned him on.

Everything about her personality drove him nuts.

Sadly, he knew Zada felt the same way about him.

Despite what she said, Rick knew he still turned her on like crazy. But he also knew his preference for order and discipline drove Zada insane. That's what was so frustrating about the whole situation.

They loved each other.

They desired each other.

There was just no middle ground.

They were either making mad, passionate love or they were yelling at each other.

Middle ground.

That's what he'd been trying to achieve by going along with Bob's madcap idea. Hoping Zada would feel the same way he did. That living together again—even temporarily—definitely wasn't an option.

He glanced down the hallway again.

Zada and her attorney were still deep in conversation.

Hopefully, Angie was talking some sense into Zada. Convincing Zada to accept his offer and put an end to the property dispute once and for all.

Zada suddenly glanced back over her shoulder at him.

Damn! Rick didn't like the gleam in her eye.

Forget middle ground!

Try shaky ground.

That's the ground I'm standing on now.

As if to prove it, Zada walked back in his direction.

Rick felt the earth shake slightly beneath his feet.

"I'll accept your *Survivor* challenge," Zada announced, "as long as you agree to a few conditions."

Did she imagine it?

Or did Rick pale slightly beneath his deep tan?

He actually gulped. "What kind of conditions?"

Zada held up the first finger. "No other women in *my* house."

Rick didn't answer.

He just kept standing there, staring at her like some zoned-out zombie.

Bob finally spoke up and said, "My client will agree to that condition. But he demands the same courtesy from you. The house will also be off limits to any of your male friends."

"Agreed," Zada said, but she looked directly at Rick when she added, "The guy I'm dating and I can always go back to *his* place."

It was a cheap shot, and she knew it.

She'd never even looked at another man.

But the slapped-silly look on Rick's face?

Priceless!

Zada held up finger number two.

"Moving back in today isn't an option," she said. "I need time to rearrange my things. You'll have to wait until tomorrow to move back in."

Bob looked over at Angie and frowned. "Your client was supposed to have her things ready to move out today."

Rick spoke up and overruled him. "Tomorrow's fine," he said. "I'll stay at the training center tonight."

"I could care less where you stay," Zada was quick to tell him. "My only concern is that you wait until Saturday to move back in."

Rick's blue eyes darkened.

Darker.

Darker.

Crap!

No more zombie.

His my-way-or-the-highway glare was back.

"I wasn't implying that you *cared* where I stayed," Rick said curtly. "But you can expect me at the house first thing in the morning, Zada. And I don't mean noon. That's *your* idea of morning. I'll be up at oh-five-hundred hours as usual, and ready to move back in by oh-seven-hundred hours."

Angie frowned and looked over at Bob. "Would you please instruct your client to speak in civilian terms? None of us, including your client, happens to be in the military at the moment."

Bob translated, "He'll be up at five AM and at the house by seven AM."

Angie said, "Then why didn't he just say that?"

Bob shrugged.

"Anything else?" Back-in-control Rick wanted to know.

Zada held up a third finger. She thought for a second. Then put her hand back down.

"I guess that's it," she said.

"That's it?" Rick seemed relieved.

She knew she should have thought up a few more conditions just to annoy him, but Zada was too rattled herself at the thought of Rick moving back in. Plus, Rick's eyes were so blue now they almost looked black.

Not a good sign!

Zada slipped the purse strap off her shoulder, reached inside for her keys, and removed the key to the *new* lock on the front door from her key ring.

She handed Rick the key and said, "Since you've already established it's unlikely I'll be up at *your* idea of morning, take the guest bedroom at the *end* of the upstairs hallway. You know the one. The bedroom that happens to be as far away from *my* master bedroom suite as possible."

"That happens to be *my* king-size bed in the master bedroom," Rick said with a frown. "I had that bed before we were married. I say we flip a coin to see who stays in the master suite."

Zada shook her head. "Not a topic for discussion," she said firmly. "*My* bed. *My* bedroom."

"For now," Rick vowed through clenched teeth.

"Game on," Zada told him, eyes narrowed.

Before Rick had a chance to get in the last word, Zada turned and walked away. And she did so with a confident swing to her hips that she hoped made Rick's damn brooding blue eyes pop right out of his thick, stubborn skull.

When Zada walked away, Rick knew without a doubt—thanks to his big shot attorney—that he had just put his own stupid neck in a hangman's noose. The imaginary pressure on his windpipe caused him to reach up and loosen the tie Zada had given him for Christmas last year.

"I expect a fifty percent discount on my legal fees," Rick informed Bob as he watched Zada sashay down the hallway. "That's the least you can do for this mess you've gotten me into."

Bob laughed. "Are you kidding me? Thanks to me, you're going home instead of going out to look for another apartment. And also thanks to me, you have a good chance of keeping Simon and the house. Maybe I should double my fee."

"I have a *slim to none* chance of keeping Simon and the house," Rick corrected. "And you know it."

"Still, slim to none is better than no chance at all," Bob said. "And you said yourself reaching a compromise with Zada never would have happened."

Rick kept watching Zada.

Bob followed his gaze.

"Stubborn or not, that Zada sure is one fine-looking woman," Bob said. "No one can argue about that."

Rick didn't try to argue.

Except "fine looking" didn't do Zada justice.

"And speaking of fine-looking women," Bob said, nodding toward Angie who was heading down the hall in the opposite direction, "I haven't called that particular fine-looking woman in a couple of days. Which means I have some fast talking to do if I don't want to spend my Friday night alone."

"What?" Rick was stunned. "Isn't that illegal or something? Attorneys sharing the same bed when they're representing opposing clients?"

"Nope," Bob said and grinned.

"Well, dammit, it should be," Rick grumbled.

"You know, Rick," Bob said with a wink, "if you'd try turning off the testosterone and turning on the charm, that pretty wife of yours might welcome you back to your big king-size bed. Remember. Even a cobra can be charmed, buddy."

"I said get out of here," Rick warned.

"Gladly," Bob said. "But watch this. Charm works every time."

Bob hurried down the hall after Angie.

Rick started down the hall in the opposite direction,

but he smiled when he glanced back over his shoulder. Bob had caught up with Angie. The lift of her chin said Angie wasn't interested. Until Bob dipped her backward and kissed her silly.

When Angie's I-forgive-you laughter echoed down the hallway, Rick frowned.

The big idiot, Rick thought.

Sure, charm might work for a self-proclaimed ladies' man like Bob. But Rick had personally never understood why women couldn't see right through a man who said one thing, and did another, yet expected to be forgiven just because he turned on the charm.

Maybe I do have boot-camp mentality.

But at least I'm honest.

A man was only as good as his word.

Right?

If I give my word, I mean it!

But Rick frowned again when *till death do us part* crossed his mind.

"Dammit," Rick said aloud, "*I* didn't file for the divorce. She did!"

Several people in the hallway looked in his direction.

Rick didn't care.

He stalked off down the hallway, looking for the signs that would take him back to the main lobby of the courthouse.

Turn on the charm.

Yeah, right!

As if charm would work on Zada now.

I'd have better luck charming a cobra.

Game on. Those had been Zada's parting words.

Outwit. Outplay. Outlast. Those stupid words, of course, had been his.

What the hell was I thinking?

Zada, give in?

Not in ninety days.

Not in a million f-ing years!

Pressure constricted around his throat again.

This time, Rick jerked Zada's tie from around his neck.

Keeping Zada's *hands* from around his neck?

Gulp!

That was going to be his ultimate ninety-day challenge.

Chapter 4

Zada walked across the courthouse parking lot, heading for the Simon mobile—the name she called her sporty, black Lexus SUV. The car was classy, yet equipped with a let-down backseat that provided sufficient room to haul around a 120-pound part-Belgian Malinois, part-German shepherd dog.

She punched the keyless entry button on her key ring, and slid behind the wheel. But Zada sat there in the driver's seat for a second, thinking about how tragic it would be if she did have to hand over the dog that had changed the course of her life forever.

Simon was far more than just a dog to her.

Simon was her inspiration.

Simon loved her unconditionally.

But more importantly, she could depend on Simon.

Zada couldn't say that about another living soul.

He was larger than most mixed-breeds of his type, but Simon was as gentle as a lamb, and he had certainly been more loyal to her than the man who had trained him, thank you very much!

Simon also had more natural instinct than many humans

she'd encountered in her thirty-two years of life—her mother and her sister immediately coming to mind. Only Zada didn't have time to dwell on that hopeless situation.

She had her own hopeless situation to worry about.

Damn you, Rick!

Why can't you just leave us alone?

Zada sighed.

God, what an idiot she'd been.

She thought she'd married Mr. Right.

Until she realized his name was Mr. *Always Right!*

I never had a chance, Zada thought. Meeting Rick had hit her like a cosmic explosion. *Boom!* One look, and she had to have him.

She'd been visiting Simon at the vet clinic that afternoon when just-out-of-the-hospital Rick walked in, his broken arm still in a cast, his head still bandaged from the concussion he'd suffered when he and Simon were injured.

"I hear you're Simon's number-*two* fan," he'd said, stealing her heart with one sexy grin.

She'd insisted on taking him to lunch.

Mainly to ask permission to keep seeing Simon.

Over lunch, she'd told Rick how Simon was her inspiration for a new children's book series she wanted to write. Lunch had progressed into dinner. And dinner had progressed into going back to his apartment and sitting up all night talking.

By the end of the first week, she was crazy in love.

"Crazy" being the operative word.

Crazy enough to go to Lake Tahoe with Rick two months later while he met with one of the major ski resorts interested in detection dogs as a security option.

The trip to Tahoe had been the most magical time of

her life. She'd never deny that. But the state of Nevada—
where all you had to do to get married was say "I do"—
had been the perfect place for "crazy" to take on a whole
new meaning in her life.

Rick had proposed the first night they were there.

She'd said yes the second he proposed.

The hotel had arranged for everything else.

One gondola ride up to the top of the Heavenly Ski Resort, and they'd literally been on the top of the world, a
breathtaking view of Lake Tahoe below them as they exchanged their vows in a sunset wedding ceremony.

They'd stayed in Tahoe an extra week, locked in a honeymoon cabin, away from the rest of the world. Two months
later, they were moving into Simon's eight-hundred-
thousand-dollar doghouse.

That's when reality set in. When they realized they
should have *lived* together first. That love was blind—but
that marriage was a real eye-opener!

Rick had certainly opened her eyes today.

And she intended to open his eyes tomorrow!

Zada jammed the key into the ignition and pulled the
gearshift into reverse, irritated all over again.

It was just like Rick to come up with some way to put
himself back in her life, back in her face. Well, she had
news for Rick. She'd outwit him. Outplay him. And outlast him.

Rick wants reality?

I'll show him reality!

Zada drove out of the parking lot, heading back to
Woodberry Park and the house on Owls Roost Road that
she *was not* going to hand over without putting up one hell
of a fight. By the time she drove into the busy downtown

traffic on Washington Street, Zada had her cell phone to her ear.

"Jen," Zada said when her neighbor answered, "I'm going to have to cancel dinner plans with you and Tish tonight."

She heard Jen gasp.

Jen Marshall and Tish Jones were her best friends. Jen lived next door. Tish lived across the street. Like her, they were both in their early thirties.

Unlike her, Jen and Tish were *happily* married.

Jen said, "Oh, God. Please don't tell me you're canceling dinner because the judge ruled in Rick's favor."

"No," Zada said, sighing over the absurdity of the whole situation. "The judge didn't rule in Rick's favor."

"Zada, you poor thing," Jen said. "I was afraid you'd lose your bravado after the fact. That's why I insist you let Tish and I take you to dinner tonight just like we planned. We're here for you, Zada, and we want you to know that. It's only natural to feel sad and let down after a divorce. You probably even feel like a failure right now, but . . ."

"Jen!" Zada said, cutting her off. "I don't feel like a failure. What I feel like right now, is mad as hell."

"Completely understandable," Jen said, talking over her again. "Anger is also a natural response to . . ."

"Having the husband you thought you were divorcing today, move back in tomorrow?"

That comment got Jen's attention.

"What did you say?"

"The judge delayed the divorce," Zada said. "He's giving us ninety days to settle the property dispute between us before we appear back in his courtroom."

"And he ordered Rick to move back home?"

"I'll explain everything when I get there," Zada told her. "You and Tish did make arrangements for your kids tonight, didn't you?"

"Yes," Jen said. "Sonya's spending the weekend with my parents and Tish has a babysitter for the twins."

"Don't cancel the plans for the kids," Zada said. "Just because I'm canceling dinner doesn't mean I'm not going to need your help. I'll call you as soon as I get home and change out of this dress I blew a bundle on, thinking it would be the last time I saw Rick."

"You need our help for what?" Jen wanted to know.

"I have a lot to do before Rick shows up on my doorstep in the morning," Zada said. "You and Tish need to help me give Rick a homecoming surprise he won't soon forget."

Rick swiped his ID card across the pad of the security lock. When the security bar lifted, he drove his spruce-green Hummer into the training center's parking lot. The two-story red brick building had once been the old fire hall in the West Chicago suburb of New Hope—back before New Hope had grown substantially in size and was able to afford a new facility.

He'd opened the training center shortly after the devastating terrorist attack on September 11, when all available resources for dogs trained in explosive detection had basically been depleted overnight. Private bomb dog companies had instantly sprouted up all over the country—many of them more interested in the money than they were in the quality training of their canines.

Rick vowed his company—Security Detection Services
—wouldn't be one of them.

He'd jumped at the chance to purchase the old fire hall,
knowing the building couldn't be any more perfect for
the type of bomb dog training center he had in mind. The
kitchen and upstairs sleeping quarters, once used by the
firemen, provided adequate accommodations for dog han-
dlers while they were undergoing extensive training courses
at the center. At the back of the building, there was plenty
of space for the dog kennels and for a first-class obstacle
course and training area for the dogs.

His experience with a canine unit during his military
service had given him the background he needed in the
bomb detection field. But Rick had been the first one to
admit he lacked the experience needed to train the dogs
himself.

For that reason, he'd hired a team unmatched anywhere
when it came to training and expertise. Like the experts
he'd hired, Rick firmly believed explosive detection dogs
were a special category of detection canines—dogs who
should only be trained for one specific task.

At SDS dogs weren't cross-trained in reckless combi-
nations, mixing explosive training with training in firearm
and drug detection. A bomb-sniffing dog needed to be
calm, patient, and completely focused. Being trained in
only one area lessened the chance of a dog becoming confused in dangerous situations and putting lives at risk.

The mission statement at SDS was simple: "Dedicated
to delivering properly trained explosive detection canines
fully capable of going forth into life threatening situations."

Rick's belief in that statement had saved his life.

Had Simon not been properly trained, there was no

doubt in Rick's mind that he and Simon would have been killed in the explosion at O'Hare.

It had been four years since he first opened the center. Now he was thirty-six years old. He had sufficient training experience under his belt. And SDS had become one of the top explosive detection operations in the nation.

The accredited certification plaques hanging on the wall in his office backed up the claim. The Department of Defense, Homeland Security's Transportation Security Administration, and the Department of Alcohol, Tobacco and Firearms commissioned his dogs on a regular basis.

At least my business is successful.

Too bad my marriage wasn't.

Rick thought this as he drove the Hummer into the bay of the building that had once housed much larger vehicles than the one he was riding in now. The second he turned off the engine, one of the main reasons his business had been so successful started walking in his direction.

Rick waved to the man.

Stewart "Scrappy" Adams waved back.

Scrappy was a top-rate kennel master who had earned his nickname during his tour of duty in Vietnam—the nickname was self-explanatory. Though in his late fifties now, Scrappy was still in better physical shape than most men twenty years his junior.

One look at his close-cut gray hair and his camouflage fatigues told you he was military to the bone, and apt to stay that way. One look at his résumé proved why his consultation services were frequently sought by the US Customs Service, the US Secret Service, and even the FBI.

Or as Scrappy often liked to brag—he'd already forgotten more about explosives than Rick would ever know.

Rick had been able to recruit a man of such caliber, mainly because Scrappy lived rent free at the center on a full-time basis. This was Rick's reason for renting the apartment rather than staying at the center himself and risk invading his kennel master's space.

Scrappy claimed he preferred living at the center because he didn't like nosy neighbors, didn't have time to take care of a place of his own, and he didn't want any damn lawn to mow. But Rick suspected the barracks-like feel of the training center was what appealed most to an old vet like Scrappy who had no close family, no children, and had been married and divorced three times—what Scrappy referred to as "three tours of duty in the middle of hell."

A big fan of marriage, Scrappy wasn't.

Which is why it didn't surprise Rick when the first words out of Scrappy's mouth when he walked up to the Hummer were, "Next time, Rick, just pick out a pretty girl walking down the street and offer to buy her a house. It'll save you a whole lot of bullshit all the way around."

Rick laughed, but he didn't have the energy to explain.

"I don't want to talk about it, Scrappy," Rick said.

"Then we won't talk about it," Scrappy agreed.

And that, Rick thought *is the beauty of being a guy!*

But not women. Hell, no!

All *women want to do is talk about it.*

Twisting words around so you forget what you've said, like the big fight he'd had with Zada the day he left. Her, accusing him of using sex to end any argument. Him, just trying to put an end to the yelling.

Jesus!

Scrappy backed away from the Hummer.

Rick opened the car door and said, "But I do need to bunk with you tonight Scrappy, if that's okay."

"Glad to have the company," Scrappy said. "I just made a pot of chili so spicy I'll never know if the tears running down your face are over losing your ass in the divorce, or from the *bad*ass jalapeños I tossed into the mix."

Scrappy headed for the upstairs kitchen.

As an afterthought, Rick yelled out, "Hey, Scrappy. Tell me the truth about something. Do you consider me obnoxious?"

Scrappy turned back around to face him.

He thought the question over carefully for a second.

"Intense," Scrappy finally said. "Guys like us are intense, Rick." He shook his gray head. "Hell, in our line of business, how can anyone expect us to be anything else?"

"Intense," Rick mumbled as Scrappy disappeared up the staircase.

Hell, yeah!

Scrappy was right.

I'm not obnoxious.

I'm intense.

Like Scrappy said, how could anyone in their line of business be anything else?

For the first time since Zada uttered those fatal words "game on" Rick actually felt a little more confident. Why should he even be worried at all? He faced danger every day, worked with explosives far more dangerous than Zada.

He'd outlast her if it killed him.

As for that smart remark she'd made about hanging out at some guy's place, he'd deal with that, too, when the time came.

Or not.

A guy even talking to Zada made Rick want to puke. He couldn't let himself think about *more* than talking. Not unless he wanted to spend his life behind bars.

Damn you, Zada!

You knew that remark would make me crazy!

Rick let out a long, tortured sigh.

He'd had enough angst for one day compliments of Zada. Tonight, he wasn't going to think about Zada at all. Definitely not that tongue thing she did, which also drove him crazy.

In places he *didn't* want to think about.

Or the silky feel of her long, tanned legs.

Or the taste of her full, sweet lips.

Or the feel of her breasts pressed against his chest.

Or the funny little noise she made that told him she was getting close, and he could stop holding back and take them both straight to nirvana.

Or . . .

Dammit!

When I'm six feet under.

Rick knew then—and only then—would he ever stop thinking about Zada.

"What on earth were you thinking, Zada?" Jen wailed. "You've been avoiding Rick the entire six months you've been separated because of your so-called fatal attraction to him. And now you've agreed to let him move back in! Rick's right. You'll end up in bed in five minutes flat."

"Not this time," Zada vowed. "I realized after I got so flustered when I saw Rick again that we'd never have any closure unless I faced him head-on. And believe me, trying to live together again will bring both of us plenty of closure."

"That's ridiculous," Jen said, looking over at Tish for support. "Almost as ridiculous as you expecting us to help you trash your own house."

Exactly the response I expected from you, Jen.

Zada had known her winner-takes-all battle plan wouldn't appeal to logical-to-a-fault Jen.

Jen was petite, short black hair, big doe-brown eyes. She was dressed in the standard summer 'burb uniform like Zada was wearing now—shorts, flip-flops, a simple cotton T-shirt. A stay-at-home mom, Jen was the perfect mother to her seven-year-old daughter, Sonya, and the perfect wife to her corporate executive husband, Charlie.

In Zada's opinion, Jen needed to lighten up a little.

Just as Jen thought Zada was way too blasé.

The only thing they did agree on was that their friendship brought out the best in both of them.

"What you're suggesting really is pretty extreme, Zada," previous beauty queen Tish chimed in.

Tish had made it all the way to the Miss America Pageant her junior year in college, and never had a hair out of place on her auburn head. Even the shorts she was wearing, like her blouse, were pressed with a razor-sharp crease. The majority of her time was spent trying to keep her eight-year-old twins, Mike and Mark, just as freshly pressed—a task she never quite achieved.

Still, Tish was the marvel of Woodberry Park.

How Tish managed to keep herself looking like a runway model 24/7; supervise twin boys by herself during the week while her salesman husband, Joe, traveled; and still stay involved in every school function and civic organization available, would always be one of those unsolved mysteries.

And the thing Zada liked best about Tish?

Tish could always be lured to the "dark side"—as Jen called it—without too much persuasion.

"I don't call what I'm suggesting extreme at all," Zada said. "By Rick's standards, the house is already trashed."

Tish laughed. "By Rick's standards, even Jen's house is trashed."

Which was absurd.

Jen's house was always spotless.

"My point exactly," Zada said before Jen could intervene. "And pushing Mr. Neat-and-Tidy's buttons as hard as I can push them is my only hope if I want to keep Simon and the house."

Zada looked around her living room, hands on her hips.

"I want this room so messy," Zada said, "that Rick won't even put his bags down when he walks through the front door in the morning."

Jen said, "And you wonder why the judge called you self-absorbed and childish. The judge was right. You and Rick are being ridiculous. You know you still love each other. If you'd stop trying to match each other tit for tat, you might be able to save your marriage."

Zada groaned. "I'm too stressed out for another lecture about saving my marriage, Jen. And," Zada added, "it was being called immature that made me angry, not self-absorbed. This *is* all about me, Jen! My house. My dog. My life!"

Jen rolled her eyes.

"And don't roll your eyes at me," Zada said. "It's a funny thing to me that in the nineties if you stood up for yourself and went after what you wanted, people called you assertive. Today, you're considered self-absorbed and shallow."

"Maybe you should start your own support group," Jen quipped. "You could call it Self-absorbed Unanimous."

"Maybe I should," Zada said, not the least bit offended by Jen's comment. "It's time self-absorbed people got the recognition they deserve."

Tish said, "And that kind of recognition would be?"

"You just had to ask," Jen mumbled.

Zada said, "Who do you think buys everything from luxury automobiles to Botox injections? Self-absorbed people keep up the demand, so workers supplying the goods can earn a paycheck every week."

"That's pretty deep thinking for someone claiming to be shallow," Jen said.

"Well, contrary to popular belief," Zada said, "shallow people are extremely bright. That's why we don't waste time contemplating the true meaning of life. We're smart enough to know life is exactly what you make of it. And I intend to make my life right here in Woodberry Park. Not in some condo Rick picks out for me!"

"Blah, blah, blah," Jen said.

"But," Zada said, "do you know the absolute best thing about us hopelessly self-absorbed people?"

"I'll pass," Jen said.

Zada told her anyway. "You'll never catch us talking about anyone other than ourselves."

Tish laughed.

Zada grinned at her own joke.

Jen rolled her eyes again.

"Well?" Zada asked. "Now that I've explained the virtues of the self-absorbed, are you going to help shallow me trash this room?"

Jen said, "How likely is it that just for once, you would look at this situation from a logical point of view and forget the whole trash-the-room idea?"

Zada thought for a second. "I'd say about as likely as you successfully nailing Jell-O to a tree in my backyard."

"That's what I thought," Jen said. "And no! I will not participate in some juvenile delinquent prank to help you trash your house."

Tish's smile was deviant. "But you will stay and keep us company, won't you?"

"I'll stay as a stand-in for the conscience the two of you obviously don't have," Jen huffed.

"Excellent!" Zada exclaimed. "Just stay out of our juvenile delinquent way."

Zada's enthusiasm, however, prompted a loud bark.

Simon was sitting stoically in the archway that led into the dining room, waiting patiently for her to notice him.

"There's my big boy," Zada said happily.

She walked over, bent down, and scratched the big dog lovingly between the ears. Simon returned the affection by lifting his head and giving Zada a few sloppy doggy kisses on the side of her cheek. Satisfied with the attention, he trotted back through the house, heading, Zada knew, for his favorite chair in the den, just off the kitchen.

"That reminds me," Zada said when she turned back around. "We can't put anything on the floor that Simon could bump into."

She walked back to where her partner-in-crime Tish

was standing, awaiting her instructions. "And I think for optimum effect, we need to focus on the things that really drive Rick up the wall."

"Like parking on *his* side of the garage?" Tish said with a giggle.

Zada grinned. "Perfect. I hadn't thought of that."

She pointed to the two floor-to-ceiling bookcases flanking the living room fireplace. "I want those bookcases to look like one of Rick's dog training bombs exploded right in the middle of them," Zada said. "And there's nothing Rick hates more than magazines littering the coffee table."

Tish walked over and began removing magazines from a magazine rack sitting by one of the matching chairs that were positioned in front of the room's large bay window.

"Those will do for now," Zada said. "But I have tons more stored in boxes in the garage."

"Of course you do, you pack rat," Tish chirped, reminding Zada that her refusal to throw anything away was another one of Rick's big pet peeves.

In minutes, Tish had magazines all over the sofa, on the chairs, and a ton of magazines strewn across the coffee table in total disarray.

"You have to admit this really is kind of fun," Tish said as she tossed the last magazine onto an end table.

Busy at the right bookcase, Zada giggled.

Standing in the middle of the room shaking her head in disgust, Jen said, "I have to be insane to stand here and watch this."

"Welcome to Woodberry Park," Zada quipped. "The official insane asylum of the suburbs."

Jen snorted. "That's the first intelligent thing I've heard you say today."

It took another hour and a few trips to the garage for more magazines before no further havoc could possibly be wreaked in Zada's living room. They all three stood in Zada's foyer, where Zada insisted they all should stand in order to get Rick's first impression when he walked through the front door.

"*Extreme Makeover: Home Edition,*" Zada said proudly.

Jen said, "Poor Ty Pennington would swallow his freaking megaphone if he saw this place."

"And his tool belt," Tish added.

Jen said, "Please tell me the living room is the *only* room you've chosen for your master disaster plan."

"For now," Zada said. "I truly think this little welcome home statement will be more than enough to send Rick right back out the door."

Tish nodded. "I agree. One look at the living room, and Rick will realize he'd never last a full ninety days with this mess staring him in the face."

Jen raised an eyebrow. "And if Rick decides to clean the mess up himself and stay?"

Zada shrugged. "He cleans up. I mess up. Not a problem."

"Oh," Jen said. "You mean the same way it was before you and Rick separated."

"Jen!" Tish scolded.

"No, Jen's right," Zada said. "It's no secret I'm not the neat-freak type. But I sure don't feel the need to apologize for it. My idea of a home is where I can leave the Sunday paper spread out on the floor all day without once feeling the need to pick it up. I *live* in my house," Zada stressed for emphasis. "And if you can't live in a house, what's the point in having one?"

Jen blushed slightly.

Like Rick, Jen was the neat-freak type.

And they all three knew it.

"I didn't mean to sound judgmental," Jen finally conceded. "I was just trying to point out that your plan might not be as foolproof as you think."

"Well, look on the bright side," always-the-diplomat Tish said. "If Rick does clean this mess up, at least we won't have to be the ones who carry all those magazines back to the garage."

"He'll fold," Zada said. "I'm sure of it."

Jen still wasn't convinced. "Everything happens for a reason, Zada. You should have been divorced today, but you aren't. Doesn't that make you wonder, even a little, if you've been granted an extra ninety days because you and Rick really are meant to stay together?"

"Not even a little," Zada said.

Jen frowned. "Do you know the number one cause of divorce, Zada?"

"Yes," Zada said. "Marriage."

"Lack of communication," Jen said, frowning at her again. "There are always two sides to a divorce."

"True," Zada said. "My side. And shithead's. Who, you keep forgetting, walked out on *me*."

"How could anyone forget Rick walked out on you?" Jen's hands were on her hips now. "You've practically worn a sign around your neck for the last six months that said 'Rick Clark walked out on me!'"

I. Beg. Your. Pardon!

Zada was speechless.

"Girls!" a nervous Tish said. "Kiss and make up right now, or I'm going to throw cold water on both of you."

Jen said, "Be honest with yourself, Zada. It was almost a relief when Rick walked out. You'd been waiting for him to disappoint you like your father did from the moment you married him. He did disappoint you, and he apologized for that. But you'd rather sacrifice your marriage than take him back and admit you're every bit as human as your mother and your sister."

"Well, thank you, Dr. Phil!" Zada exclaimed.

But Jen was right on target as usual.

Zada finally reached out and put her arm around Jen's shoulder. "Look," she said, giving Jen a let's-not-argue hug. "I know you love me. And I know you're equally fond of Rick. I also know you only want what you think is best for both of us. But if you really want to be a good friend, Jen, you're going to have to respect my decision, whether you agree with it or not."

"Okay, you win," Jen said with a sigh. "I give up."

"Thank you," Zada said. "Let's just hope Rick gives up when he arrives to play *Survivor* in the morning."

Chapter 5

When her alarm sounded at Rick's idea of morning on Saturday, Zada opened one eye long enough to slap the clock back to sleep. Why anyone would get up at such a ridiculous hour would always be a mystery to her. She glanced toward the large bay window on the other side of the bedroom, looking for any signs of early morning light.

Black as pitch.

At 0500 hours, even Mr. Sun was still snoozing.

Bay windows, Zada thought.

She knew it was silly, but she'd always been a sucker for bay windows. This house had a bay window in every major room, including her master bath.

She'd fallen in love with the house the second she saw it. She'd loved the distressed white brick, the English cottage look, and the flower boxes beneath every window across the front of the house.

The fact that the developer had stayed true to the Woodberry Park name he'd given to the subdivision, was also a selling feature for her. Unlike many new subdivisions that were often stripped bare, only a minimal amount of trees had been cleared from the lots. That country, woodsy kind of atmosphere also complimented the private golf course that meandered throughout the subdivision.

The golf course had been the selling feature for Rick.

That, and the New Hope location.

Woodberry Park was less than ten miles from SDS.

The reason she'd set her alarm for 5:00 AM: She planned to be up, fresh and frisky when Rick arrived. Standing at the top of the stairs. Smiling at his shocked expression when he saw the mess in the living room. *And* waving good-bye when he said "I give up, you win," just as Jen had said the night before.

Waving good-bye.

Zada sighed.

Her heart warned her she'd regret letting Rick go.

Her pride reminded her she had no other choice.

She didn't want to be every bit as human as her mother and her sister, dammit! What had being human ever done for either of them?

Her mother had ended up with a husband who cheated on her and left her for another woman—a woman who was so worthless she threw him out twelve years later when the brain tumor appeared. And what had her mother done? She'd taken him back and cared for him right up until the day he died—as if twelve long years of him ignoring her and his children never happened.

Then there was her sister Sally, who after nine years, was still trying to hold on to a man who couldn't decide from one day to the next if he wanted a family or his freedom.

Did she intend to follow in their *humanly* footsteps?

Hell, no!

She intended to be stronger. Smarter. Independent and totally self-sufficient. The way she'd always been—before

Rick Clark walked into her life. Had Rick not been the first man she truly couldn't resist, she never would have gone along with their spur-of-the-moment wedding in the first place.

Yesterday's news, Zada reminded herself.

She yawned and stretched, waking Simon in the process.

The dog moved from his position at the foot of her bed, crawling on his belly until his head was on the pillow next to hers. When Simon rolled over on his back, Zada gave him a belly rub, his favorite doggy thing in life.

"It's been a long time since you were awake this early, hasn't it, buddy?" she cooed to the dog.

Before Rick moved out, he'd always taken Simon with him on his early morning run. But after Rick left, Zada found it didn't take much persuasion to lure Simon over to the dark side, either.

They took their daily walk every morning on the walking trail around the golf course around ten—her true idea of morning—instead of *noon* as Rick had exaggerated.

It was on those peaceful morning walks that she got most of her ideas for her children's books. Like the morning Simon had sniffed out an injured baby bunny, and had brought the bunny to her, holding it as gently in his mouth as a mother cat would hold one of her kittens.

She and Simon had taken Thumpless—the name she'd given the bunny in her book—to the vet to have his broken back leg splinted. After the bunny's leg healed, they'd set Thumpless free in the same place where Simon had found him.

The Bunny Who Lost His Thump had been her best selling book in her *Simon Sees* children's series so far—all thanks to one gentle, blind dog whose insight more than compensated for the things he couldn't see.

"He's a good boy, that's what he is," Zada cooed.

Simon curled himself into a ball against her.

"Just don't get too comfortable, buddy," Zada mumbled. "I'm going to close my eyes for five more minutes. Then we have to get up. And I have to get beautiful. I want Rick to see the true meaning of irresistible when he walks back through the front door this morning."

Zada wasn't sure if the sound of a car door slamming, or Simon's low growl snapped her eyes wide open. But one look at the clock jerked her out of bed.

No! No! No!

She'd only closed her eyes for a minute.

How could it possibly be 7:00 AM?

Zada flew to the bay window, knowing what she'd find sitting in her driveway, yet praying that she wouldn't. The large grill across the front of the ominous green Hummer seemed to be grinning up at her with a big gotcha smile.

Crap! Crap! Crap!

Just when she'd accepted yesterday, along came today!

Now there would be no time to shake, shake, shake her beauty into irresistible—no time to shower or dress.

And if she didn't hurry?

She'd even miss the shocked look on Rick's face when he saw the mess waiting for him in the living room.

Her head jerked around when Simon whimpered.

He was sitting up on the bed now, ears pricked to attention, signaling he knew exactly who had just arrived on the premises.

"Stay," Zada ordered and ran for the bathroom.

The taste of victory would be sweet.

But victory wouldn't taste near as sweet if she didn't at least take time out to brush her teeth.

The absence of Zada's Lexus in the driveway was Rick's first clue that Zada hadn't been kidding when she'd said "game on." She never parked in the garage. Mainly because her side of the garage was always filled with all of the junk she refused to throw away.

Rick pushed the garage remote, just to make sure.

There was the Lexus, all right.

Parked on his *junk-free* side of the garage.

Rick slowly counted to ten.

He was *not* going to let Zada rattle him before he even got out of the car. He was stronger than that. He could take anything Zada could dish out. And he intended to prove it to her!

Back in control, Rick took his keys from the ignition and got out of the Hummer. Minutes later he was walking up the sidewalk with a duffel bag in each hand, the same way he'd walked down the sidewalk with a duffel bag in each hand six months earlier.

He'd hired a lawn service to take over his yard work after he left, and as he made his way up the walk, he made a mental note to call the service. The shrubbery lining the sidewalk needed more mulch. He intended to point that out.

An intense thing to do? Probably. But guys like him were intense kind of guys.

He used his new key in the new lock, already smiling to himself. At least Simon was going to be happy to have him back home. His happy smile faded, however, the second Rick walked into the foyer.

Game-on clue number *two* was waiting for him.

Holy Mother of God.

The mass destruction that used to be his living room would have made his mouth drop open—had Rick's jaw not been immobilized in a damn-you-Zada! clench.

So this is how she's going to play the game, is she?

Down and dirty.

No holds barred.

Well, he had news for Zada. Explosive detection was his line of business.

It had only taken a second to detect that Zada had blown up the damn living room, but he could dodge as many magazines as Miss Outwit-Outplay-Outlast wanted to throw in his direction!

But what a damn mess.

All Rick could do was stand there and stare.

One look in the bathroom mirror told Zada she had more to worry about than the sweet taste of victory. With her up-too-early bloodshot eyes and her overnight bed-head curls in a tangle, she looked like one of those bizarre doctored photos on the front of *The National Enquirer.* HALF-WOMAN HALF-MONSTER FOUND LIVING IN SUBURBIA could have been the caption under her picture.

Hopeless! Zada decided.

She only smeared toothpaste across her teeth and only raked through the tangles with her fingers.

She still looked monstrous, even wearing a sexy black

lace teddy. But it didn't matter; she was *not* going to miss Rick's reaction when he walked through the door!

Zada flew out of the bathroom and into the bedroom.

Simon was still on the bed where she'd left him.

"Stay," Zada repeated for good measure.

Seconds later, she had flattened herself against the upstairs hallway wall, and was leaning forward only far enough to peek into the downstairs foyer below.

Rick.

Already in the house.

A duffel bag in each hand.

And . . .

Yes!

A shocked expression on his now frowning face.

Zada kept watching.

Rick kept standing there, motionless. So still, in fact, he could have been a statue. Except, Zada decided, for that muscle that kept twitching uncontrollably in his tightly clenched jaw.

He finally shook his head disgustedly.

Several times.

Atta boy. You get the idea. Stay, and this is what you'll be facing every day for the next ninety days.

He let out a long sigh.

I don't blame you a bit. I don't want to live in this mess, either.

He turned toward the door.

That's it.

He walked to the door.

Don't disappoint me. Keep walking.

Zada licked her lips, the taste of victory, sweet.

Until . . .

Bam!

What?

Rick had kicked the front door shut with his foot! He wasn't leaving at all.

Holy freaking hell!

Now he was coming up the stairs!

Zada sprinted back down the hallway to safety. She closed her bedroom door and leaned against it. The f-word she said out loud *wasn't* "forward," but Simon evidently decided it was close enough. He jumped off the bed and ran forward. In seconds, he was scratching at the door like crazy.

"Simon, sit!" Zada commanded.

Simon's bark said he was tired of taking orders.

"Please," Zada begged, her back still against the door.

Rick knocked.

Zada jumped.

"Come on, Zada. Let Simon out. He knows I'm here."

Simon barked again, agreeing with that suggestion.

"Traitor," Zada grumbled, but she opened the door.

She stood there in the doorway, telling herself the sight of a grown man—down on his knees while a happy dog licked his face—didn't tug at her heartstrings.

The lie threw its head back and laughed in her face.

Rick loved Simon as much as she did.

That was a given.

That she loved Rick as much as Simon did?

That would probably be her downfall.

Rick finally got Simon out of his face long enough to look up at Zada. The expression on her face was tender, as if even she were a tiny bit happy to see him. The tender look disappeared the second their eyes met.

His gaze traveled downward.

Black. Lace. Teddy.

Rick gulped.

Another ploy to drive me insane?

That thought quickly cleared his head.

"I like what you did with the living room," Rick couldn't resist saying.

Slam! went the bedroom door.

Damn!

He shouldn't have said that, but how could he not? Zada had already set the stage for the game. She'd already proved by her actions that her strategy was going to be doing everything in her power to purposely drive him crazy.

But who am I kidding?

I'm already insane.

Or I never would have come up with the Survivor *idea.*

But here he was, prepared to stay.

Whether Zada realized it or not, it was going to take more than using his side of the garage and dumping a truckload of magazines in the living room for him to walk away and declare her the winner.

"Don't worry, boy," Rick told Simon, patting the dog's head as he rose to his feet. "I'm home to stay."

Simon wagged his tail happily.

Rick smiled.

Man's best friend.

Insane or not, Simon was worth it.

"Let's go get my stuff," Rick said, smiling again when Simon fell in beside him.

The next hour, Rick spent making multiple trips up and down the stairs, unloading his clothes from the Hummer. The hour after that, Rick spent hanging his clothes in the closet, putting his socks and underwear into dresser drawers, and basically getting settled into the guest bedroom at the far end of the hall—as far away from Zada and her damn master bedroom as possible.

Simon never left his side.

The dog followed every step he made.

Thirty more minutes spent organizing his personal items in the bedroom's adjoining guest bath, and Rick stepped back from the medicine cabinet, thoroughly pleased with himself. He was officially settled back into *his* house, with *his* dog sitting faithfully beside him. Nothing Zada could say or do was going to force him to leave home again.

Game on?

Absolutely!

Rick looked down at Simon. "How about it, boy? Do I dare go downstairs and see what's waiting for me in the kitchen? Zada knows there's nothing I hate more than a messy kitchen."

Simon barked as if he understood the question.

Rick took a deep breath, then headed downstairs.

The only thing he found waiting for him in the kitchen, however, was Zada sitting calmly at the kitchen table. And looking like a million bucks in a tight pair of jeans and a skimpy little top. And . . .

Geez!

Eating one of her disgusting Dove ice-cream bars.

Ice-cream for breakfast, Rick thought. *Like that makes perfect sense.*

He glanced at the leash across her lap.

Zada ignored him completely, looked directly at Simon and said, "Ready for our walk this morning, buddy?"

Walk?

When did exercise-phobic Zada start taking Simon on a morning walk?

Rick said, "Now that I'm back home, I thought I'd take Simon on a run with me this morning. Get him back on schedule."

Zada looked directly at him this time.

She even smiled.

Lethal-like.

"Simon has a *new* schedule now," she said. "One he's been enjoying quite nicely for the last six months. It wouldn't be fair to confuse him. Or is *consistency* no longer your sacred golden rule over at the training center?"

Sacred golden rule. Cute.

Rick scrambled for an equally wiseass answer.

The front doorbell saved him the trouble.

Zada, however, didn't budge. She sat there, as if she didn't hear the chime.

Teasing him.

Taunting him.

Driving him truly insane as he watched her pink tongue lap, lap, lap at the last bit of ice cream on her Popsicle stick.

Do. Not. Think. About. The. Tongue. Thing.

Rick forced himself to look away when she made one more exaggerated lick up and down the length of the stick.

"Well?" Rick finally said.

"Well, what?" said Zada.

"Aren't you going to answer the door, Zada?"

"Are *your* legs suddenly broken, Rick?"

Alicia Greene pushed the doorbell again, then adjusted her low-cut top so the only way Rick Clark could miss her cleavage was if he had suddenly gone as blind as his bomb-sniffing dog.

The dog had never liked her. And the feeling was mutual. But was a mere dog going to deter her from her mission?

Not!

She'd deal with the dog. Even if it meant keeping doggie treats in her pocket, and shoving one in the mutt's mouth every time Simon growled at her.

Still, winning Rick over wasn't going to be easy by any stretch of the imagination, and Alicia knew it. Of all the husbands in Woodberry Park, Rick was the husband who had paid her the least attention—something a woman with her looks usually didn't have to worry about.

But he's gorgeous.

On the rebound.

And ripe for the taking.

Alicia smiled to herself.

She was sure Rick had been faithful to Zada, even during their separation. Rick was just that kind of guy— another reason he intrigued her. One look and you knew he was straight-up and honest. So unlike most of the men she'd come in contact with during the course of her life.

But Rick was also one hundred percent male. And no doubt lonely for female company by now.

Lonely.

Available.

And living right across the street!

With Zada out of the way now, she might have a chance.

That would make Jen and Tish regret letting Zada push her out of the loop. After all, Jen and Tish had been her friends first. Well, semi-friends, if you wanted to be technical about it.

Before her nasty divorce from Edward. And before her big settlement made the headlines.

That's when wives started getting nervous around her. And when Jen and Tish had dropped her in favor of just-moved-into-Woodberry-Park Zada.

Alicia frowned.

Zada and her infamous "Housewives' Fantasy Club."

Ex-housewives excluded, of course.

Their club was the talk of the neighborhood.

"Wouldn't you love to listen in?" everyone said.

"Wouldn't you kill to be invited to one of their Fantasy Club meetings?" everyone agreed.

Well, that situation was about to change.

Zada was the *ex*-housewife now.

And I'll be more than happy to fill her empty slot.

Besides, once she and Rick were an item, she'd no longer be the out-of-the-loop divorcée, watching life in the suburbs pass her by from her upstairs bedroom window, the way she'd been doing yesterday.

She'd watched Zada zoom into her driveway; watched Jen and Tish rush over to console her. After they'd declined another invitation from her. This time to a bunko party—the new millennium replacement for bridge. Sorry, but they were taking Zada out to dinner, Jen and Tish had informed her, to console poor Zada after her big day in divorce court.

Snobs!

All of them.

Where were Tish and Jen when she had her day in court?

They certainly hadn't offered to console her. Much less take her out to dinner!

Alicia shook her head. She wasn't even sure why she bothered.

Since her divorce, she'd completely exhausted herself trying to think of ways to keep Jen and Tish from avoiding her. She'd tried to start a book club, with no success. She'd also hosted every type of makeup, home interior, cooking utensil, and jewelry party available.

Have it and they will come.

That's what she'd kept telling herself.

Alicia sighed.

I've had it, all right!

She'd had it with playing nice to get their attention.

I'll give them a reason to notice me.

And I'm standing at his front door right now!

She'd come up with her new Seduce-Rick-Clark plan late yesterday evening when she'd noticed all of the frantic activity going on at the Clark house. All of the running back and forth to the garage, gathering up box after box of Zada's belongings.

That's when she'd realized what was really going on.

That Rick had won the house in the divorce.

That Rick, not Zada, was going to be her neighbor!

She'd been so excited, she'd hardly closed her eyes all night. This morning, Zada's Lexus was missing from its usual place in the driveway, and Rick's Hummer had taken its place. This was the reason she was standing at Rick's front door now.

The proverbial early bird, worming my way into the Housewives' Fantasy Club.

The front door opened.

Alicia snapped to attention.

Rick seemed surprised to see her, but he smiled.

"Hi, Alicia," he said. "Is there something I can do for you?"

Alicia smiled back.

Her best femme fatale smile, to be exact.

"Actually, Rick," she said, "I came over to see if there was anything *I* could do for *you*."

Zada's dark brown eyes narrowed.

Alicia's breathy voice always made her gag.

Simon growled in agreement.

She'd clipped the leash to Simon's collar and headed out of the kitchen after Rick left to answer the door. But she'd come to a screeching halt in the foyer when she heard Alicia's voice.

What the hell is she doing here?

Friends, they weren't.

Alicia had always blamed her for breaking up the friendship Alicia had with Jen and Tish before she moved to Woodberry Park, which was absolutely ridiculous. She'd had nothing to do whatsoever with Jen and Tish's decision to avoid Alicia whenever possible.

After her divorce, Alicia simply no longer fit into the suburban couples scene. Add that to the fact that men couldn't keep from falling all over themselves in Alicia's presence, and it didn't take a genius to figure out why the former Alicia Carlton—now Alicia Greene—was *not* at the top of Woodberry Park's married couple guest list.

Or as Tish put it, "Alicia Greene is what you'd get if you put Anna Nicole Smith and Pamela Anderson in a blender. Except with ten times the class. Old family money. And a freaking MBA from Harvard."

In other words, every wife's nightmare.

The nightmare said, "I couldn't help but notice Jen and Tish coming over to help Zada pack up all her things from the garage last night. That's when I realized you got the house in the divorce."

Dammit!

You just implicated Jen and Tish.

I didn't want Rick to know they were here last night!

"I know how devastating a divorce can be, Rick," she gushed on, sugar dripping from every word.

Zada rolled her eyes.

Please.

Taking your wealthy neurosurgeon ex-husband for a cool two million dollars does NOT *qualify as devastating!*

"That's why I wanted to be the first one to welcome you back home. After all," she said, her flirty little giggle echoing through the foyer, "you and I are the minority here in happily-ever-after land, you know."

You're about to be the first FATALITY here in happily-ever-after land!

"If you ever need to talk to someone who's already gone through what you're going through now," she said, "don't forget I'm right across the street."

I'm sure you'll remind him on a daily basis!

"And for you, Rick," she added, her voice low and sexy, "I'll always be available. Any time. Day or *night*."

Can the woman be any more obvious?

She's a man-eater, you idiot.

Surely you can see that!

"That's really sweet of you, Alicia," the idiot had the nerve to say. "Thanks a lot. I appreciate the offer."

Alicia?

Sweet?

That does it!

Zada marched forward, pulling Simon with her. Simon growled again when they reached the door. She didn't know who looked more startled—Rick or Alicia. But Zada definitely knew who she wanted to strangle. It *wasn't* the blond bombshell with the low-cut top that showed everything but the nipples of her (all *real*, dammit) 38DD!

Rick said, "Alicia just came by to . . ."

"I heard," Zada said.

She reached out . . . and *slam!* went the front door, right in Alicia's supermodel-perfect smirking face.

Rick's mouth dropped open in shock.

He looked at the closed door, then back at Zada.

"That was rude," he said, frowning at her. "Everyone knows you can be ornery as hell when you want to be, Zada, but I've never known you to be rude before."

"And I've never known you to have amnesia before," Zada said right back. "We had an agreement, Rick. No other women in *my* house. Remember that conversation?"

"*My* house," Rick corrected. "And if I decide to take Alicia up on her offer, I'll do what you said you'd do. We'll hang out over at *her* place."

His smirk said he knew he'd just made a major coup, throwing her own words back in her face like that. Even worse, the twinkle in his damn blue eyes said he was loving every minute of it.

Damn. Damn. Damn.

Paybacks are such unequivocal bitches!

"Why don't you hang out over at Alicia's place *permanently?*" Zada told him, refusing to be outdone. "You'd save us both a lot of trouble."

"Nah," Rick said, grinning at her now. "I think I'll stick around here. It's good to be back *home.*"

"Enjoy it while you can," Zada warned him. "You're the one who's going to be leaving soon. *I'm* not going anywhere."

"Oh, I'm not I going anywhere, either," Rick vowed. "Except to take Simon on his morning *walk.*" He held his hand out for the leash. "You were right about consistency being one of my golden rules," he added. He was even smart enough to drop the irritating grin. "We shouldn't confuse Simon by changing his routine."

Zada handed the leash right over. She didn't even put up a fight. But the perplexed look on Rick's face?

Almost worth giving in.

"Thanks," he said.

He sent another suspicious look back over his shoulder as he led Simon out of the foyer toward the kitchen and the nearest route to the jogging trail—a look that said he was still waiting for her to change her mind.

Zada was waiting, too.

Waiting for Rick and Simon to leave.

The back door opened.

The back door closed.

Zada hit the *front* door running.

She had a more important agenda bleeping on her radar.

Mayday Mayday.

Desperate Housewife to Bombshell Control.

Simon's morning walk was the least of Zada's worries.

Chapter 6

—————◆—————

"Alicia, wait!"

Alicia turned around when Zada yelled.

She was already walking up the steps to the most expensive home in Woodberry Park. The house was a sprawling Tudor-style manor, with more money tied up in the landscaping than Zada had made on her last book.

Short of money—or cramped for space—Miss Right-Across-the-Street *wasn't*. Nor was Alicia lacking in the men-magnet department. Namely, thirty-eight, twenty-four, thirty-six.

Zada squared her shoulders and started across the street, but it was Angie's warning about Rick knowing the one thing that would make her walk out and never look back, that put urgency in her step. She didn't like to think about Rick with any woman. But Rick romancing Alicia right under her nose was another story.

Angie was right.

I'd never survive it.

I'd walk out the door and never look back.

Her only choice was to win Alicia over to her side be-

fore things got out of control. Before Rick realized what
an excellent weapon Alicia would be to use against her.

I can do this, Zada assured herself.

She made her way up the expensive flagstone walkway.

Alicia was standing at the top of the stone steps now,
hands on her hips, and an icy glare that threatened to
make frost of the early morning dew.

Zada marched up the porch steps anyway.

Be nice. Be nice. Be nice.

Even if it kills me, I have to be nice.

"I was rude, Alicia," Zada said when she stepped onto
the porch. "I came to apologize."

Alicia looked her up and down. "You were *extremely*
rude," she corrected.

"Oh, don't push it, Alicia," Zada said, forgetting all
about her be-nice speech. "How did you expect me to
react? You were trying to *seduce* my husband!"

Alicia's eyebrow arched. "Don't you mean *ex*-husband."

"No, I mean *husband,*" Zada assured her. But she added,
after a long sigh, "At least for the next ninety days."

"Well, excuse me," Alicia snipped. "I thought your divorce was final yesterday."

"Look, Alicia," Zada said, "I'm in a real sticky situation
where Rick is concerned right now, and I need your help.
Until we're divorced, I'm asking you woman to woman to
stay on your side of the street. I'm serious, Alicia. Will
you do that for me?"

Up came the eyebrow again.

"Maybe," Alicia said. "If you tell me what's really
going on."

Common sense warned Zada Alicia couldn't be trusted.

But desperation whispered: Keep your enemies close. Zada opted for the latter.

A quick two-minute rundown later, Zada said, "So that's the whole story. Now do you see why I'm asking that you not make the situation any more complicated than it already is?"

Alicia's pink-painted lips curved in a catty smile.

"I'm not stupid, Zada," she said. "If you really wanted Rick out of the picture, you'd be delighted I was in the mood to take him off your hands. You're obviously not through with him, yet. And even if you were, we both know the last person you'd want Rick to end up with is *me*."

Busted.

But Zada said, "Be careful, Alicia, I can go from zero to bitch as fast as you can."

Alicia smiled again.

Hiss-like this time.

"I don't doubt that for a minute," Alicia said.

Zada said, "So, what's it going to be, Alicia? Are you willing to back off, or aren't you?"

Alicia said, "I could be persuaded to back off. *If* you'll tell me the truth about something else."

"Name it," Zada said.

"Tell me what really goes on at your Housewives' Fantasy Club meetings."

What?

Zada laughed.

It had all started over a silly conversation they were having with the guys about why men couldn't just tell the truth about whether or not a woman's butt looked fat in whatever she was wearing.

"You can't *handle* the truth," Rick had joked, doing his best Jack Nicholson imitation from *A Few Good Men*.

"I agree," Zada had said, laughing. "Forget the truth. Give me a fairy godmother!"

After that, the guys had started calling them the Housewives' Fantasy Club, teasing them that *only* a fairy godmother could ever make their butts look skinny enough to suit them. Zada, Jen, and Tish had laughed themselves silly over the outrageous rumors that quickly spread through Woodberry Park after the nickname got out—everyone putting their own twist on the true meaning behind why they were called the Housewives' Fantasy Club.

But Zada wasn't going to admit that.

Not to Alicia any-time-day-or-night Greene!

"Well?" Alicia said.

"What do you think goes on, Alicia?" Zada asked.

The catty smile was back.

"What do I think personally?" Alicia asked.

Zada nodded.

"Nothing," Alicia said smugly. "Absolutely nothing."

Busted. Again.

"You're wrong," Zada lied.

Alicia tossed her shimmering (*naturally* blond, dammit) hair over one tanned shoulder. "Then the rumors about the three of you sharing your sexual fantasies are true?"

Zada only nodded. The foot in her mouth wouldn't let her speak.

Alicia said, "Invite me to your meeting tonight and prove it."

Life's a bitch.

Then it has puppies!

"I can't do that," Zada said.

Alicia looked pointedly at Zada's house.

Zada frowned.

"No invitation," Alicia said, "no backing off."

Zada was tempted to give in, but only for a second.

Invite Alicia so she can expose us as frauds?

Not one of my fairy godmother wishes!

"Maybe you're right," Zada lied. "I should be glad you're in the mood to take Rick off my hands. Go for it, Alicia. You'll be saving me a lot of trouble."

Zada whirled around and started down the steps.

"You make a lousy liar, Zada," Alicia called after her.

Frack!

Zada didn't even bother calling out an answer. Fists clenched, she stomped back across the street. And she cursed desperation with every step she took.

Unleashing Alicia on Rick was just plain stupid!

Alicia waited until Zada was out of sight before she went inside the house. The second she closed the door behind her, Alicia did a wild Snoopy dance all around her foyer. Her dancing came to a screeching halt when she looked up and saw her cleaning lady, who was standing at the top of the stairway, staring at her as if Alicia had suddenly gone mad.

"Is there a problem, Roberta?"

Roberta shook her head, then went about her business.

To hell with Roberta!

Let the woman think she was crazy. Alicia was too excited to care. She wasn't interested in Rick Clark. Never had been. Rick had only been the means to an end. The end of her being treated like the piranha of Woodberry Park.

Alicia smiled to herself.

All she had to do now was make Zada *think* she was pursuing Rick. Within the week, she'd have that invitation. Most likely served up on a freaking silver platter!

And what a relief not having to throw herself at Rick. Rick had been cordial enough to her, sure, but Alicia knew he wasn't interested.

Alicia laughed out loud.

It was the first time in her life another woman seeing her as a threat might actually work to her advantage.

And women had always seen her as a threat.

Or as her twin brother Alfie had told her more than once, "Face it, sis. All you have to do to piss other women off is walk into the room."

Well, dammit, she was tired of women acting pissed off. And even more tired of getting pissed on! Her famous ex-husband quickly came to mind. What a laugh her marriage to Edward Carlton had been. Except "tragic" was a better word.

And as for her big two-million-dollar settlement?

Nothing but Edward's hush money.

As if she had any interest in telling the world she'd caught the charming neurosurgeon—not with another woman—but going at it with their twenty-something Latino pool guy!

She'd accepted the money only because she'd known how Edward agonized over parting with a penny. And though his betrayal screamed for revenge far exceeding a measly two million dollars, she was simply a better person than he.

What Edward had done to her was unforgivable, but he was still a gifted neurosurgeon who saved people's lives daily. Even her own wounded pride and her shattered faith in men, didn't, in her opinion, justify ruining his career.

She had to believe Edward would get what was coming to him in his own good time. She just hoped she lived long enough to see it happen.

Alicia sighed.

The brunt of everyone's joke; that's what she'd always been. Too smart. Too pretty. Too rich to fit in. And obviously too stupid to realize Edward was gay.

Well, dammit, she was over it! It was time she stopped feeling sorry for herself, and took control of her life.

Too menacing NOT to be included!

From here on out, this was going to be her new motto!

Rick looked up to see Charlie Marshall and Joe Jones heading down the path in his direction. Simon's head came up instinctively when Rick stopped walking, his nose sniffing the air. The dog wagged his tail when he picked up the scent.

When Charlie and Joe walked up and stopped in front of them, Charlie said, "Good to have you back, Rick. How does it feel to be home?"

"Ask me later," Rick said, "after I haul all of Zada's junk out of the living room and back to the garage."

He shook hands with Charlie first.

Then with Joe.

That people often mistook them for brothers when they were together, was understandable. They were both around six feet tall, both had dark hair, dark eyes. Like him, they both worked out regularly and kept in shape.

The three of them had formed an instant bond from the first day he and Zada moved to Woodberry Park. It had been the same for the wives—best friends on sight.

Charlie said, "Yeah, I heard about Zada's welcome home present."

"What present?" asked Joe.

Charlie looked at Joe. "Didn't Tish tell you?"

Joe shook his head. "Tish gave me a rundown about the whole *Survivor* scenario, but it was late when I got home last night. She didn't mention any present."

Rick said, "The girls trashed the living room last night. Zada's way of letting me know what I'm facing if I try to stick it out over the next ninety days."

"Jen didn't help," Charlie was quick to say. "Jen was there, but she tried to talk Zada and Tish out of trashing the living room."

Joe looked at Rick in shock. "Tish really helped Zada trash your living room?"

Rick shrugged. "Hey. Don't worry about it. No real damage was done."

Joe frowned. "I'll do more than worry about it," he said. "If Tish helped trash the place, I'll make sure Tish helps clean up the mess."

Charlie said, "Why clean it up?"

Rick and Joe both looked at him.

"Forget I said that," Charlie said quickly, glancing over his shoulder for a second. He looked back at Rick. "Jen has already given me strict instructions we're not taking sides in this game you and Zada are playing."

"But?" Joe asked.

Charlie sent another nervous look behind him.

"But," he said, after he was sure the coast was clear, "if I were you, Rick, I'd beat Zada at her own game. If you clean up the mess, she'll only make another one. I say, leave the mess. Show her you're not playing into her hands."

Rick said, "Good point."

"Or," Joe said, grinning, "fight fire with fire and do a little trashing of your own. Zada isn't the only one capable of making a mess. She wants messy, I say give the lady what the lady wants."

Rick cringed at the thought.

Charlie burst out laughing.

"What?" Rick demanded.

"Sorry," Charlie said. "I was just trying to imagine you neatly organizing the mess you were trying to make."

"I'm not that anal," Rick grumbled.

"Yes you are," Charlie and Joe said at the same time.

"Okay, dammit, maybe I am," Rick admitted, "but I didn't move home to lose this bet to Zada. I came home to win."

"Damn right," said Joe.

"That's the spirit, soldier," Charlie said.

"*After* we play eighteen holes," Joe threw in. "We have a tee-time in an hour. Zada told us where you were. That's when we came to find you."

"You saw Zada?"

"Briefly," Charlie said. "She was coming back across the street from Alicia's house."

Rick laughed.

"What's so funny?" Joe asked.

Tongue in cheek, Rick said, "Alicia dropped by to wel-

come me back home this morning, and to offer me—
Well, let's just say she made it a point to let me know she
was available for anything I needed. Day or night. Zada
slammed the door in her face. I hope she went over to
apologize."

Joe let out a low whistle. "Wow. I don't even want to
think about what Tish would have done. But apologizing
isn't one of them."

"Even Jen wouldn't have taken a welcome home visit
from Alicia in stride," Charlie admitted.

"Women," Rick said, shaking his head. "One hundred
percent comprehendable-proof."

"Which is why we should stick to playing golf instead
of trying to figure them out," Joe said.

"I bet Simon agrees with that statement," Charlie said,
bending down to ruffle the dog's fur. "Don't you, boy?"

Simon's bark was affirmative.

"Good boy," Rick said. "Let's go home and get my golf
clubs."

As they started back toward the house, Charlie said,
"Tell us the truth, Rick. What is your real strategy for
coming up with the *Survivor* game? Do you really want
Zada to move out? Or is the game just a tactic to convince
Zada she should call off the divorce and let you move
back in permanently?"

Good question.

But Rick said, "Zada's too stubborn to call off the
divorce."

"Be fair," Charlie said. "Zada isn't the only stubborn
one."

"True," Rick admitted. "We're both too stubborn for our
own good. Which is exactly why we can't live together."

Joe spoke up. "You and Zada could live together if you joined leagues with the rest of us husbands and used the magic phrase all us married men rely on to keep the little woman happy."

Rick laughed. "What magic phrase?"

"'Whatever you say, dear,'" Joe told him.

Rick shook his head. "Sorry. I'm not a whatever-you-say-dear kind of guy."

"Like your dad, you mean?" Charlie asked.

Rick said, "What does my dad have to do with this?"

"Just an observation," Charlie said. "You told me once your dad always gave the orders and you and your mom always followed them to the letter. I hate to burst your bubble, Rick, but your mom came from a different generation. Today's woman is better at giving orders than she is at taking them."

"And that's when you appease her with the magic phrase," Joe said. "Then you go about your business and basically do whatever you want."

Rick sent them both a puzzled look.

"But that seems so . . . so dishonest," he said.

"I'm not saying honesty doesn't play a major role in marriage," Joe said. "It does. Just reserve honesty for the big stuff. Like your commitment to the marriage."

"And fidelity," Charlie threw in.

Joe nodded. "Use the magic phrase for those little day-to-day battles that really don't matter one way or another."

"That's just it," Rick argued. "There are no *little* battles where Zada and I are concerned."

"That's because you haven't figured out you have to be man enough to use the magic phrase," Joe said.

Man enough?

Or dishonest enough?

Rick wasn't sure.

But as they continued walking back toward the house, Rick had already decided he would file Joe and Charlie's out-mess suggestion in his strategy file for future reference. Unfortunately, even if he could force himself to ignore the mess in the living room, he would never be able to out-mess Zada. And whether his friends believed it or not, once Zada filed for the divorce, it had become way too late for the friggin' magic phrase.

Besides, he had his own idea for the type of challenge Zada wouldn't be able to survive.

Out-tease. Out-tempt. Out-tantalize.

Zada could deny any chemistry still existed between them if she wanted, but he intended to prove she was lying.

Turning up the sensuality meter a few notches was bound to send Zada running to safety. And in his way of thinking, the sooner she ran, the better. The madness over the last six months hadn't been productive for either of them.

It was time to settle the property dispute. Time for both of them to get on with their lives, even if it meant going their separate ways.

"I give up. You win."

That was the *only* magic phrase Rick was interested in hearing at this stage of the game.

Jen, Tish, and Zada stood at Tish's kitchen window, watching as the guys placed their golf bags into the back of Joe's four-seat golf cart that was sitting in Tish's driveway.

Within seconds, all three of them were scuffling over who was going to drive the cart.

"Isn't that cute?" Tish said. "They're having a Larry, Moe, and Curly moment."

Joe finally won the scuffle and slid behind the wheel.

Charlie jumped in beside him.

Rick hopped onto the backseat.

But as they drove off, Rick glanced up at the window for a second and looked directly at Zada. He had the nerve to send her a big smile and a friendly little wave.

"Zada!" Jen scolded.

"I waved back," Zada said in her own defense.

"Try using *all* of your fingers next time," said Jen.

"I can't help it," Zada said, turning away from the window. "I'm wicked pissed at Rick right now."

Tish looked at Jen.

Jen looked at Tish.

They both followed Zada across the room.

When Zada sat down at Tish's kitchen table, Tish said, "You're wicked pissed at Rick as opposed to say—the last six months?"

Zada let out a long get-this-over-with sigh.

Damn Rick and his hanging-out-at-her-place rotten hide!

"I have something to tell you," Zada said.

Neither Jen or Tish said a word after Zada finished telling them about Alicia's visit that morning.

Ten seconds.

Fifteen seconds.

Zada couldn't take the silence any longer.

"Well, at least yell at me or something," Zada wailed. She looked at Tish, then back at Jen. "You think I don't already know that inviting *Pubic* Enemy Number One to go after Rick takes first place on the stupid human tricks top-ten list?"

"You aren't stupid, Zada," Tish said, "you're just hard of thinking sometimes."

Jen said, "See? I told both of you when the rumors started, we should tell everyone the truth. I can't believe you talked me into letting everyone think we actually sit around and discuss our sexual fantasies on Saturday night."

Zada said, "Well, I was certainly tempted to invite Alicia over to share sexual fantasies with the infamous Housewives' Fantasy Club. Especially when she said we were nothing but boring housewives who were so clueless we wouldn't know a fantasy if it walked up and pinched us on the ass."

Jen's mouth dropped open. "Alicia said that?"

"She didn't have to say it," Zada said. "The smug look on her face said it for her."

Jen said, "Well, thank God you didn't invite her over to share any fantasies! I have no intention whatsoever of sharing sexual fantasies with the likes of Alicia Greene."

"Nor do I," Zada said and sighed. "The only sexual fantasies I'm having right now are of the Lorena Bobbitt variety."

"I'll swap sexual fantasies with Alicia," Tish said.

The room fell as silent as an old maid's bedroom.

Zada sent Tish a look that said, *Now, you tell me!*

Jen sent Tish a look that said, *Who are you?*

"I don't know about the two of you," Tish said, "but I intend to go to my grave without admitting all we do on Saturday night while the guys play poker, is sit around stuffing our faces with appetizers, drinking wine, and moaning about what the guys are or aren't doing to piss us off. I vote for keeping our hot and spicy reputation. It sure beats bland and boring."

"This isn't a freaking cook-off, Tish!" Jen yelled.

Unruffled, Tish said, "Oh, please. I'm sure even you have at least one sexual fantasy, Jen."

Jen's hands flew to her hips. "What do you mean *even* me? I'll match my sexual fantasy against your sexual fantasy any day of the week, Tish Jones."

Zada said, "If I'd known how eager you two are to share sexual fantasies, I would have invited Alicia over tonight!"

Jen said, "I was only trying to make a point. Whatever my sexual fantasies are, I am *not* interested in playing super-nympho for Alicia *or* for Tish." She glared back at Tish. "Got it, Miss Suddenly-Turned-X-rated?"

Tish grinned. "Sticks and stones may break my bones, Jen, but whips and chains excite me."

Jen paled.

"I'm *kidding*," Tish said, laughing.

Zada looked at Tish and said, "For my sake, I hope you aren't kidding. If Alicia does decide to go after Rick in a big way, I might be begging you to share your sexual fantasies with her."

"Sounds like fun to me," Tish said.

Not me, Zada thought.

Sharing sexual fantasies would be torture for her.

Rick, sleeping at the end of the hallway.

Wearing nothing but naked—Rick always slept nude.

His hard, lean body sprawled across the bed.

The bedsheet kicked off as usual.

His legs splayed just enough to be dangerous.

What she *didn't* need to think about in full view.

Arousing her.

Teasing her.

Mocking her with heated memories.

Warning her of cold regrets.

"You know," Tish said, "just in case we do have to invite Alicia over to save poor Rick from her greedy clutches, maybe we should practice sharing our fantasies tonight while the guys play poker."

"No!" Zada and Jen said at the same time.

"Why not?" Tish argued. "This boring cul-de-sac of ours could use some spicing up, if you ask me."

"I like our boring cul-de-sac just the way it is," Jen said, nose in the air.

"I agree," Zada said. "Boring is definitely the way I need to keep things as long as Rick and I are sleeping under the same roof."

"I'd rethink that, if I were you, Zada," Tish said. "Boring isn't exactly what you need to be with hot and spicy Alicia living right across the street."

Zada didn't answer.

But Tish's point was well taken.

Chapter 7

———●———

Zada looked at herself in the mirror. She was way over-dressed for a walk across the street. But Tish was right; now was *not* the time to turn into a frumpy hausfrau.

Not with Alicia lurking in the shadows.

She adjusted the thin straps of her lime-green satin camisole, then turned around to check out how her butt looked in the low-cut white capris she was wearing. They'd fit perfectly when she bought them, but now they felt a bit snug. Had she gained weight? *Did* her butt look too big?

To hell with it.

I'll never be able to handle the truth!

A few fluffs to her hair later, Zada took a deep breath and opened her bedroom door. As luck would have it, the bedroom door at the opposite end of the hallway opened at the same time. She and Rick stood there for a moment, staring at each other. Each of them waiting for the other one to make the first move.

Zada kept staring at Rick.

Rick kept staring at Zada.

Rick, she noticed, wasn't overdressed. It didn't matter, Zada decided. Rick looked better in a T-shirt and jeans than most men looked in Armani—too damn good. So good, Zada's mind flashed back to that image of him sprawled out naked on the bed.

To hell with that!

She started down the hall.

So did Rick.

They both reached the staircase at the same time.

"Wow," he said, taking in her appearance.

And to hell with you!

Zada ignored his comment and made a sweeping gesture with her hand for Rick to go down the stairs first.

He didn't.

Instead, he said, "You look incredible."

"Don't do this," Zada told him.

"Don't pay you a compliment?"

"Don't act like everything's back to normal because you moved back in."

"If everything were back to normal," Rick said with a teasing grin, "we would have come out of the same bedroom."

Zada stamped her foot. "And don't make comments like that one!"

"Don't say you haven't thought about it, Zada."

"About what?"

"About how hard it's going to be," he said. "The two of us sleeping under the same roof. In separate bedrooms."

Zada's chin came up. "I thought that was the whole point of playing *Survivor*," she said. "A game worthy of the settling the property dispute, didn't you say? Winner takes all?"

"True," he said. "I just didn't realize my first challenge would be waiting for me when I arrived this morning."

"Game on, Rick," Zada reminded him happily.

His eyes instantly changed to brooding-blue mode.

"Game on," he repeated. "But I'll play fair and give you a choice. Do you want your first challenge now? Or do you want it later when we get back from Tish and Joe's?"

Zada laughed. "Later? As in after I've had a few glasses of wine later?" She laughed again. "You wish."

Rick shrugged. "It's your call."

He took a step forward.

Then another.

Zada gulped.

"What do you think you're doing?"

He grinned a sexy grin.

"Challenging your remark that you no longer find me irresistible."

Zada willed herself not to back up. When she didn't, strong arms slid around her waist. He pulled her roughly against him.

Mercy!

He was already hard—willing to prove her a liar.

She was already finding it hard not to let him.

Outwit. Outplay. Outlast.

Outwit. Outplay. Outlast.

His head inched forward.

Zada held her breath.

She kept watching his lips. His teasing, slightly parted lips. Amazing lips that had kissed every inch of her body. Lips that were only inches away from her lips now.

Closer.

Closer.

Closer.

Zada turned her head at the last minute. His hot mouth

found the hollow of her neck, instead. She managed to stifle a moan, but a traitorous shiver of desire outran her. A tingle ransacked her entire body, yelling Rick's name.

"See how challenging I can make this game over the next ninety days?" Rick whispered against her ear. "Are you sure you can survive it?"

"Are you sure *you* can survive it?" Zada eked out between ragged breaths. "You're the one who has to walk across the street with that bulge in your pants."

He held her close for a few more seconds.

Then he released her, and stepped back.

Zada grabbed for the banister, steadying herself.

"Congratulations," Rick said. "Looks like we've both survived our first challenge."

"I intend to survive all of them," Zada told him.

"And I intend to see that you don't," he said.

Without warning, Rick grabbed her shoulders.

The kiss he delivered almost brought Zada to her knees.

"Game on," he said when their lips broke apart.

Rick smiled again and walked down the stairs.

He and his bulge walked right out the door.

Zada walked right back to the bathroom, and splashed cold water on her just *out*-kissed face.

When Zada blew into Tish's kitchen, Tish said, "Hi."

Jen said, "What's wrong with you? You look flushed."

Zada ignored the question and headed straight for the island in the middle of the kitchen and the bottle of pinot sitting on the bar. She poured herself a glass, downed it in one gulp, then poured another glass just as quickly.

"Still wicked pissed?" Tish asked.

Try wicked kissed!

"I don't want to talk about it," Zada said.

Jen didn't try to hide a superior I-told-you-so smile.

"And don't you dare look so pleased," Zada warned Jen.

Jen laughed. "Surely you realized what you'd be facing when Rick moved back in, Zada."

Zada drained the glass again.

"No," Tish said, "Zada believed Rick would back out of the bet the second he saw the mess in the living room. Remember?"

"Zada didn't believe that for one minute," said Jen.

"Okay, okay," Zada said. "I didn't stop to think how hard it would be when Rick moved back in. He threw down the gauntlet and I couldn't ignore it. I should have realized he'd go right back to his old tricks. Always using sex to get the better of me."

"Rick propositioned you?" Jen asked.

"He might as well have," Zada fumed. "He waylaid me on the staircase and kissed me silly. My first challenge, he called it."

Jen shook her head. "Why you two would rather play silly games with each other, than admit you aren't ready to give up on your marriage, is beyond me."

Zada sent her a suspicious look. "How do you know Rick isn't ready to give up on our marriage? Did he say something to Charlie?"

"Oh, no you don't," Jen said, shaking her finger at Zada. "Charlie and I agreed we are not taking sides. Nor are we carrying messages back and forth between you. If you want to know how Rick feels about your marriage, you'll have to ask him yourself."

"Great idea, Jen," Zada said. "I'll just run down to the

basement right now and interrupt the poker game to find out how Rick feels about our marriage."

"I have a better idea," Tish said. "Maybe you should call Rick's bluff. You can make advances toward him, too, you know."

Zada shook her head. "No way. I'd advance myself right into bed with him. I'm not willing to take that chance."

Tish said, "But I thought you were prepared to meet Rick head on, Zada. So you both could have closure."

"That was yesterday," Zada admitted. "When I was talking big and still feeling confident."

"And," Jen threw in, "when you were positive Rick would take one look at the living room and walk right back out the door."

"I thought you and Charlie agreed you were staying out of this," Zada reminded Jen with a don't-rub-it-in frown.

Tish looked at over Jen. "I wouldn't be so smug about Charlie not taking sides, Jen. Joe wasn't happy when he learned Zada had help trashing the house. He couldn't wait to tell me he and Charlie didn't intend to let us women gang up on Rick. Joe said he and Charlie both gave Rick a few suggestions on how to beat Zada at her own game."

Jen frowned. "But I didn't help you trash the house."

Tish said, "No, but you were there. I guess that gave Charlie the excuse he needed to toss out a few suggestions to Rick."

Jen's lips pressed together in a thin line.

"What kind of suggestions?" Zada wanted to know.

Tish laughed. "Like Joe would have told me, even if I'd been stupid enough to ask. Jen might be naïve enough to think guys don't stick together like we women do, but I know better."

Jen said, "So Charlie gave Rick a few suggestions, did he?" She reached for the wine bottle and poured herself a glass of wine.

"Seriously, you two," Zada said, "the last thing I want to do is cause any problems between you and your husbands."

"You aren't causing any problems," Jen was quick to say. "But now that I know where Charlie stands on the issue, you can be sure my days of staying neutral are over."

"Thatta girl," Tish said, grinning. She thought for a second. "I think I have an idea," she said. "An idea that will make Rick back off and put Joe and Charlie in their places. *And* that will add a little sizzle to the dribble we pass off as conversation every Saturday night."

Sizzle?

Yup.

"Sizzle" pretty much described Rick's blistering kiss.

Zada reached for the wine bottle again.

"Maybe I lied," Charlie said. "Maybe it isn't so good to have you back home."

Rick laughed and spread his cards out on the game table. "Read 'em and weep, boys. Read 'em and weep."

"That's the third game you've won in a row," Charlie grumbled.

Rick happily raked the pennies in his direction.

"But don't let it go to your head," Joe said, taking a few puffs from his poker-night cigar. "Charlie and I haven't played much poker since you've been gone. Give us a chance to warm up, and you'll be the one who's weeping."

Rick was surprised. "Why haven't you played since I've been gone?"

"We more or less lost interest," Charlie said. "It wasn't much fun beating Joe every game."

Joe said, "Tell the truth, Charles. You win only when I feel sorry for you and let you win."

"Shut up and deal," said Charlie.

Joe shoved the cigar between his teeth, shuffled the cards, then tossed them around the table. He looked up and smiled when Tish came down the stairs with a platter of their favorite nacho cheese appetizers.

"Thanks, hon," Joe said when she placed the platter on the table. He frowned when she placed the baby monitor on the table beside the appetizers.

"Ah, come on, Tish," Joe protested. "How can I concentrate on the game if I'm glancing at the twins every few minutes?"

Tish folded her arms across her chest. "The same way I concentrate on everything I have to do around here and keep up with the twins when you're traveling all week."

Rick looked up from his cards. The monitor screen showed the twins' bedroom. They were sitting on the floor, controls in hand, a video game on their TV screen.

"I'm getting ready to go up now and tell them lights out," Tish said. "And I'm depending on you to make sure they stay in bed after I tuck them in."

"Okay, okay," Joe grumbled.

"And keep the monitor on," Tish ordered. "No just checking on them every now and then."

"Whatever you say, dear," Joe said.

Tish disappeared back up the stairs.

Joe reached over and switched off the monitor.

"See how well the magic phrase works?" he said, grinning over at Rick. "Agree with your wife. Then do exactly what you want."

"But shouldn't you leave the monitor on?" Rick asked.

Joe snorted. "Hell, no. The twins are eight years old, not infants. This obsession Tish has of watching them every minute is ridiculous. She's made me install cameras all over the damn house."

"She made *us* install cameras all over the house," Charlie corrected. "One in the playroom, after the twins crawled out the upstairs window onto the roof last year. One in their bathroom a few months ago, after they stuffed a pillow in the toilet and flooded the entire upstairs. And the most recent one was last weekend in the kitchen, after the twins decided microwaving the hamster might be a fun thing to do."

Joe frowned. "The twins were only trying to *cremate* the hamster," Joe corrected, "so they could keep Wuzzy's ashes in their room. And that's Tish's fault for explaining cremation to them in the first place, and for keeping her favorite aunt Ida's ashes in that urn on the mantel."

Rick couldn't help but laugh.

So did Charlie.

"God, I'm glad I have a daughter," Charlie said.

Joe grinned. "I'll remind you of that in a few years when one of the twins shows up to take Sonya out on a date."

Rick really laughed that time.

Charlie didn't.

"Enough about the twins," Joe said. "Are we playing

poker? Or are we going to sit around gossiping like the girls are doing upstairs?"

Charlie said, "And I guess you already know who they're gossiping about tonight."

Joe looked at Rick.

Rick looked at Joe.

They both looked back at Charlie.

"Alicia," Charlie said, looking at Joe. "Didn't Tish tell you?"

"No, Tish didn't tell me," Joe said. "And I wish you'd stop pointing that out. Tish only tells me what Tish wants me to know."

"Not Jen," Charlie boasted. "Jen tells me everything."

"Yeah, well, I'm not in touch with my feminine side the way you are," Joe said. "And just for the record," he added, "I happen to like it that way. There are some things guys are better off *not* knowing."

Rick said, "You mean like why the girls are gossiping about Alicia tonight?" He brought his beer bottle to his lips.

Charlie and his feminine side said, "Alicia asked Zada to invite her over tonight to share sexual fantasies with the Housewives' Fantasy Club."

Rick spewed beer all over the table.

"But Zada refused to invite her," Charlie said. He frowned at Rick, then grabbed a napkin from a stack sitting by the snack tray Tish had brought them and handed it to him. "I guess Zada was still pissed about her coming over to welcome you back to the neighborhood."

Rick took the napkin and started mopping up the beer.

Joe said, "Too bad. I can't think of anything sexier than a bunch of women sitting around sharing their sexual fantasies. That's one conversation I'd sure like to hear."

Rick knocked the whole bottle over this time.

"Geez, Rick," Charlie grumbled. "What's your problem?"

Joe teased, "Yeah, Rick. What's your problem? Other than no sex for six months. Man, I'd shoot myself. It's hard enough going without all week while I'm traveling."

"Yeah, but you make up for it on the weekend," Charlie said.

Joe said, "How do you know?"

Charlie grinned. "Remember? Jen tells me everything."

"Would you drop the sex subject?" Rick said, looking at Charlie. He looked over at Joe. "And aren't you supposed to be keeping an eye on the twins?"

"Whatever you say, dear," Joe joked, and turned the monitor back on.

Except laughter blared through the speaker this time, and it *wasn't* the twins. They all three stared at the monitor screen. It was Jen, Tish, and Zada, sitting around the kitchen table.

"Sorry, wrong channel," Joe said and pushed a button.

The picture changed. They were back to the twins' room again. Both boys were in bed now, the TV off.

Joe looked at the monitor for a second, then back at Rick and Charlie. A sinister grin spread across his face.

"Are you thinking what I'm thinking?"

"Oh, yeah. I'm thinking it," Charlie said.

Rick's blank look said he didn't have a clue.

Joe said, "You told us earlier how you plan to outplay Zada by turning up the sexual tension, Rick. One push of the button on that monitor and you'll have the inside information on what she's planning to do to you."

"No way," Rick said, finally getting it. "There's no way I want any part of eavesdropping on the girls."

"Technically, it wouldn't be eavesdropping," Joe argued. "Technically, I'd only be doing what my lovely wife instructed me to do. Being in charge of the monitor tonight. It's not my fault Tish forgot about the new camera in the kitchen."

Rick said, "Wrong. *Technically* what you'd be doing is called unauthorized surveillance."

"Dammit, Rick," Joe complained, "just once, could you switch off that straight-as-an-arrow side of your brain and be a regular guy like the rest of us?"

Rick flinched.

For the second time in two days a good friend had complained about him not being a *regular* guy.

First, boot-camp mentality.

Now, straight as an arrow?

When Rick didn't answer, Joe switched the channel.

"I'm outta here," Rick threatened.

"Rick's right," Charlie said. "I don't think we should eavesdrop on the girls."

"Then I guess I'll see you both later," Joe told them. "I'm not stupid enough to pass up an opportunity like this one."

Rick pushed his chair back from the table and stood up.

Charlie did the same.

"Do you know how you can tell if a man is ready to have sex?" a voice asked.

Charlie frowned. "Hey! That's Jen talking."

"Yes," another voice said. "He's breathing."

The cackles that followed were deafening.

"And that comment came from Zada," Rick said dryly.

"Maybe you two wimps *should* leave," Joe said, grinning at them. "We wouldn't want your iddy-biddy feelings hurt, now would we?"

Wimps?

I might have a boot-camp mentality.

And I might be straight as an arrow.

But I'm no damn wimp!

Rick looked at Charlie.

Charlie looked at Rick.

They both sat back down.

"Okay," Tish said. "Enough of the man-bashing jokes. It's time the Housewives' Fantasy Club lived up to its reputation. I officially call this meeting to order."

Tish looked at Zada, then back at Jen.

Her bad-girl grin was more than mischievous.

"If I remember right, Jen," she said, "you were the one who said you would match your sexual fantasy against mine any day of the week. Why don't you go first?"

Jen rolled her eyes.

"Isn't that right, Zada?" Tish looked over at Zada. "Didn't you hear Jen say those exact words?"

Zada said, "Yes. Jen said those exact words."

Jen retorted, "Why don't you go first, Tish? Then I'll see if I really can top your fantasy."

"I thought you'd never ask," Tish said and reached into the pocket of the palazzo pants she was wearing.

When she pulled out a sticky note, Jen laughed and said, "Only you would sticky note a fantasy."

Zada lifted her wineglass. "Let's hear it for our beloved Queen of Sticky Notes."

Tish said, "And the Queen of Sticky Notes wants you to sit back, get comfortable, and close your eyes."

Jen said, "Tish wants us to close our eyes so we won't see her blush."

Zada laughed.

Tish said, "Don't be silly. I want you to close your eyes so you can visualize the fantasy better."

Jen closed her eyes.

Zada squeezed her eyes shut tight.

Going in the sexual fantasy direction could backfire, and possibly put her in serious jeopardy. She'd argued that point, but Tish wouldn't listen.

Please, Rick, Zada thought.

Please be asleep when I get home.

"Your back is pressed against the cold marble column in a darkened section of the museum," Tish said, her voice dropping low and sultry. "He has your arms pinned above your head with one hand, while he runs his other hand under your skirt and slowly up your thigh.

"He grins when he finds you aren't wearing any panties, just as he instructed.

"You whisper, 'We can't. Not here.'

"He ignores you and slides his hand between your legs.

"You bite down on your lower lip to keep from crying out as his fingers keep exploring. His hot mouth stays buried against your neck. His fingers grow bolder. Move faster. Probe deeper.

"You finally give in and lose yourself in the moment, unsure of what excites you more—his willingness to pleasure you in public, or the danger of you being caught.

"He increases the tempo.

"You arch your back, pressing harder against his hand.

"The sensation overcomes you, the pleasure enhanced even more as your eyes stay glued to the full-length mirror you're facing on the opposite side of the room.

"The mirror that allows you to see the handsome security guard standing just around the corner. The same security guard who could glance over his shoulder at any second and see the reflection of the two of you, there in the shadows, hidden from view.

"Slowly, the guard turns his head.

"Your breath catches in your throat.

"His eyes meet yours in the mirror.

"You know you should push your lover away, but you don't. You're much too selfish to be cheated. Much too close to fulfillment to care.

"Your breathing becomes faster now.

"Your heart pounds harder.

"Still, the guard keeps watching.

"His lustful look says he knows what you want.

"The smile on his lips dares you to take it.

"Yes. Oh, God. Yes!

"Your head snaps back.

"Your body stiffens.

"Spasm after delicious spasm rocks your entire body.

"Satisfied at last, you look back in the mirror.

"The security guard is gone."

No one said a word for at least a full minute.

"Wow, Tish," Jen finally said. "I don't think there's any

danger of you ever losing your hot-and-spicy reputation. And I take it back. I don't think I can top your fantasy."

Zada said, "I'm still shocked shitless you got all of that on a sticky note."

Tish held up the sticky note. "I used the front and back sides, silly." She turned the note over as proof.

She looked over at Jen. "Okay, Jen," Tish said. "Your turn."

Jen picked up a napkin and pretended to fan herself. "No way," Jen said. "After that performance, I think we need a serious break."

Zada said, "I was thinking more along the lines of a cold shower."

"And a cigarette," Jen said. "And I've never smoked a cigarette in my life."

Chapter 8

---❦---

Rick could use a cold shower, himself. And the fact that Joe and Charlie suddenly seemed to be extremely interested in the cards they had snatched up from the table the second Tish finished her fantasy, suited Rick just fine.

He didn't want to look at them right now, either.

"Well," Charlie finally said.

He didn't expound on "well" what.

"Trust me," Joe said, his eyes still fixed on the cards he was holding. "That security guard was older than dirt, blind as a bat, and he wouldn't have been able to hear an elephant fart if he was standing under its tail. There was never any chance of him catching us."

Rick and Charlie both burst out laughing.

Joe said, "And that's all I'm going to say. The subject is closed."

"I think we should close the subject for good," Rick said. "No more eavesdropping on the girls. I've proved I'm not a wimp. I say we turn the monitor off."

"Wrong," Joe said. "I sat here and took it like a man through Tish's fantasy. Let's see if the two of you are man enough to do the same when Jen and Zada take their turns."

Will Zada take a turn?

It surprised Rick when he realized he wasn't sure. He and Zada had always been so hot for each other, they'd never had time for fantasies. Or maybe fantasies didn't kick in until after you'd been married for a few years.

Married for a few years.

Sadly, something he and Zada would never know.

What if Zada did share a fantasy with the girls? And if, say, Zada's fantasy didn't involve him? Could he take it?

"Jen won't go there," Charlie said with confidence. "So I don't have to worry about whether or not I can't take it."

"Meaning what?" Joe thundered. "That Jen is more sophisticated than Tish?"

"No, I didn't mean that," Charlie started, but his head jerked toward the speaker again.

"It's late," Jen began. "And you finally hear the garage door open, signaling he's home."

"Turn it off," Charlie yelled.

He grabbed for the monitor.

"Over my dead body," Joe said, laughing.

Joe jerked the monitor out of Charlie's reach.

And wasted no time turning up the volume.

Jen said, "You're alone tonight, but he doesn't know that yet. You haven't told him the grandparents are babysitting.

"You slip out of the silky robe you're wearing and walk barefoot through the house, wearing nothing but the skimpy black panties you purchased especially for this occasion.

"Everything else you need is already waiting in the garage. The pail of warm, soapy water. The soft sponges. A fluffy dry towel for later.

"He's still sitting in the car when you open the kitchen door and step into the garage.

"He looks up and sees you.

"His eyes widen as they travel over your bare breasts.

"You let him look for a second, then turn off the light, knowing the full moonlight streaming through the garage windows will be perfect for what you have in mind.

"He starts to open the door.

"The look you give him tells him to stay where he is.

"And he does.

"You dip one of the sponges into the soapy water, then squeeze the sponge over your bare breasts, enjoying the feel of the warm water as it trickles between your breasts and runs down your stomach.

"You enjoy the desire you see in his eyes even more.

"He loosens his tie as you walk toward the car.

"You lean forward and run the sponge, slowly, seductively over the hood of the car.

"He begins unbuttoning his shirt just as slowly.

"You ease yourself onto the hood of the car and lie back, your head turned to face him.

"He smiles as you run the soapy sponge down your neck.

"You move the sponge lower.

"Between your breasts.

"Down past your stomach.

"His eyes stay fixated on the sponge.

"You spread your legs wide.

"You move the sponge even lower.

"You hear him moan from inside the car.

"He moans again when you arch your hips and move your body against the sponge.

"Slowly, at first.

"But his enjoyment at watching you increases your tempo.

"Faster.

"Faster.

"Faster.

"The sensation finally overtakes you.

"Your eyes meet as you shudder with pleasure.

"He smiles and opens the car door.

"This time, you don't try to stop him.

"He's beside you in an instant.

"He grabs you by the ankles and pulls you forward.

"You gasp as your wet body slides across the hood.

"A hot, hungry kiss covers your mouth.

"A forceful tug rips off your panties.

"He unzips his pants.

"Grabs your hips.

"And plunges deliciously deep . . ."

"Jesus, that's enough!"

Charlie grabbed the monitor and turned it off.

"Holy shit," Joe said. "I know exactly when that happened. I came over the next morning and you gave me some lame excuse about why you didn't finish washing your car."

"No comment," Charlie mumbled.

Rick frowned. "Now do you see why this wasn't a good idea?"

"That's easy for you to say," Charlie said. "You're off the hook now."

"And not a moment too soon," Rick agreed.

Joe shrugged. "Oh, well," he said. "I guess it doesn't hurt to have one wimp in a group of real men."

He was clearly trying to piss Rick off.

It worked.

"I am *not* a wimp," Rick said. "I didn't turn the monitor off. Charlie did."

"Does that mean you're ready to face the music like we did?" Joe challenged.

"Whatever," Rick said with disgust. "Turn the monitor back on, or leave it off. It doesn't matter to me."

Joe took him at his word and turned the monitor back on.

In time to hear Tish say, "Okay, Zada. Your turn."

"I'll pass," Zada said.

Hallelujah!

There is a God!

Tish said, "Not acceptable, Zada. We've told you ours. Now, you tell us yours."

"Okay, okay," Zada groaned.

Okay?

Rick gulped.

"I do have one Rick-inspired fantasy I'll share."

Really?

Rick-inspired, did you say?

Zada said, "Remember that Halloween party we had last year?"

"I know exactly where you're going with this," Tish spoke up. "Rick wore that Zorro costume. Right?"

"Right," Zada said.

Charlie and Joe laughed.

"Shut up," Rick said. He leaned closer to the monitor. "I want to hear this."

"Of course you do," Joe said, laughing. "Now that you know Zada's fantasy is all about you."

Zada said, "You awake from a deep sleep, sensing someone else is in the room.

"You sit up in bed, clutching the sheet to your breast.

"As your eyes slowly adjust to the darkness of your bedroom, you tense.

"There. In the shadows. You see the silhouette of a man, dressed all in black.

"Black hat.

"Black shirt.

"Black cape.

"Sinister black mask, hiding his face.

"He moves toward the bed.

"You want to cry out, but you don't.

"Your excitement quickly overrides your fear.

"He stops by the side of your bed.

"Dark blue eyes peer out at you through the mask.

"But the look in his eyes leaves you no doubt what this man has in mind.

"He reaches out and pulls the sheet from between your clutched fingers.

"Slowly. Methodically. Inch after inch, he pulls the sheet down until he has you fully uncovered.

" 'Who are you?' you whisper.

"His only answer is to pull a sword from the sheath tied at his waist.

"The glint of the sharp blade flashes in the darkness.

"A small excited cry escapes your lips.

"His blue eyes never leave your face, but he toys with you.

"Lightly. Seductively. Purposely, he runs the tip of the cold steel in and out between the toes of your right bare foot.

"The sensation is incredible.

"The danger posed by the sharp tip of the blade more of a turn-on than you'd ever imagined.

"Upward the icy blade moves.

"Frightening you, yet tantalizing your tender flesh.

"Upward.

"Along the inside of your right thigh.

"Across your taut abdomen.

"Right up to the valley between your breasts.

" 'Take the top off,' he orders. 'Slowly,' he says. 'We have all night.'

" 'And if I don't?' you ask breathlessly.

" 'I'll take it off for you,' he threatens.

"Your hands shake slightly.

"Your fingers fumble with the buttons.

"Your silky pajama top slides away from your shoulders.

"His gaze travels downward.

"Now, to the lacy, black thong you're wearing.

"His smoldering look says he still isn't satisfied.

"The tip of the sword moves downward.

"Lower.

"Lower.

"Stopping at the strip of fabric between your legs.

"You close your eyes and bite down on your bottom lip.

"The thong is the only thing protecting the most intimate part of your body from the razor-sharp steel.

"The danger of it makes you shiver.

"The feel of the sharp tip tracing the intricate patterns on the see-through lace takes your breath away.

"You gasp, and open your eyes.

" 'Off,' he commands. 'Slowly.'

"Again, you obey.

"You lift your hips and slide the thong down slowly.

"Down past your thighs.

"Down past your knees.

"Slowly, you slip the thong off both feet.

"When you toss it aside, you're fully exposed, completely naked under his penetrating stare.

"He admires you openly, his lust for you obvious.

"You want to look away.

"But you can't.

"Those dark blue eyes keep holding you captive.

"He lowers the weapon and places the sword on the bed.

"In a low, sexy voice, he whispers, 'You are the slave, I am your master. Always.'

"He takes off the hat and sails it across the room.

"His billowing black cape falls to the floor.

"He pulls the shirt over his head.

"You can't help it, your pulse races at the sight of his bare, muscled chest.

"Your gaze drifts downward to the tight black trousers that fit him like a second skin.

"In anticipation of what's coming next, you lick your parched lips.

"He doesn't disappoint you.

"He steps boldly out of the pants, daring you to look as long as you like.

"You accept the challenge, and stare at him openly.

"The fact that you do, excites him even more.

" 'Lie back on the bed,' he orders, but the urgency in his voice finally betrays him.

"You smile inwardly, knowing the truth.

"*You*, not he, are in complete control now.

"When it comes to sex, he is *your* slave.

"You are *his* master.

"Always.

" 'Leave the mask on,' you command.

"He obeys his master and does as he's told."

" 'Obeys his master' my royal ass!" Rick grumbled. He reached over and switched off the monitor. He looked at Charlie. Then at Joe. "Is that typical Zada? Or is that typical Zada?"

Charlie shrugged sheepishly.

Joe said flatly, "Leave me out of this."

"Can you believe that?" Rick said, talking more to himself than he was to Joe and Charlie. "Zada can't even have a fantasy without making sure I know she's completely in control."

"Whoa!" Joe said. "Zada had no idea you were listening to her fantasy, and don't you forget it. If the girls find out we were eavesdropping on them, we'll all end up in divorce court."

"Amen to that," Charlie said, looking rather nervous.

"I may be anal," Rick said, "but I'm not stupid."

"Keep it that way," Joe said. He looked over at Charlie. "And that goes for you, too, Mr. Jen-Tells-Me-Everything."

Charlie winced. "Hey, don't make me feel any more guilty than I already do." He motioned to Rick, who was sitting there with a forlorn look on his face that matched his own. "Rick feels just as guilty as I do about eavesdropping on the girls. Don't you, Rick?"

Rick didn't answer.

Joe said, "I don't think guilty is what Rick's feeling right now. I think he just figured out that what Zada said is true. When it comes to sex, the woman is always in control."

Charlie looked over at Rick. "You didn't know that?"

Charlie seemed shocked.

"I'm a slow learner, okay?" Rick grumbled. "But Joe's right. I just realized trying to intimidate Zada with sex is like playing a game of Russian roulette with all six bullets in the chamber."

"What kind of game did you say you were playing?"

Rick froze at the sound of Tish's voice. He was glad he was sitting with his back to the stairs; Tish couldn't see the guilty look on his face.

Joe and Charlie weren't as lucky. GUILTY AS SIN might as well have been stamped in big block letters on their foreheads.

Thankfully, Tish didn't seem to notice. Nor did she press an answer to her previous question. Instead, she placed a new snack tray on the table, and removed the empty tray in one simple swoop.

"Joe!" she scolded, glancing over at the monitor. "I told you to keep the monitor on."

She and Joe reached for the monitor at the same time.

Joe was smart enough to knock it to the floor. He finally came up with the monitor, thankfully changed back to the correct channel: The picture on the screen showed the twins, snoozing peacefully in the their bedroom.

"I thought you meant to keep it on until they went to sleep, sweetheart," Joe said, sending Tish a passable *innocent* look.

Tish rolled her eyes and held out her hand.

"Sorry," Joe said, handing over the monitor.

"Men," Tish grumbled as she headed back up the stairs.

Joe eased himself out of his chair and walked to the foot of the stairs. When he was sure Tish was out of hearing range, he looked back at them and said, "Was that a close call? Or was that a close call?"

"What that was, was a great save," Charlie said. "Knocking the monitor on the floor so you could switch the channel back to the twins' room was brilliant."

Rick looked around the room. "Wait a minute. There isn't a camera installed down here, is there?"

"No, thank God," Joe said.

Rick still wasn't convinced. "And you really don't think Tish suspected anything?"

"Not a chance," Joe said with a big grin as he headed back to the table. "If Tish suspected we were listening in on their conversation, she'd still be down here kicking my butt all over this game room."

Charlie said, "And not without good reason."

"Don't get sanctimonious on us now, Charles," Joe said. "No one twisted your arm to stay and listen."

Charlie ignored him and looked over at Rick. "Were you serious, Rick? Are you really thinking about changing your strategy and backing off on turning up the sexual tension?"

Joe said, "Maybe you should rent that Zorro costume before you back off on the sexual tension, Rick. Zada said seeing you in that costume inspired her fantasy. Who knows? Show up as Zorro and she might even forgive you for walking out on her and call off the divorce."

Charlie stared at Rick, waiting for his reply. "Would that even be an option for you, Rick? Would you be willing to give your marriage another chance if Zada agreed to call off the divorce?"

For the second time that day, Charlie had quizzed him about calling off the divorce. Rick decided to ask why. "Has Zada said something to Jen to make you believe she wants to call off the divorce?"

"No," Charlie said with a sigh. "Just wishful thinking on my part."

Rick let out a sigh himself.

He looked back at Joe.

"There's one big problem with your Zorro idea, Joe," he said. "If I show up in Zada's bedroom in the Zorro costume, and she asks how I knew about her fantasy, what do I say? Do I have your and Charlie's permission to confess we were listening on the kids' monitor tonight?"

Joe choked on a nacho.

Charlie turned as pale as a ghost.

"Forget playing Zorro," Charlie said.

Joe snorted. "Like Rick dressing up as Zorro to act out Zada's fantasy was ever going to happen anyway."

Rick frowned. "What's that supposed to mean?"

Joe laughed.

So did Charlie.

"I'm not that straitlaced, you morons," Rick told them.

"Yes you are," the morons said in unison.

* * *

Tish walked back into the kitchen and placed the monitor on the kitchen counter.

"Well?" Zada demanded.

"Mission accomplished," Tish said with a big grin.

Jen glanced at the monitor of the sleeping twins.

"How do you know?" Jen asked.

Tish laughed. "You should have seen their faces when I walked into the basement. Joe almost had a heart attack when I reached for the monitor. I'm sure the big dummy knocked it on the floor only so he could switch the channel back to the boy's room."

Jen said, "That still doesn't prove . . ."

"No?" Tish said, cutting her off. "Then how about me overhearing Rick say he'd just realized that trying to intimidate Zada with sex was like playing a game of Russian roulette with all six bullets in the chamber?"

Zada squealed. "You're a genius!" She hurried over to give Tish a big hug.

Jen wasn't as jubilant. "I can't believe Charlie Marshall sat there and listened in on our conversation."

"Oh, please," Tish said. "Would you really want Charlie to be that emasculated? Would you rather he had come running up the stairs with the monitor to tattle on those bad boys down in the basement who were going to listen to our fantasies?"

Jen didn't answer.

Tish said, "Look, they're all three really great guys, but they're only human. And we set them up. Don't try to tell me we wouldn't have done the same thing if the situation was reversed."

"I might have been tempted," Jen admitted. "But I wouldn't have gone through with it."

"Well, I would have listened, just the way they did," Tish said. "And I sure would have liked to have been a fly on the wall so I could have seen the look on Joe's face when I started describing a scene that was very familiar to him."

"That really was clever of you," Zada said, "suggesting you and Jen should make the boys squirm by describing something private you had done with them in the past."

"Yes, that was pretty clever of me," Tish said grinning. "But you're the one who deserves the applause. Your performance was spectacular."

"Unless Zorro shows up in her bedroom," Jen said.

Zada laughed. "We're talking about Rick, remember?"

"Yes, we are," Jen said. "Rick. The same guy who just let you know that sex was the strategy he was planning to use to win the game."

Zada said, "It doesn't matter. Rick Clark would never dress up as Zorro to fulfill any woman's fantasy. I'm positive about that."

"You hope," Jen said.

"Besides," Zada added, "how would Rick show up as Zorro without exposing all of them for eavesdropping?"

"That's the beauty of this whole situation," Tish said. "The guys won't dare say anything about what they overheard, so we have no explanations to give them and nothing to worry about."

"Which means," Zada said, looking over at Jen, "this is one time you can't go running to Charlie and tell him everything like Tish and I know you always do."

"I do not tell Charlie *everything*," Jen said.

"Yes you do," said Zada and Tish.

"Not this time," Jen vowed. "Charlie drew the line in

the sand when he listened to our conversation. For the next ninety days, it's strictly us against them."

Tish laughed. "Finally, we've converted you. Welcome to the dark side, Jen."

Zada said, "Which reminds me, I need the force to be with me in the morning. Trashing the living room didn't work, but trashing the kitchen will. There's nothing Rick hates more than a messy kitchen. We can do our dirty work around ten. Rick agreed we should keep Simon on his new schedule. When he takes Simon on his morning walk, we'll have a surprise waiting for him when he gets back."

Zada walked back to the table and filled the wine-glasses. After she passed the glasses around, Zada lifted her own in a toast.

"To the dark side of the Housewives' Fantasy Club."

"Hear, hear," Tish said.

Jen clinked her glass against theirs, but she said, "I want you both to understand that I'm only visiting the dark side right now in support of Zada. Don't either of you think for one minute you've finally won me over."

Zada looked at Tish.

Tish looked at Zada.

"Oh, don't kid yourself, Jen," Tish said. "We've defi-nitely won you over to the dark side."

To prove it, Zada lowered her voice to a sultry octave and mocked, "He unzips his pants. Grabs your hips. And plunges deliciously deep inside you, over and over and over again until . . ."

"Okay, okay!" Jen shouted, her face beet-red. "You've made your damn point!"

Chapter 9

———❦———

Zada had purposely waited almost an hour after Rick left Tish and Joe's before she started home herself. It had seemed like a good idea at the time—waiting to give Rick plenty of time to go on to bed, so there would be no risk of him springing another unexpected challenge on her.

She still wasn't convinced Tish's big fantasy-fest idea wasn't going to backfire on her. Even if her slave-and-master fantasy had left Rick cold in the water, that didn't mean her own raging hormones had returned back to normal after the heavy sexual content they'd conjured up for the guys' benefit.

But staying an hour longer meant more glasses of wine.

And more glasses of wine meant . . .

Zada jumped when the door opened before she could use her key.

Rick was standing with his hands at his waist.

Wearing nothing but his boxer briefs.

And an amused look on his face.

Zada swooned slightly. From the sight of his near nakedness, not the wine. She blushed slightly, too, wondering if Rick's amused look had anything to do with her Zorro fantasy.

"You gave me your key yesterday," Rick said. "I was afraid you didn't have one."

Zada held her key up, but she hiccupped when she did it. "'Scuse me," she said, covering her mouth.

She was every bit as tipsy as she sounded, and his right arched eyebrow said Rick knew it. But was his right eyebrow really arched? Or was she just seeing two of him?

Zada closed one eye, trying to decide.

"Did you just wink at me?" Rick said and grinned.

Zada's eye popped back open.

"Get over yourself," she said, and pushed him out of her way.

Zada staggered across the foyer and started up the stairs, mentally thanking whoever it was who invented the banister. Some poor drunk most likely, she decided.

Rick was following so closely behind her, she could feel his warm breath on the back of her neck.

She was almost to the top step. And she would have made it, but Rick reached out and pulled her backward. Zada gasped when she fell against his chest.

"If this is another challenge," she slurred, "you are *not* an honorable man. An honorable man would *not* take advantage of a compromised woman."

"This is not another challenge," he said. "I told you earlier we both survived our challenges today. You'll get your second challenge tomorrow."

So will you.

Bright and early.

Zada said, "And your arms are around me because?"

"Because you missed the step," Rick said. "And I caught you."

He knew it was a lie.

And he knew she knew he knew it was a lie.

Or, whatever.

Zada also knew she should move away, but she didn't. His strong arms felt so good around her. Fantasies were still swirling around in her head. And six months without sex had been a long damn time.

"Do you need any help getting to bed?" he whispered against her hair.

Zada almost laughed.

I need help staying OUT of bed, and you know it.

Damn Tish Jones and her brilliant ideas!

Or maybe this was the time to test Tish's idea.

"Will you be my slave and do exactly as I say?" Zada whispered back.

She felt Rick tense.

Zada smiled.

She'd chosen her words perfectly.

Rick picked her up. And he put her back down in the middle of the hallway, whirling her around until she was facing her own bedroom door.

Whoa!

Way too much motion when the room is already spinning!

Zada wobbled off in the direction of her bedroom, but she stopped before she reached the door. She turned back around. Rick was already at the end of the hallway.

"Where's Simon?" she called out.

He turned back around to face her. "He's in my room,"

Rick said. "I think it's only fair that we take turns keeping him at night."

"Whatever," Zada said, with a pooh-pooh wave.

She was too tipsy to argue.

And smart enough to know it.

She made it inside her bedroom and closed the door behind her. She didn't even take off her clothes before she crawled onto the bed. She was asleep practically by the time her head hit the pillow—with visions of swords, and masks, and one hot naked man in particular dancing happily through her dreams.

On Sunday morning, Zada avoided Rick completely.

She took her time bathing and dressing, then waited patiently in her bedroom until ten o'clock sharp. At precisely ten o'clock, she walked to her upstairs bedroom window and watched Rick and Simon head across the backyard for the walking trail. If there was one thing you could say about Rick, he was always punctual.

And predictable.

Just like him backing off last night.

All she'd had to say was "slave." Just one little word, and he'd dropped her like a hot potato. Not that she wasn't happy about it—that had been the plan, after all. Pushing his "control" button so he'd back off and any threat of them ending up in bed would be over.

Yet, the mind was a difficult thing to turn off.

And watching Rick from her bedroom window now certainly conjured up some very dangerous memories.

Like how great he had looked in that Zorro costume.

Stop it!

Zada shook her head, trying to clear her mind.

It didn't work.

Not while Rick was roughhousing with Simon. Not with his T-shirt riding up every time he threw the beeping sensor ball Rick had developed himself for Simon to chase.

Zada sighed.

Those six-pack abs would make any woman's mouth water.

Any woman?

Or one woman in particular?

Zada stepped closer to the window.

Crap! Crap! Crap!

Alicia had suddenly appeared from out of nowhere.

Zada leaned even closer to get a better look.

Hot pink spandex halter top! Cleavage up to her eyebrows! Pancake-flat stomach! Hot pink freaking running shorts! Mile-long legs, tanned and toned!

Maybe it's time to start a Bimbo Elimination Club!

Except Alicia wasn't a bimbo, which made her even more dangerous.

A low, guttural growl rumbled in Zada's throat. Simon must have reacted the same way because Alicia stepped backward, away from Rick.

"Good boy," Zada said aloud.

But her eyes narrowed when Rick laughed at something Alicia said. And Zada clenched both fists when they walked off together, heading for the walking trail.

Dammit! Dammit! Dammit!

She was one second away from heading after them.

Until the doorbell rang.

Jen and Tish.

Right on schedule.

Zada turned and stomped off to answer the door.

To hell with Rick and Alicia! she decided.

She only had an hour at best before Rick returned. With Jen and Tish helping, an hour should be plenty of time for them do their dirty work.

Tish hurried through the front door first.

Jen was right behind her.

"We've got to make this quick," Tish said. "Joe's tossing the ball around in the backyard with the twins. He doesn't even know I'm gone."

"That goes for me, too," Jen said. "I sent Charlie to pick up Sonya from my parents. But that won't take long."

When Zada didn't answer, they both said, "What's wrong?"

Zada said, "Guess who just showed up half-naked to take a morning walk with Simon and Rick?"

"You've got to be kidding me!" Tish exclaimed.

Zada said, "I'm tempted to forget trashing the kitchen, in favor of pulling Miss Hot Pink's halter top up around her neck and strangling her with it!"

Jen laughed.

It was the wrong thing to do.

"Dammit, Jen, this isn't funny!" Zada wailed.

Jen said, "Sorry. But you're the one who gave Alicia permission to take Rick off your hands."

"I was using reverse psychology, dammit!" Zada argued. "I assumed if Alicia thought I didn't care, she'd back off."

"No," Jen said. "What you were doing was covering your own butt because you told Alicia the big lie about us sharing our sexual fantasies."

"Which, after last night," Tish said brightly, "really isn't a lie now, is it?"

Zada stamped her foot. "This is *not* cheering me up!"

"Sorry," Tish said.

Zada said, "Oh, to hell with it! Forget Alicia. We've got work to do."

They headed down the hall to the kitchen.

Zada screeched to a halt when she reached the door.

The domino effect followed.

Thud. Thud. Oomph.

Tish peered over Zada's shoulder. "Oh. My. God."

All Zada could do was stand there and stare.

The living room was spotless compared to the mess they found waiting for them in the kitchen.

Every cabinet door was open, every drawer pulled out. The sink was stacked high with dishes. An entire bag of her favorite cookies appeared to have been crumbled into a chocolate chip pyramid on the kitchen table. The cushions on the six kitchen chairs had been untied and removed from the chairs. Three cushions were stacked on top of the stove. The other three on top of the refrigerator.

A paper towel banner ran from the paper towel holder, across the valance above the kitchen sink window, back down to the kitchen counter, coming to a draped end over the coffeemaker. Simon's dog bowl was running over with food. The large bag of dog food had been left turned over on the counter, most of the contents spilling onto the kitchen counter tile.

Jen pushed Tish forward. "What's wrong?"

Tish pushed Zada farther into the kitchen.

When Jen stepped into the kitchen, Zada wheeled around to face her. "Let me guess," Zada said. "Your conscience finally got the better of you and you just had to confess everything to Charlie."

"I did not!" Jen said. "I swear," she added, looking around the kitchen in shock. "Charlie and I hardly said two words to each other after we went home last night."

"Joe and I didn't say much, either," Tish said. "But the sex was fabulous."

"Same here," Jen said, cheeks flushing.

"Would you two give me a freaking break already!" Zada wailed. "I am not in the mood for a repeat performance about your fabulous sex lives. I'm in serious trouble here."

"No one had to tell Rick anything," Jen said, stating the obvious. "It only makes sense Rick would realize the kitchen was your next target."

"True," Tish said. "But who would have ever believed Rick Clark could bring himself to make a mess like this one?"

"Not me," Zada said with a sigh.

So much for Rick being predictable.

"So?" Tish said. "What now?"

"Give me a minute, okay?" Zada said, running both hands through her hair. "Can't you see I'm speechless right now?"

Jen said, "I hope this makes you realize how childish you and Rick are being with this whole *Survivor* game, Zada."

Zada sent Jen a well-duh look.

"That isn't a news flash, Jen. Of course, we're being childish. Childish is what Rick and I do best. I've been trying to explain that to you for months. We're not mature enough to be married."

Jen said, "You have to grow up sometime."

"And I will," Zada said. "The minute Rick signs over the house and Simon."

"You're hopeless," Jen said.

Tish said, "So is this kitchen."

"His bedroom!" Zada exclaimed. "Rick might trash the kitchen, but he'd never trash where he sleeps."

"And the madness continues," Jen said with a groan.

Tish hurried out of the kitchen first.

Jen followed.

Zada ran forward, bringing up the rear.

"Too late," Tish called over her shoulder when she opened the guest bedroom door.

Too late?

What the hell do you mean, "too late"?

Zada pushed Tish aside and walked into the bedroom.

The bed was unmade—unbelievable for Rick. Clothes were strewn around the room—also unbelievable for Rick. His bureau drawers were open, socks and underwear hanging from every drawer. The closet door was open, clothes half on the hangers, half off. Even his precious golf clubs were out of the bag. Some were on the bed; others were propped against the wall here and there.

Unfreakingbelieveable!

Zada hurried into the adjoining bath.

Nothing but calamity awaited her there.

She walked back into the bedroom, shaking her head.

"I just can't believe Rick would do this," Zada said.

"Neither can I," Tish said. "I guess this proves how serious Rick is about keeping Simon and the house."

Zada's eyes narrowed.

Jen sent Tish a mean look. "You just had to say that, didn't you? Don't you realize you're only making Zada more determined to continue this nonsense?"

"I'll *show* him serious," Zada vowed.

"So?" Tish said, ignoring Jen's scathing look. "Like I said before. What now?"

Alicia glanced over at Rick as they walked along the trail. Her better judgment told her not to confess to Rick that she really wasn't interested in him. But Rick was in a vulnerable position at the moment; she also didn't want to lead him on.

She decided to test the waters a bit. See if Rick would be interested in a collaboration. Making Zada jealous could benefit both of them.

Alicia said, "You seem nervous, Rick. Are you uncomfortable with me taking a walk with you?"

He looked back over his shoulder for a second.

"A little," he admitted when he turned back around. "Can I ask why?"

He sighed and said, "I made a stupid comment after Zada slammed the door in your face yesterday. I was only trying to get back at her for something she'd said to me."

He stopped walking and faced her. "Look, Alicia," he said, "I don't know any other way to say this. I'm not interested in you personally."

Alicia laughed. "That's the same thing I was getting ready to tell you."

He looked puzzled.

Alicia said, "I didn't know you and Zada weren't divorced when I came over yesterday morning, Rick. And the only reason I came over was because I'm tired of being treated like a leper by the women in this neighborhood."

He still looked puzzled.

Alicia said, "I was hoping if you and I went out occasionally, maybe everyone would stop seeing me as the threatening divorcée waiting to pounce on their husbands."

Rick laughed. "I see," he said.

They started walking again.

"And then Zada rushed over and asked me to back off where you were concerned."

His head jerked in her direction. "Really?"

"I told Zada I'd do her a favor, if she'd do one for me and invite me to join the Housewives' Fantasy Club. The minute it spreads through the neighborhood that Jen, Tish, and Zada have accepted me, I'll be taken off the Woodberry Park blackball list."

Rick said, "But I heard Zada refused to invite you to their meeting."

Alicia said, "Exactly. And that's why I'm strolling down the walking path with you right now."

Rick stopped walking.

The expression on his face said he knew exactly where the conversation was heading.

"Look, Alicia," he said. "I might have teased Zada about you yesterday, but I'm not interested in purposely making her jealous in any way, shape, or form. I wouldn't do that to her. First, because that's not who I am. Second, Zada had a womanizer for a father, and I don't think she's ever gotten over it."

Alicia wasn't ready to give up yet.

"Not even if it means you keeping Simon and the house?"

"No," Rick said. "I know Zada and I are playing games

with each other right now, but that's one game I'm not interested in playing."

Alicia gave in and said, "You're a good guy, Rick. Zada obviously doesn't know you very well or she wouldn't have asked me to back off."

"That's been our problem all along," Rick said. "We should have waited until we knew each other better before we got married."

"I can certainly identify with that statement," Alicia said, but she had no intention of elaborating any further.

Nor did she have any intention of telling Rick, that regardless of his refusal to play her let's-make-Zada-jealous game, she *wasn't* ready to back off yet. She'd accomplished exactly what she'd wanted to accomplish when she saw Rick leave the house and head for the walking trail: She'd let him know exactly where she stood.

She was also willing to bet Rick would never repeat one word of their conversation. Not to Zada. Or anyone else. Rick was just that kind of guy. Straight up and honest.

"Well," Alicia said, confident that her mission was over. "Since I can't persuade you to help me further my cause with an invitation to the Housewives' Fantasy Club, I can at least let you enjoy the rest of your walk in peace."

Rick laughed. "I didn't say you couldn't walk with us, Alicia. I just said I wasn't interested in making Zada jealous."

Simon growled in disagreement.

Alicia jumped back.

"Simon!" Rick scolded, jerking on his leash.

Alicia said, "There's no need to keep scolding poor Simon. Dogs and kids never like me. I think they can sense I'm uncomfortable around them."

"Seriously?" Rick asked.

Alicia nodded. "I was bitten by a dog as a child. And I've never really been around kids."

"I'm an only child, too," Rick said.

"Oh, I'm not an only child," Alicia said. "I have a twin brother. We just have a hypochondriac for a mother. My mother's germ phobia kept us away from other kids. And her allergies prevented us from ever having pets."

Rick said, "You never thought about getting a pet as an adult?"

Alicia laughed and shook her head. "A goldfish, maybe," she told him. "But that would be the only acceptable pet on my list."

Rick's cell phone rang.

Alicia saw her chance.

She waved good-bye and hurried off.

But she couldn't keep from smiling as she walked away. She'd seen Zada watching from the window. Felt those dark-brown daggers aimed at her back.

Too damn bad.

Zada could have completely avoided any angst from her.

All she'd asked Zada for was a simple invitation!

Rick placed his cell phone to his ear when Alicia walked away. Joe didn't waste any time filling him in on the scoop.

"I thought you'd like to know I just watched my wife and Jen go through your front door a few minutes ago."

"Perfect," Rick said. "At least someone's there to call 911. Zada's probably passed out on the floor."

Joe said, "You really went through with it?"

"Yup," Rick said proudly. "The kitchen. The guest bedroom where I'm sleeping. Even the guest bathroom."

"I have to tell you, Rick," Joe said. "I truly didn't think you had it in you, buddy."

That makes two of us.

But Rick said, "Maybe you don't know me as well as you think you do, Joe."

"I'm sure that's what Zada's thinking about now," Joe said and laughed.

"Guaranteed," Rick said.

"What do you think Zada's next move will be?"

Rick said, "We could both avoid going into the living room, but we can't avoid using the kitchen. She might hold out for the rest of today, but Zada will fold by tomorrow and clean up my mess. Then maybe we can sit down like two rational adults, and I can remind her that I'll gladly buy her a place of her own anywhere she wants."

"And you really think she'll accept your offer?"

"No," Rick said. "But I can always hope."

"Hey, the girls are coming back out," Joe said. "Gotta run."

Rick closed his cell phone. He dropped it back into his shorts' pocket. And looked down at Simon.

"I think we'd better extend our walk longer than usual this morning for safety's sake, boy," Rick told the dog. "After the mess I've made and Alicia showing up, we need to give our master plenty of time to calm down before we go back home."

Zada stood watching at the kitchen door.

When she saw Rick and Simon start through the backyard, she jumped back from the door and hurried across the kitchen to the table. When Rick and Simon walked into the kitchen, she was sitting calmly on one of the now cushionless kitchen chairs, thumbing through her latest issue of Oprah's *O* magazine.

From the corner of her eye, she saw Rick bend down and unfasten Simon's leash from his collar. Simon immediately trotted over and placed his big head on the magazine she was holding in her lap.

"Did you have a good walk?" Zada asked sweetly, rubbing Simon's head.

"We had a great walk," Rick said.

I just bet you did! Zada fumed.

But she said, "I was talking to Simon."

"In case you haven't noticed," Rick said, "Simon can't talk. I was answering for him."

"Simon talks to *me* all the time," Zada said in baby talk. "Don't you, my sweet buddy?" She gently stroked the big dog's ears, still never once looking at Rick. And if he thought for one second she would give him the satisfaction of even uttering Alicia's name, he was as crazy as she'd been for egging Alicia on in the first place.

Two seconds.

Five seconds.

Ten seconds.

"Well?" Rick said, just as she knew he would.

Zada finally looked at him. "Well, what?"

"Cut the crap, Zada. Don't you have anything to say?"

"About what?"

Rick's ears turned deep red.

Zada almost laughed out loud.

"About your challenge today," Rick said. "As if you didn't know exactly what I meant."

Zada blinked innocently. "What about it?"

Rick said, "Don't lie and say you weren't shocked that I beat you to the punch and trashed the kitchen before you and your domestic diva buddies could trash it yourselves."

"Do I appear to be shocked?"

"Yes," Rick said. "You appear to be so flipping shocked you can't even carry on a simple conversation."

Zada's face turned red this time.

Rick did laugh out loud.

"And in case you haven't gone upstairs yet," Rick said, "I also beat you to my bedroom and my bathroom."

Zada tossed her hair nonchalantly.

"Then that was your mistake," she told him. "We agreed the bedrooms were off limits."

The look on his face was priceless.

"When did we agree to that?" he boomed.

It was a lie, of course.

But Zada was counting on Rick not remembering the conversation they had in the courthouse hallway word for word. He had, after all, been standing there like a zombie.

"We agreed the bedrooms were off limits while we were arguing over the king-size bed," Zada said with a straight face. "I said flipping a coin for the master bedroom wasn't a topic for discussion. *My* bed, I said. *My* bedroom. And that bedrooms were off limits. You agreed, and said, quite *smugly* if I remember correctly, 'For now.'"

The truth she'd sprinkled in with the lie worked.

"Damn," Rick mumbled under his breath.

"What did you say?" Zada couldn't resist asking.

"Nothing," Rick grumbled. "I didn't say a thing."

He walked out of the kitchen shaking his head.

Zada stuffed a hand in her mouth to keep from laughing.

"Gee, was it something I said then?" she called out as he headed down the hallway.

Simon's ears pricked. He whimpered, then trotted after Rick.

Turncoat, Zada thought. Until she heard the doorbell.

"Don't worry," Rick yelled out. "My legs still aren't broken. I'll get the door."

That better not be Alicia! Zada vowed.

Until she heard the last voice she was expecting.

"You obviously won the house in the divorce, Rick. But what have you done with Zada?"

Zada jumped up from the chair.

Mom!

No! No! No!

Yes, her mother had left a dozen messages on her voice mail since Friday. And yes, she did intend to call her mother back. *After* she figured out a way to explain what had happened in court. A way that would keep her mother and her sister from whispering behind their hands that she was every bit as human as they were, and had taken Rick back.

"Calm down, Nora," she heard Rick say. "Zada's in the kitchen. Go see for yourself."

The kitchen!

This kitchen?

Have you lost your freaking mind?

Nora Thornton breezed into the kitchen before Zada could take the first step forward to stop her. Zada's sister, Sally, breezed in right behind her, dragging her two squirming sons by the hand. The eight-year-old managed to wrangle away from his mother first. The six-year-old quickly followed.

Sally didn't seem to notice the boys had jerked free from her grasp. Neither did Grandma Nora. They were both standing in the middle of Zada's destroyed kitchen, shocked expressions on their faces.

"Boy, were you wrong, Mom," eight-year-old Tommy said, looking around the kitchen. "Me and Timmy could never be as messy as Aunt Zada."

Sally's face flushed.

"Timmy and I," she corrected. She looked back at Zada and shrugged. "Kids."

"Yeah, kids," Zada said, frowning at her sister. "Funny how they only repeat exactly what you *never* should have said."

"This is no time for bickering, you two," Nora scolded.

The boys ran off down the hall calling Simon's name.

"Well?" Nora said, frowning at Zada. "Can I assume a pack of burglars ransacking your house is the reason you haven't returned my calls? You had to know Sally and I have been worried to death about you. The last we heard from you, you were headed off to divorce court."

Before Zada could answer, Nora continued, "And what's Rick doing here if you're here? You did get the house, I hope."

"Not exactly," Zada said.

"You mean Rick got the house?" Nora frowned again. "Then what are you doing here? I thought if Rick got the house, you had to move out immediately."

"Mom," Sally said. "Give Zada a chance to answer."

"I," Zada said. "Well, I mean Rick and I . . ."

Sally's eyebrow came up.

"You see," Zada began again.

"Yes," Sally said with a knowing smile. "I think I do see what's going on here."

Zada said, "Rick and I are not back together, Sally."

"So you are divorced?" Nora asked.

"Not exactly," Zada said.

"Well what *exactly* is going on, Zada?" Nora demanded. "Stop talking in riddles!"

Zada said, "The judge won't grant the divorce until we reach a property settlement."

Nora looked around the kitchen. "So you've decided to do what? Divide everything right down the middle? Including Simon's dog food? Grain for grain?"

"Very funny, Mom," Zada told her. "Rick and I have ninety days to reach a property settlement. Rick moved back in to . . ."

Sally gasped. "What did you say?" She looked at Nora, then back at Zada. "My ears must be playing tricks on me," she said. "*You?* The woman who swore she would *never* let any man move back in if he moved out, let *Rick* move back in?"

"*Temporarily,*" Zada stressed.

Sally laughed. "That's your story and you're sticking to it. Right?"

Zada groped for an answer.

Sally reached out and grabbed Nora's arm.

"Come on, Mom," she said, pulling Nora out of the kitchen. "We know Zada's safe now. Let's give the lovebirds some privacy."

"'Lovebirds'?" Nora repeated. "Oh," she said when she realized what Sally was implying.

Lovebirds?

Lovefreakingbirds!

"Sally, come back here!" Zada yelled.

Zada hurried down the hall after them.

Sally pushed Nora through the open front door.

"Sally!" Zada yelled again.

But Rick stepped out of nowhere, blocking her path.

"Is there a problem?" he asked, grinning at her.

"Yes," Zada said. "I'm looking at it."

She pushed Rick out of her way.

"Get in the car!" she heard Sally yell.

The boys stopped wrestling on the front lawn. They both sprinted for the driveway. Zada reached the minivan just as Sally was backing up. Sally's window slid down before she drove off.

"We're really happy you took Rick back, Zada," Sally called out, waving madly. "Call us in a few days when your second honeymoon is over."

Second honeymoon?

Second honeyfreakingmoon!

Zada was livid.

So livid, she pitched a mad stomping fit, right in the middle of her driveway. She'd never been any more angry, until she glanced over her shoulder.

Rick was walking toward her, grinning from ear to ear.

"Just curious," he said, fishing his keys out of his jeans pocket. "But was that some mystic tribal fertility dance you were doing? You know, for our second honeymoon?"

Zada took a threatening step in his direction.

Rick threw his hands up and stepped back.

"Hey!" he said, still grinning. "I was only kidding."

The look on her face must have scared him.

Rick's grin disappeared.

"Not that you care," he said, his expression serious now. "But I'm going to the training center, and I won't be back until late. We have a new class starting tomorrow morning. I need to help Scrappy get things ready."

Zada didn't answer.

She whirled around.

She stomped down the driveway.

And marched across the street.

Jen caught up with her as she reached Tish's porch.

"Was that Sally's minivan I just saw driving off?"

"No," Zada said. "That was my worst nightmare driving off. Sally *and* Mom. Both of whom Rick happily invited into the kitchen-from-hell to see me, which humiliated me to no end. And then Sally, of course, came to the immediate conclusion I had taken Rick back."

"You poor thing," Jen said as Tish opened her front door. "I'd kill myself if anyone saw my kitchen in such a mess."

"You'd kill yourself if someone found a measly crumb on your kitchen counter," Tish teased.

Her expression turned serious when she looked at Zada.

"What's wrong?"

Zada looked back over her shoulder as the Hummer backed down the driveway. She pointed. "He's what's wrong!"

"Surprise, surprise," Tish said, but she stepped aside.

Zada and Jen walked through the door.

"I'm so angry right now," Zada said, "you may have to bail me out of jail for first-degree murder."

They all three headed for Tish's kitchen.

"Joe and the boys are at the clubhouse pool," Tish said when Zada flopped down at the table. "Take a deep breath. Calm yourself down. And tell us what happened."

Chapter 10

Rick felt like a first-class jerk.

First, for sending Nora and Sally into the kitchen.

Second, for teasing Zada about Sally's assumption.

He knew Zada gave Sally a hard time about her husband. He knew Sally was loving rubbing Zada's nose in the fact she had let him move back in.

But the hurt look on Zada's face had said it all.

He'd crossed the line, embarrassing her in front of her mother and sister.

The realization that he'd hurt Zada by walking out— far more than he'd ever made her angry—hit Rick like being mowed down by a two-ton truck.

He started to turn the Hummer around and go back to apologize. But he knew Zada would never listen. Not right now. Not when she was still so angry at him.

He'd apologize when he got back from the center.

Tell her he was sorry. Ask her to forgive him for being such an ass.

And for being insensitive.

And self-centered.

And most of all, immature.

He hated to admit it, but after the comments his own buddies had been making over the last couple of days, he'd started to realize maybe he wasn't the easiest guy to live with, after all.

Zada had a combative personality, sure.

But so did he.

Which only added more fuel to the raging fire that kept them apart—that burning desire they both had to constantly prove each other wrong.

But was his expectation of marriage really that far-fetched? Was it really so unreasonable to want to be the king of your own castle? To have a wife who loved you in spite of all your flaws?

Charlie had flaws, but he and Jen got along.

Joe and Tish had their differences, and still made it.

Was the magic phrase really the key to married bliss?

His father had never used the magic phrase.

He was positive of it.

And his parents had recently celebrated their fortieth anniversary!

Rick pulled his cell phone from his pocket. First, Nora and Sally showing up, and now thinking about his parents, reminded Rick he also hadn't called them to let them know what was going on. At least he didn't have to worry about his parents showing up the way Nora and Sally had just done. They would never think of showing up on anyone's doorstep without calling first. But then, the relationship Zada had with her mother and her sister had always been a mystery to him.

Rick shook his head.

The three of them were always in a squabble about something, yelling at each other one minute, all hugs and smiles the next. Funny thing was, he also knew they loved each other dearly.

Zada treats me like she treats her mother and sister.

And maybe that was part of the problem.

They'd come from such different family lifestyles. Zada's life had always been nothing but chaos. He was used to life being neat and orderly.

Rick hit the speed dial for his parents' number.

His father had recently retired from the military. For the past year, his parents had been living the good life in Phoenix, Arizona—a place where his father could play golf year round, and the climate kept his mother's asthma at bay. Maybe after the divorce was final, he'd fly out and pay them a visit.

Rick smiled when he heard his mother's sweet voice.

"Hi, Mother," he said. "I should have called you Friday after I went to court, but things have been pretty hectic around here."

Mary Clark said, "I knew you'd call when you were ready to talk about it, Rick. I'm so sorry you and Zada couldn't work things out. You know your father and I adore her."

Rick hesitated before he said, "The divorce isn't final yet, Mother."

"You mean there's a chance you're going to reconsider?"

Rick heard the hope in her voice. False hope was something he didn't want to give her.

"No," Rick said. "I don't think there's any chance of a reconciliation. There are still some problems with the property settlement. But we're trying to work those problems out."

He grimaced at her sigh of disappointment.

"I just wanted to let you know to call me on my cell phone if you need me," Rick said. "I gave up the apartment. That number's already been disconnected." Rick avoided his mother asking where he was staying with another question. "Is Pop around?"

His mother laughed. "Oh, he's around, all right. We're having the patio extended. Your father's out back barking orders to the poor contractor who didn't realize what he was getting into when he agreed to do the job to a drill sergeant's military standard of satisfaction."

Barking orders.

Rick grimaced again.

"I've come to realize I'm a lot like Pop," Rick admitted to his mother. "Too much like him, if you want to know the truth about it. And since Zada isn't anything like you, I guess our marriage was pretty much doomed from the start."

"What do you mean Zada isn't anything like me?"

"Your personalities," Rick said. "Zada's in my face every second, Mother. That's our problem. You've always accepted Pop's take-charge personality and lived with him in spite of it. Zada doesn't have that capability."

Mary laughed. "Where did you ever get the impression I accept your father's take-charge personality? I put your father in his place on a daily basis."

Rick was stunned.

"But, but . . ." he stuttered. "I've never seen you and Pop have an argument in my life."

"Well, of course, we never argued in front of you," Mary said. "Claude Clark might wear the pants in this family,

Rick, but don't you ever doubt that I tell him which pair to wear."

My father?

Fondly known as Claude the Conqueror?

Taking orders?

Rick went from stunned to downright angry.

"Well, I hate to point this out, Mother," Rick said sharply, "but if you and Pop *had* argued in front of me every now and then, I might have had a more realistic idea of what to expect in my marriage."

He heard her gasp.

Uh-oh.

"Now you listen to me, Richard Avery Clark," she said, proving she could be every bit as feisty as she claimed.

Richard Avery Clark?

You haven't called me that since I was a kid.

"If you'd been present for every knockdown drag-out fight your father and I had when you were growing up, and still have in case you're wondering, you'd be complaining our *arguing* was responsible for your marriage not working out."

"Now, Mother," Rick said. "I was only saying . . ."

"Oh, grow up!" Mary snipped. "Take responsibility for your own actions like an adult. And don't call me back until you're ready to apologize!"

Rick looked at his cell phone when the line went dead.

He couldn't believe it.

His mother had *never* talked to him like that.

Never!

Rick started to call her back, then thought better of it. He'd call his mother back and apologize later, after he apologized to Zada.

Dammit!

There was just no winning with the women in his life!

"Go ahead and have a good cry, sweetie," Tish said, after Zada finished a rundown of the humiliating visit from her mother and her sister.

"Don't be ridiculous," Zada said. "Tears are nothing but a big waste of time and energy."

Jen looked at her funny. "I think you're serious."

Zada sent Jen a puzzled look back. "Why wouldn't I be serious?"

"Because," Jen said. "It's a woman's nature to cry. Tears are all tied up in our emotions. We cry when we're happy. We cry when we're sad. We cry when we're hurt or embarrassed. Sometimes we cry for no other reason than the fact that we're long overdue for a good, hard cry."

"You maybe," Zada said. "Not me."

"You never cry?" Tish asked.

Zada shook her head. "No. I don't."

Jen and Tish exchanged worried looks.

Tish said, "Through this whole divorce? You've never cried once?"

Again, Zada shook her head.

Tish and Jen kept staring at her.

"I swear," Zada said laughing. "I can't even remember the last time I cried."

"Try," Jen said.

What?

Maybe it was the whole situation: Her losing face with her mother and Sally. Her being so angry at Rick. Maybe even her feeling threatened by Alicia. Whatever the reason, painful memories surfaced.

This time, Zada couldn't hold them back.

Her, holding Sally's four-year-old hand, both of them crying as her mother followed her father to the car, begging him not to leave. Her father, finally taking her mother by the shoulders and shoving her out of his way so he could get into his car.

Her, standing by her mother's bed, tears streaming down her six-year-old face, begging her mother to get up. Sally sitting on the floor, crying because their mother had been in bed for two days and she was scared and hungry.

Her, going to the wall phone in the kitchen. Pushing a kitchen chair up to the wall so she could reach the phone. Going down the list of numbers on the bulletin board by the phone like her mother had taught her to do in case of an emergency.

Her, calling her father at work. Begging him to come home. Telling him her mother was sick. Him, saying he would come. Her watching out the front window for hours. Him never coming.

Her, finally drying her tears. Vowing she would never cry again. Leading Sally back to the kitchen. Fixing both of them another peanut butter sandwich.

The mental filmstrip ended.

Zada burst into tears.

She cried.

She sobbed.

With her hands over her face, she wept her heart out.

Twenty-six years worth of pent-up rage spewed forth, allowing bitter tears to wash away the anger she'd kept buried deep inside. Only then, did Zada finally forgive her father for being the incredible jerk that he was. And she finally forgave her mother for still loving him in spite of it.

Through her anguish, Jen and Tish had comforted her. Murmuring words of encouragement. Holding her hand and patting her back. Staying with her until there were no tears left to cry. When she finally pulled herself together, Zada didn't know what to say.

"I'm so embarrassed," she admitted. "I never expected to have a nervous breakdown on you."

Tish handed her another tissue. "If it makes you feel any better, I have a nervous breakdown at least once a month. I'd say you were well overdue."

"And whether you believe it or not," Jen said, patting her hand, "a good cry always makes you feel better."

"I already feel better," Zada said. "So much better, the first thing I'm going to do is call my mother and Sally and apologize for being the incredible ass I've been my entire life. I'm beginning to realize men can make a liar of you no matter how strong you think you are."

Jen said, "You mean like letting Rick move back in?"

Zada nodded. "Does that sound mature enough for you?"

Jen smiled. "Extremely mature. And now I want you to tell me the second extremely mature thing you're going to do is sit down with Rick tonight and put an end to the madness."

"Don't push it, Jen," Zada said, getting up from the table. "I think one mature thing a day is a good place to start. Besides, I'm still too angry at Rick to be mature about anything where he's concerned."

Zada walked into Tish's half bath off the kitchen. She took one look in the mirror, and almost passed out.

Crap! What a dirty trick.

Her eyes were so red and swollen, she looked like she'd been in a fist fight.

"I know why crying makes you feel better now," Zada yelled out to Jen and Tish. "Crying makes you feel better so you can handle looking like pure hell afterwards."

She heard them both laugh.

"And speaking of pure hell," Jen said when Zada walked back into the kitchen. "Please tell me you aren't going to live in the hellish mess you and Rick have made in your house."

Zada said, "Does that mean I can borrow your Queen of Clean title for the afternoon?"

"Absolutely," Jen said.

Zada grinned. "How much damage do you think a caustic cleanser could do to an expensive set of wood drivers?"

Tish gasped. "Oh, Zada. You wouldn't dare! Joe would kill to have a set of drivers like Rick's."

Zada said, "I bought Rick those clubs. I can do whatever I want with them."

Jen shook her head. "You really are mad at Rick, aren't you?"

Zada looked at Jen. "How mad would you be if Charlie invited your mother and sister into a kitchen that looked like mine does right now?"

"Use a Brillo pad," Jen said. "A Brillo pad will do more damage to the wood."

Chapter 11

—🍎—

Alicia wasn't sure what happened after Rick's walk.

Only that it wasn't good.

She'd glanced out the window in time to see Rick and Zada in a face-off in their driveway. She'd watched Zada stomp across the street to Tish's house, Jen right beside her. Watched Rick back down the driveway and zoom off.

Guilt tugged at her conscience for a second. But only for a second. She had nothing to feel guilty about. All she'd done was tell Rick the truth. Zada's assumptions were her own.

Assumptions.

How Alicia hated assumptions.

People had made unfair assumptions about her all her life. Assumed she was rich, spoiled, and conceited. Never giving her a chance to prove otherwise. Never taking time to get to know her as a person.

She'd spent her whole life wishing she hadn't been born into money. Wishing she was dumb as a stump. Wishing she was average-looking enough not to stand out from the crowd. But no more. From now on, she was going to take advantage of every asset she had.

And she was going to start with Zada.

Zada saw her as a threat, so she was going to be a threat. Until Zada gave her what she wanted.

Alicia's head jerked toward her bedroom phone.

She smiled as walked across the room.

Maybe Zada's ready to give me what I want sooner than I expected.

Alicia frowned when she saw the caller ID: her twin, Alfie. Calling, she was sure, with his latest crisis du jour.

"Still in Woodberry Park exile?" were the first words out of Alfie's mouth when she answered the phone.

"For now," Alicia said, "but I'm working on it."

Alfie said, "I still don't know why you don't sell the house and move back to the city with me."

Alicia said, "You know exactly why I'm not selling the house."

"What's the big deal about giving Edward half of the proceeds?" Alfie argued. "It's not like we've ever been desperate for money. Dear old real estate mogul Dad saw to that before we were ever born."

"It's the principle of the matter," Alicia said.

Alfie said, "And speaking of dear old Dad, he's still on me every minute about talking you into coming back to the bosom of the family business."

"Why? So I can meet another devious neurosurgeon who wants to destroy my life?" Alicia quipped. "No thank you."

"You didn't know Edward was devious when you sold him the commercial property for his office building, sis," Alfie said. "You also didn't know he was devious when you married him. Edward had us all fooled. Not just you."

"It doesn't matter," Alicia said. "The answer is still no!"

Alfie sighed. "Then at least come to a party in my building tonight. I just got dumped again, so I don't have a date. I want you to go with me."

"Whose party?" Alicia wanted to know.

"Eddie Salvo," Alfie said.

"Public Dick Eddie?" Alicia laughed. "Again, no thank you."

"The term is 'Private Dick,'" Alfie corrected. "And Eddie has the reputation of being the most successful private detective in Chicago. Plus, he has a major crush on you."

"Eddie has a major crush on anything wearing skirts," Alicia said. "Which is why *public* dick suits him much better. I repeat. No thank you."

"At least you wouldn't have to worry about Eddie's sexual preference," Alfie said right back.

"I'm hanging up now," Alicia told him.

"Seven o'clock," Alfie said. "Sixth floor. Eddie's apartment number is six B."

"I said I'm hanging up now."

And Alicia did just that.

It was nine PM when Rick pulled into the driveway. He slammed on the brakes when he saw Zada's Lexus, out of the garage, and parked back in its usual place on the turn-around.

Rick sat there for a second, contemplating exactly what this meant. A bomb, maybe? Ready to explode if he tried to reclaim his junk-free side of the garage?

He eased the Hummer up the drive and stopped again. It took a second before he found the courage to use the

YOUR BED OR MINE? 161

garage door opener. When he did, and the garage light came on, what Rick saw blew his bomb theory all to hell.

He couldn't believe his eyes.

Not only was his side of the garage free of debris, Zada's side of the garage was basically spotless. All of her boxes of God only knew what were neatly stacked in one corner. Her yard sale junk for that yard sale she insisted she was going to have some day, had disappeared. She'd even gotten rid of that old refrigerator from her college dorm days that she insisted still held sentimental value.

Rick didn't know whether to be ecstatic or terrified.

Common sense told him to lean toward the latter.

His fear only mounted when he entered the house through the garage and walked into a pristine kitchen. Sweat broke out on his brow when he hurried down the hallway and found a neat and tidy living room. He held his breath as he tiptoed up the stairs and down the hall, switching on the lights in his immaculate bedroom and his squeaky clean bath.

Terror arrived when he glanced at his golf bag.

The grips were sticking up out of the golf bag, instead of the heads. Panic propelled Rick forward. Rage took over when he pulled the first driver out of the bag.

Zada was sitting up in bed, pretending to be reading when the loud banging started on her bedroom door.

"Go away," she yelled. "It's Simon's turn to sleep with me."

"Dammit, Zada," Rick yelled back. "This isn't about Simon and you know it."

Simon sat up on the bed, wagging his tail.

"Stay," Zada whispered. "I may need you for protection."

When Rick barged through the door, Zada realized how true those words were. A new vein she didn't even know he had popped out on Rick's forehead. Zada didn't like the way he was holding on to his ruined golf club, either.

Rick held the club up.

Zada glanced at it nonchalantly, then back at him.

"I can't believe you did this!" he yelled.

"And I can't believe you invited my mother and sister in to see the mess from hell you made in the kitchen!" Zada yelled back.

Rick lowered the club and looked at her.

"I owe you an apology for that," he said. "It was a rotten thing to do."

"I accept," Zada said, and calmly went back to reading.

One second.

Two seconds.

Three seconds.

"You accept?" Rick exploded. He held up the club again. "Aren't you going to apologize for this?"

"No," Zada told him. "You deserved it."

He stood there for a moment.

Zada stared him down.

Rick whirled around and stomped out of the room.

The bedroom door slammed so hard, the pictures on the wall rattled.

Zada let out a slow sigh of relief.

Until Rick stormed right back into the bedroom.

"So, what now, Zada?" he thundered. "The house has been messed up. And now the house has been cleaned up. The only thing left is to *blow* the damn place up. Is that the only way we're ever going to come to an agreement on the property settlement?"

Zada closed her book and placed it on the end table.

"You could always leave," she mentioned.

"Over. My. Dead. Body," he said through clenched teeth.

Zada said, "Believe me. I've thought of that option."

Rick took a menacing step toward the bed.

Zada scooted farther back against the headboard. She worried that she might have pushed him too far, until she saw a familiar gleam in his eye.

Right back where we started.

All about sex!

Zada said, "You don't intimidate me."

He grinned. "Then why is that little pulse point at the base of your throat going ninety miles a minute?"

Zada's hand flew to her throat to cover it.

Rick took another step forward.

"I want you out of my bedroom," Zada said. "Now."

"Liar," he said.

He had the nerve to sit down on the edge of the bed. He was testing her, and she knew it. Zada refused to move an inch.

"Would it intimidate you if I did this?" Rick asked, moving the covers back to reveal her lacy red teddy.

"No," Zada said, but her voice quivered slightly.

Their eyes met.

Rick smiled and said, "Did I ever think to tell you how much I appreciate your taste in sexy lingerie?"

Zada said, "You always had me out of my sexy lingerie so fast, I didn't think you noticed."

His eyes turned a deeper blue.

His grin turned more aggressive.

"What if I did this," he said, slowly moving the cold end of the golf club across her bare foot, up the inside of her left thigh, stopping only when he couldn't go any farther. "Would that intimidate you?"

Their eyes met again.

Zada knew exactly what he was doing: playing out her fantasy. And substituting the golf club for a sword. Too bad for him. Rick had no clue she knew what he was doing.

Zada smiled and said, "I don't remember you ever needing a golf club to help you drive it home, Rick."

Oops!

There was that new vein on his forehead again.

Rick got up from the bed and headed for the door.

His now worthless golf club was clutched in his hand.

"Can I assume I survived another challenge?" Zada called out after him.

Bam! went her bedroom door.

Crash! went the pictures on each side of her dresser.

To Zada's relief, after their Sunday night golf club episode, the week had been uneventful. Partly due to the new training class Rick was tied up with at the center—he left home early and came home late. And partly due to the fact that they were both purposely avoiding each other.

Which suited Zada just fine.

Except avoiding each other meant no challenges.

And no challenges meant no sole survivor.

Jen and Tish had speculated the reason Rick hadn't delivered any challenges all week was because he was trying to regroup after she'd made it clear his sex intimidating scheme wasn't going to work. But Zada had the unsettling feeling that maybe Rick was right: They'd already exhausted all of their challenge options.

Was blowing up the house the only way they'd ever solve the problem to each other's satisfaction?

Zada was contemplating that dilemma late Friday afternoon when the sound of the garage door opening signaled Rick was home early for the first time all week.

Dammit!

She was not in the mood to retreat to her bedroom in order to avoid him all night. And she was positive she was beginning to wear out her welcome where Tish and Jen were concerned.

But, wait a minute!

Maybe that had been Rick's plan all along. He knew she'd get tired of having him around, so he'd hold out long enough to make her leave.

Well, it isn't going to happen, mister!

She was tired of scurrying away like a scared mouse.

Tonight, Rick was *not* going to force her to retreat to her bedroom. Nor was he going to force her out of her own house. She was going to sit right there in her own kitchen and ignore him completely. Let *him* find some place to go if he wanted to avoid seeing her I'm-not-giving-in face!

Zada had just headed for the kitchen to stake out a claim at the kitchen table when the telephone rang.

"Bombshell alert," Tish said the second she answered.

"Excuse me?"

"Alicia!" Tish exclaimed. "Hurry. Go to your front window."

Zada hurried through the house, phone to her ear.

Spit!

Skintight jeans! Low-cut top! A sexy take-me-anytime look on her face!

Maybe I will start a Bimbo Elimination Club!

Alicia really *was* a bimbo if she thought she was going to get away with seducing Rick!

Zada said, "Why that rich, conniving . . ."

"Bitch," Tish finished for her. "And just when we'd convinced ourselves Alicia was backing off because we hadn't heard a peep out of her all week."

"What a piece of work," Zada said. "She practically has her ass in Rick's face bending over like that."

Tish said, "And how convenient that she didn't realize her tire was flat until she backed out into the street."

Zada snorted. "I guarantee you she punched a hole in that tire the second she saw Rick pull into the driveway."

"No doubt about it," Tish agreed. "I was on the front porch when she came prancing across the street and way-laid Rick at your mailbox. Has the woman never heard of the Triple-A Club?"

"Why bother," Zada said, "when you can get the idiot across the street to change the tire for you?"

Tish said, "Surely Rick can see she's openly coming on to him."

"Right now Rick can't see anything," Zada said. "Alicia has both of her double D breasts shoved in his face."

"Well, do something!" Tish ordered.

"What can I do?" Zada wailed.

"Stomp out there and invite her to our meeting tomorrow night," Tish said.

"Jen would kill me!"

Tish said, "A guy can only take so much, Zada. We've

already tortured him with our fantasies last weekend. And you've made it clear you aren't having sex with him. Could you really blame a guy who hadn't had sex in six months if he . . ."

Zada cut her off. "Don't even say it. You know that's the one thing that would make me walk out the door."

"Then do something!" Tish ordered again. "Alicia's already used the ass pass and the bust thrust. Get out there, Zada. Now!"

"I don't mind changing your tire, Alicia," Rick said. "But I thought I'd made myself clear that I wasn't going to get involved in whatever's going on between you and Zada."

Alicia was only half listening. She was too busy glancing at Rick's front window, gloating over the fact that Zada was watching.

"Did you hear me, Alicia?"

"Yes," Alicia said, looking down at him with a flirty smile for Zada's benefit. "You made it crystal clear you had no intention of trying to make Zada jealous."

"I mean it, Alicia," Rick warned. "No more stunts." He walked behind her Mercedes to open the trunk.

Alicia looked back at the window.

Dammit!

Zada was gone.

She'd truly hoped all it would take was one more nudge and Zada would give in. Especially since Rick wasn't an easy guy to track down. She'd watched for him all week, but he'd come home after dark every night.

She could have easily gone over and asked him to fix her tire anyway, but it wouldn't have had the same effect.

She'd wanted Rick to fix her flat tire in broad daylight. Wanted Zada to watch as she came on to Rick. Wanted those brown eyes of Zada's to turn grass green with jealously.

She'd obviously misjudged Zada. Maybe Zada was a better adversary than she realized.

And dang it! It's already Friday.

That meant another week without an invitation.

Another week of scheming and planning.

Another week of exile in suburbia.

"Alicia, can you help me a minute?"

She glanced over at Rick. He was now squatted down by her left rear tire. "Sure," she said.

Alicia didn't even try to stand too close to Rick when he held out the lug nuts he wanted her to hold. What was the point if Zada wasn't watching?

"I was afraid this was going to happen," Rick said, looking past her and shaking his head.

Alicia looked over her shoulder.

Zada.

Stomping toward them.

Both fists clenched.

Alicia turned around, ready for battle.

She folded her arms across her chest.

Zada ignored Rick completely when she walked up, and looked directly at Alicia.

"Alicia," she said in a voice sweet as honey, "we'd like to invite you to our Fantasy Club meeting tomorrow night."

In a voice *sweeter* than honey, Alicia said, "Tomorrow night? Sorry, I'll have to check my calendar first, Zada. Why don't I call you later and let you know if I can make it?"

There was absolutely no doubt in Alicia's mind.

If Rick hadn't been there, Zada would have slapped her!

After the encounter with Alicia, Zada did retreat to her bedroom to avoid Rick, even though she vowed that she wouldn't. She knew if she didn't, she'd punch Rick square in the nose.

Just who did he think he was?

Taking walks with Alicia.

Fixing tires for Alicia.

Next, he'd be moving in with Alicia!

Like Tish said, six months without sex was a long time. Plus, Alicia wasn't your run-of-the-mill adversary. No woman in her right mind would stand beside Alicia Greene and ask a guy to choose between them.

Zada had finally become so frustrated, she'd gone to bed. She was lost somewhere in a fitful tired-of-the-whole-situation slumber, when the dog that obviously *wasn't* tired scratched at her bedroom door.

Zada forced one eye open.

The loud bark forced her out of bed.

When Zada opened her bedroom door, Rick was stumbling down the hall in her direction, wearing nothing but a sleepy frown.

In a nanosecond, Zada went from groggy to wide awake. Awake enough to make a very important mental note: *The night-light in the hallway has to go!*

"Sorry," Rick said with a yawn. "I thought Simon wanted to go out."

Zada quickly averted her gaze back to the dog. Simon

ambled past her and jumped up on her bed. Zada slammed the door on temptation, and went back to bed.

Fifteen minutes later, she had just drifted off to sleep again, when the scratching at the door started all over again.

"Simon!" Zada scolded. "If you want to go out. Go out!"

Zada jerked the covers back and walked to the door. Simon trotted past her into the hallway. But he didn't go downstairs to his doggie door in the kitchen as Zada expected. Instead, Simon made a beeline down the hallway, heading straight back to Rick's closed bedroom door.

Two barks later, Rick was standing in the doorway.

Still naked.

Still looking sleepy.

Still driving her slowly insane.

He yawned. "What's going on now?"

"I think it's pretty obvious," Zada snipped. "Your big idea of taking turns keeping Simon at night has him all confused."

"Whatever," Rick said, yawning again. "You leave your door open. I'll do the same. Then Simon can go back and forth until he wears himself out."

Back to bed.

Almost back to sleep.

Bark. Bark. Bark.

Bark. Bark. Bark.

Zada let out a loud groan.

She put a pillow over her head to drown out the noise.

Rick dragged himself out of bed and reached for his boxer shorts that he'd folded neatly and left at the foot of his bed as usual. Seconds later, he was stumbling down the hallway, his pillow and the comforter from the bed under his arm.

Zada sat up in bed when he entered the room.

Simon trotted into the room behind him.

"Simon isn't going to be satisfied until we're all three sleeping in the same room," Rick told her. "Go back to sleep. I'll sleep on the floor."

He spread the comforter out and threw his pillow down.

"Absolutely not!" Zada said.

"Why?" Rick challenged. "You were over me by the time I backed down the driveway. Remember?"

Rick lay down on the floor.

Simon lay down beside him.

Rick closed his eyes.

Be strong. Be strong. Be strong.

Don't dwell on Zada being only king-size inches away.

Wearing nothing but one of her flimsy teddies.

Ignore the intoxicating smell of her perfume.

Forget about taking her in your arms . . .

Geez!

Just go to sleep, dammit!

Look at the clock.

12:06 AM.

Close your eyes.

Look at the clock.

12:10 AM.

Close your eyes.

Look at the clock.

12:25 AM.

Zada sat up and crawled to the foot of the bed.

The moonlight streaming through the large bay window gave her a perfect view of exactly what was keeping her awake.

She stared at the back of Rick's head.

"Are you asleep?"

"Yes," he told her.

But he rolled over on the floor to face her.

"This isn't working for me," Zada said.

"Maybe you should try counting sheep," he suggested.

"I did that already," Zada said.

Until they stopped jumping fences and started getting frisky with each other.

But she wasn't going to tell him that!

"I've been thinking," Zada said.

"That always scares me," Rick mumbled.

Zada ignored him and said, "You were right when you said we didn't have any challenge options left, short of blowing up the house. What would you say to joint custody of Simon and the house?"

Rick sat up.

"Joint custody?"

"Yes," Zada said. "You live in the house with Simon six months. I live in the house with Simon six months. And instead of buying me a condo, we'll buy us a condo. A place for each of us to stay when we're not living in the house with Simon."

"No," Rick said flatly.

He lay back down and turned his back to her again.

"No!" Zada yelled. "That's all you're going to say? Just 'no'?"

"No," Rick repeated and pulled the comforter over his head.

Zada scrambled on her hands and knees back to the head of the bed and switched on her bedside light.

"Would you just go to sleep, Zada?" Rick groaned from the floor. "I have to be at the center early in the morning."

"You're off tomorrow. It's Saturday."

"I never take weekends off during training sessions," Rick said. "And I'm surprised you forgot that. You used to bitch about it enough before we separated."

Zada ignored that remark and said, "No! I will not go to sleep. Not until you tell me why you instantly vetoed my joint custody idea."

Rick sat up and jerked back the comforter.

"The way I see it, Zada," he said with a frown, "we either stay together, or we get a divorce and make a clean break."

"Hell-o!" Zada said. "We aren't capable of living together. That's why we're getting a divorce. And that's why my idea is perfect. We get the divorce *and* we take turns living in the house with Simon."

Rick looked at her and shook his head.

"Sorry," he said. "But I want kids someday, Zada."

Whap!

His words hit her right between the eyes.

Zada seriously thought she might pass out from the pain of imagining Rick having kids with anyone but her.

"You never told me you wanted kids," Zada said.

"Don't you want kids?" Rick asked.

"Yes," Zada said. "I want a whole house full."

"Well, there you go," Rick said. "That's why your joint custody idea isn't going to work. What would we do with our families? Move them back and forth every six months? I don't think so."

Zada was too rattled to answer.

She reached over and turned off the bedside light.

Rick returned to his makeshift pallet on the floor.

And not a moment too soon.

She'd be damned if she let him see her cry.

But Rick with a wife, kids, and not in my life?

God, I really have been shallow.

Had forgiving her mother and sister changed her somehow? Is that why she was able to finally admit, that no matter how crazy he made her, she still couldn't bear the thought of Rick not being in her life?

She loved him.

She'd loved him from the second she saw him.

She'd love him till she drew her last breath.

Stay together or make a clean break.

Did that mean Rick was still open to them staying together?

Was he willing to learn to compromise?

Even make an effort to overlook each other's flaws?

Did she dare even ask?

No.

I'd be beyond devastated if Rick said it was too late.

Better to leave things as they were.

Until one of them gave up and moved out.

And at the rate they were going?

That person will most likely be me!

Rick pretended to be asleep, but his eyes were wide open.

Maybe for the first time in his life.

He hadn't missed the hurt look on Zada's face when he'd mentioned kids and families. Did he dare hope she looked so hurt because deep down she hadn't given up on them yet?

He was tempted to sit up and ask her.

Just blurt it out.

Ask her point-blank: *Do you really want a divorce?*

But if she said yes, they had nowhere to go from there, except back to their squabble over the house and Simon. Maybe he should just give in and let her have Simon and the house. Put them both out of their misery. Zada was obviously getting as tired of the game-playing as he was, or she wouldn't have approached him with her joint custody idea.

But if he gave Zada Simon and the house, then *he'd* have nowhere to go. Except to walk away from everything in his life that was important to him. Zada being at the top of the list. And he wasn't going to lie to himself about that any longer.

He loved her.

He had always loved her.

He would always love her.

If only there was some way to turn his *Survivor* idea into something that could bring them closer together instead of pushing them farther apart. A game of love, not war. Now, *that* would be a fantasy worth having.

Fantasy.

Master.

Slave.

Holy shit! That's it!

Zada insisted there was more to marriage than just great sex. But great sex sure added more to a marriage. The only problem was, he had to make Zada think she was in control of the situation. That she really was his master, and he really was her slave.

Rick sat up and looked across the bed.

Zada was buried somewhere beneath the covers.

"Are you asleep?" he whispered.

"Yes," Zada whispered back.

"I've been thinking," Rick said.

"That always *surprises* me," Zada mumbled.

But she sat up in the bed and looked at him.

Rick said, "Sex has always been the main issue between us, Zada. Our attraction for each other got us into a spur-of-the-moment marriage. And our last big fight was over you accusing me of always using sex to end any argument we were having."

Zada said, "And your point is?"

Rick answered, "Don't you think it's only fair that sex should be the challenge we use to declare one of us the sole *Survivor?*"

Zada's eyes narrowed. "Do you think I'm stupid? We have sex, and that voids our separation agreement."

"I didn't say consummation," Rick said quickly. "What I'm suggesting is everything *but* consummation. The first one to have an orgasm loses the game."

"You're certifiable," Zada said. "The answer is no!"

She flopped back on the bed, ending the discussion.

Rick sighed and fell back on his pillow on the floor.

Zada looked at the clock.

12:45 AM.

Her eyes closed.

Everything BUT consummation.

Rick really had flipped out. Who did he think he was all of a sudden, Bill freaking Clinton?

Maybe she should accept his challenge and teach him a lesson. It was common knowledge that all women craved foreplay. Hours upon hours of foreplay, to be exact. And a woman could always hold out longer than a man. Especially a man who hadn't had sex in six months.

Zada looked at the clock.

12:50 AM.

She closed her eyes.

Hours and hours of foreplay.

God, it was tempting. She hadn't had sex in six months, either. She'd be a damn fool if she didn't accept the challenge. Especially since she had the upper hand.

Wait a minute.

Rick had to know she had the upper hand. Was he really that anxious to speed things along? That anxious to get on with his life so he could find himself a new wife and have those kids he wanted?

Or, was his new plan only his way of saving face? He'd let her win, but he'd go out smiling with one last orgasm!

He wants one last orgasm?

I'll give him one last orgasm!

Zada sat back up and switched on the light.

Rick's head instantly popped up at the foot of the bed.

"Let me get this straight," Zada said. "You're proposing ninety days of foreplay as our ultimate challenge."

Rick grinned. "Eighty-three days of foreplay, if you want to be technical about it."

Zada said, "And the first one to have an orgasm loses the game?"

Rick nodded. "The first one to have an orgasm loses the game. We call our attorneys. We sign the property settlement. And the divorce will be final."

Zada said, "But if the loser has an orgasm, isn't that technically consummation? And doesn't that violate our separation agreement?"

"I'll never tell," Rick said. "Will you?"

Zada stared at Rick.

Rick stared back.

Zada decided to play along.

"I have to admit," Zada said, "I doubt there's a person on earth who wouldn't agree that enduring eighty-three days of foreplay without having an orgasm has to be the *ultimate* challenge known to man."

Rick said, "Try the ultimate challenge known to any life-form in the universe."

Zada kept staring at him.

Rick kept staring back.

Zada said, "And when do you suggest we start this challenge?"

There was that look in his eye again.

Rick grinned. "What's wrong with now?"

Zada reached over and switched off the light.

Rick was in bed before she could turn back the covers.

"Game on," Zada said when his hand ran up her leg.

"Teddy off," Rick told her with just as much confidence.

Chapter 12

———❧———

Face hurriedly washed, teeth quickly brushed, and her body haphazardly dressed in the first pair of jeans and T-shirt she could find, Zada stood barefoot in the kitchen the next morning. She was staring at Rick's side of the pullout pantry in the kitchen cabinet next to the refrigerator.

The "health food" side.

Soy breakfast bars.

Soy breakfast shakes.

Soy coffee variety pack.

Ewwwwww.

Soy coffee?

How disgusting!

But Rick obviously didn't think so, and Rick was in a hurry.

The four long hours of delicious foreplay the night before had left them both exhausted. So exhausted, Rick had overslept this morning—probably for the first time in his life. Now, he was an hour late getting to the center—another first in his life, she was sure.

The least she could do, Zada decided, was make him a

cup of coffee to help choke down one of the disgusting soy bars he ate for breakfast every morning.

And no, they definitely weren't back together.

And no, neither of them had any intention of calling off the divorce.

But it was pretty hard to switch back to combat mode after you'd teased, stroked, and licked every inch of someone's body the night before. Besides, what was the harm in being civil to each other until Rick finally gave in and orgasmed himself into a coma?

Poor baby, he doesn't have a chance.

One more night, and I'll be the sole survivor.

Zada frowned at the word "sole."

Sole.

As in "single."

As in "all by myself for the rest of my life."

She quickly pushed that thought aside, reached out, and picked the coffee variety pack package up by the corner, as if it were contaminated. After a quick apology to her beloved Mr. Coffee coffeemaker for filling him with anything but one-hundred-percent caffeine—as God surely intended—Zada dumped the contents of one of the pre-measured packets into the filter. She ran some water into the pot and dumped it into the canister. Then flipped the switch to "on."

By the time Rick made it into the kitchen a few minutes later, Zada had a cup of steaming hot soy (*yuck*) coffee waiting for him on the kitchen counter beside his nutritious soy (*gag*) breakfast bar.

Zada handed him the cup and the breakfast bar.

Rick looked suspiciously at the cup.

"Don't worry," Zada said. "It's a selection from your own *soy* coffee variety pack."

Rick grinned. "You made coffee for me?"

"Don't read anything into it," Zada told him. "I'm just trying to get you out the door so I can sleep all day."

"You are a truly evil woman," Rick told her.

"And pretty apt to stay that way," Zada assured him.

"Game back on tonight," Rick reminded her with a grin.

He headed out the door, breakfast bar and coffee cup in hand.

"Don't worry about me," Zada yelled after him. "I have all day to sleep and rest up for tonight."

But she couldn't keep from smiling after Rick left. And who wouldn't be smiling after the incredible experience they'd shared the night before? Taking time to explore each other's bodies. For once, pushing all their differences aside. Focusing on nothing but each other.

Too bad we're only playing a game.

Zada pushed that thought aside, too, as she took a coffee cup down from the kitchen cabinet for her morning walk across the street to have coffee with Jen and Tish. That is, she took a cup down *before* she remembered the mean trick she'd played on poor Mr. Coffee.

She stared at the coffeemaker for a moment, then timidly took the pot from the burner. She held the pot up to her nose for a quick sniff.

Hmmm.

The aroma isn't bad.

Zada filled her cup and bravely took a sip.

Surprisingly, the taste wasn't bad.

She reached for the empty packet on the counter, curious

to see exactly which flavor she'd randomly selected from Rick's handy dandy soy coffee variety pack.

Zada laughed out loud when she turned the packet over. AROUSE ME MOCHA was stamped across the front.

Alicia watched Zada walk across the street from her upstairs bedroom window. The same way she'd watched Jen and her daughter walk across the street to Tish's house earlier.

The regular morning coffee and gossip session.

With me as their main topic of gossip this morning. Alicia was sure of it, but she wasn't going to worry about that. She had her invitation to the meeting tonight. And she was going to that meeting, come hell or high water.

She didn't even care if Jen and Tish did snub her because she had basically blackmailed Zada into inviting her. Forget them. She'd tried to be a good neighbor, and where had it gotten her?

In fact, she was tempted to tell all three of them exactly what she thought when she did arrive for the meeting. Tell them how rude they were. Remind them other people had feelings, too. Ask them how any one of them would feel if they were the one living in the cul-de-sac, constantly being ignored by their neighbors day in and day out.

Better yet, maybe she really should turn into the neighbor straight from hell and teach them all a lesson.

Maybe she'd pitch a fit the next time the twins pulled up every tulip in her flower bed to make a bouquet for their mother, instead of being nice the way she had been last spring. This time, she wouldn't tell Tish not to worry about it. Instead of refusing to accept any money for the replacement of the bulbs, she'd hand Tish the sizable bill from the lawn service that repaired all the damage.

When Jen and her daughter showed up on her doorstep selling Girl Scout cookies again, or any other promotional fund-raising item they were always selling for the freaking PTA, she wouldn't whip out her checkbook the way she usually did and buy a ton of stuff she didn't even want. Instead, she'd send them back across the street empty-handed. Let Jen see what it was like not to have the support of a neighbor.

And as for Zada, maybe she wouldn't back off where Rick was concerned at all. Even if Rick wasn't interested, she could certainly make Zada's life miserable. Wonder how Zada would like that woman-to-woman lesson in karma!

Alicia sighed and walked away from the window.

But first, I'll see how they treat me tonight.

Whether Zada realized it or not, having another divorcée join their circle could actually work out to Zada's benefit. Jen and Tish had kids and husbands. She and Zada would have a lot in common once Zada got her divorce. If Zada would only give her a chance, they might even end up becoming good friends.

Good friends.

Something she'd never had.

Something she'd always wanted.

Funny, Alicia decided, that you never think about peer pressure carrying over into your adult life, but it does.

You feel slighted if the boss favors someone else.

Ostracized, if your neighbors avoid you.

Rejected, if date one doesn't lead to date two.

Invisible, if everyone ignores you at a party.

Well, they can't very well ignore me tonight!

Alicia smiled.

Tonight, she intended to show them exactly with whom they were dealing!

"Eighty-three days of foreplay," Tish said, a faraway look in her eyes.

Jen said, "Would you please stop repeating that over and over? It's becoming a chant."

Tish said, "I'm just trying to imagine being lucky enough to win that kind of multi-mega bedroom lottery. Eighty-three days of foreplay definitely gives a whole new meaning to the term 'Powerball.'"

Zada burst out laughing.

Jen rolled her eyes.

Jen looked back at Zada and said, "I hate to point this out, but you know, of course, that you're possibly setting yourself up for serious heartbreak here."

"Maybe," Zada said. "But foreplay sure beats making messes and cleaning them up."

Jen's lips pressed into a thin line.

The lip thing?

Jen's trademark for being pissed.

She said, "This is serious, Zada."

Zada sighed. "I know this is serious, Jen. And I know what Rick and I are doing is completely bizarre. But maybe one last big hoorah is the only way Rick and I ever will have any closure."

"And that's what you really want?" Jen asked. "Just one last big hoorah?"

"I don't know what I want, Jen," Zada admitted. "And I

don't think Rick knows what he wants, either. But as long as we play the game, that gives us a little more time to figure things out."

"Eighty-three days of foreplay," staring-off-into-space Tish said again.

Zada laughed. "If it makes you feel any better, Tish, as wickedly delicious as it sounds, it's sheer torture at the same time."

Tish sighed. "There's a very thin line between pain and pleasure."

Jen looked at Tish funny. "Tish Jones! I'm beginning to think there's more to that whips-and-chains comment you made than you're willing to tell us."

Tish only smiled.

"And speaking of whips and chains," Zada said, stealing the conversation away from doom-and-gloom Jen. "Shouldn't we be discussing how we're going to handle the sexual fantasy segment of our meeting with Alicia tonight?"

Jen groaned. "Don't remind me."

Tish said, "What do you mean? Your fantasy last Saturday was the sexiest by far, Jen."

"Forget it, Tish," Jen said. "Flattery does *not* work with me."

Jen looked right back at Zada. "Alicia is your guest, Zada. I vote for you giving Alicia a rundown of your session with Rick last night and put an end to it."

"I have a better idea," Tish said, beaming.

Now Jen had that faraway look.

"All I ever wanted," Jen said wistfully, "was to move into a nice, normal subdivision. I'm going to call a Realtor on Monday before you two really do corrupt me."

Tish ignored Jen and looked back at Zada.

"We need to remember that our main goal tonight is not to antagonize Alicia in any way," Tish said. "We don't want Alicia going back on her word and resuming her plan to seduce Rick. That means we need to be nice to her, even if it kills us."

"And on the fantasy level?" Zada quizzed.

Tish grinned. "That's where my better idea comes in."

Zada had already gone off to her Fantasy Club meeting by the time Rick got home Saturday evening. But she'd left a note on the kitchen table for him.

Only four little words: "Your bed or mine?"

Words that promised she was still in the game.

And God, how he had enjoyed finally having Zada back in his arms—even if the game they were playing was pure torture for him. Zada had no clue, but his main goal was not about keeping Simon and the house at all. His main goal was to hold out until they both had some answers. Answers about how they really felt about each other. About whether or not they really could learn to live together without arguing day in and day out.

But most importantly, an answer about whether or not Zada really wanted a divorce.

Last night had given Rick hope that she didn't.

And he'd kept a goofy grin on his face all day.

Even now, as he played poker with Joe and Charlie, Rick couldn't keep the goofy grin from occasionally tugging at the corners of his mouth. If Joe or Charlie had noticed, neither of them had said anything.

Yet.

Rick glanced at the monitor sitting beside Joe on the card table again this Saturday night, the screen showing the twins watching TV in their bedroom. Only tonight, the monitor was useless. The Fantasy Club meeting was being held at Jen and Charlie's.

"A dirty, rotten shame is what it is," Joe grumbled as he tossed the cards around the table. "If anyone has any steamy fantasies, I bet it's Alicia."

"Look on the bright side," Charlie said, scooping up his cards. "No matter where the girls gather to share their fantasies tonight, it means hot sex for us later."

Joe frowned and punched Charlie with his elbow.

"Would you cut Rick a little slack here? It might mean hot sex for us, but there's no point in torturing a guy."

"Don't worry about Rick," Charlie said, looking over at Rick and moving his eyebrows up and down. "Right, Rick?"

Joe frowned again. "What's that supposed to mean? Charlie said, "Didn't Tish tell you?"

Charlie ducked when Joe took a swing at him.

Alicia wasn't sure what was going on, but something was up. Everyone was being too damn nice.

Especially Zada.

They'd been sitting around Jen's kitchen table for the last hour. They'd had a few glasses of wine. Nibbled on Jen's artfully displayed hors d'oeuvres. Swapped enough boring chitchat to put them all to sleep. But none of them had mentioned one word about sharing any sexual fantasies.

Alicia almost laughed.

She'd known all along the fantasy part was a farce. Not

that sharing fantasies had ever been her goal—being invited to the meeting had been her goal. Being invited meant when other women in the neighborhood learned she was hanging out with the Housewives' Fantasy Club, everyone would stop treating her as if she had some dreaded social disease.

But, Alicia decided, it wouldn't hurt to do a little prodding. At least enough to watch Zada squirm.

Ha!

She'd bet money Zada hadn't even told Jen and Tish about the big fantasy lie she'd told. Poor Jen and Tish were probably clueless. They were sitting here, doing what they did every Saturday night while their husbands played poker. Absolutely nothing. Just as she'd suspected all along.

Alicia glanced at Zada.

Zada looked in her direction at the same time.

Eyes locked.

Phony smiles appeared.

Alicia was one second from jerking Zada's chain, but Tish tapped her fork against her wineglass.

"Okay, ladies," Tish said. "It's time to officially call this meeting to order."

Zada smiled and looked away.

Alicia settled back against her chair, casually crossed her legs, and leisurely swirled the wine around in her glass.

This, I gotta hear.

Tish smiled at Alicia this time. A smile not quite as phony as Zada's, but phony, nonetheless.

"Before we start the fantasy side of our meeting, Alicia," Tish said, "we have one sacred rule. What we say at the meeting, stays at the meeting. Understood?"

Alicia nodded.

"And since you're our guest this evening," Tish went on to say, "you have the honor of drawing the type of fantasy we'll be sharing tonight."

Lucky me.

Jen got up from the table.

She came back with a glass bowl.

When she held the bowl out, Alicia fished her hand into it and pulled out one of the folded pieces of paper.

Alicia unfolded the paper and read the words. When she looked back up, all three of them were staring at her. Alicia didn't like the cat-swallowed-the-canary looks on their faces.

" 'Progressive fantasy?' " Alicia said quizzically.

"My favorite kind," Zada said with a smug smile.

Tish said, "Let me explain how this works, Alicia. One person starts the fantasy and stops wherever she wants. It's up to the next person to pick up wherever she left off. However, you can go in any direction you like when it's your turn. That's why this type of fantasy is so much fun."

I'll try to contain my enthusiasm.

Zada looked over at her and said, "Usually the person who draws the fantasy starts the fantasy, Alicia, but why don't we let Jen go first tonight? By the time we get back around the table to you, you'll have a better understanding of how a progressive fantasy works."

I'm not an imbecile. I get it!

Alicia looked at Jen and said, "Is that okay with you?"

"My pleasure," Jen said, "if you'll pardon the pun."

Everyone laughed.

Except Alicia.

Something told Alicia the infamous Housewives' Fantasy Club had been rehearsing this meeting all day.

Chapter 13

—❦—

Jen picked up her wineglass. She took a leisurely sip, and looked around the table.

"You notice him the second you walk into the small boutique.

"He looks out of place in a lingerie store.

"He's tall and lean.

"Shaggy hair.

"Black leather jacket.

"Tight, faded jeans.

"Your gaze locks on the rear of those tight jeans.

"He glances over his shoulder and catches you looking.

"You blush.

"He smiles.

"Seductively.

"You quickly look away.

"You hurry past him, cheeks flaming, yet incredibly turned on by his bad-boy grin.

"He's every mother's nightmare.

"Yet, the type of bad boy every woman wants in her bed.

"You pretend to ignore him, but you sense he's still watching you.

"You can feel his eyes moving over your body, slowly undressing you, one piece of clothing at a time.

"The thought excites you as you run your finger lazily along the clothing rack, pretending to shop.

"But the feel of the sexy lingerie between your fingers takes your thoughts right back to the bedroom.

"You imagine him fisting your hair.

"Jerking your head back.

"Covering your mouth with a bruising, breathtaking kiss.

"Your finger runs across a black, floor-length, see-through negligee, and you chance another look in his direction.

"He smiles at you again.

"Approvingly.

"This time, you boldly hold his gaze.

"He watches as you take the hanger from the rack.

"Watches as you walk to the full-length mirror attached to the front of the dressing room door.

"Watches as you press the sheer fabric suggestively against your body.

"Your eyes meet in the mirror when he walks up behind you.

"You tease him and run one hand lightly over one breast, then the other.

"Your nipples spring to life and press against your blouse.

"He steps closer, the look on his face warning you he's tired of being teased.

"You panic and quickly open the dressing room door.

"You're only one step away from safety.

"But you look back over your shoulder one last time.

"And . . ."

Jen pointed to Tish.

Tish said, "You look back over your shoulder one last time, and crook your finger in his direction."

Jen said, "No! I was only playing a game. I imagined myself blowing him a farewell kiss!"

Tish said, "You've had your turn. This is my fantasy now."

Tish repeated, "You crook your finger in his direction.

"He looks around the store, puts his hand at the small of your back, and pushes you inside the small cubicle.

"You turn around to face him as he slides the lock closed on the dressing room door.

"He pulls you to him, kissing you roughly, just as you imagined.

"Your arms slide around his neck.

"The forgotten negligee falls to the floor.

"His fingers fly over the buttons on your blouse.

"He pushes the blouse off your shoulders and jerks down the straps of your skimpy, lace bra.

"Your breasts spring forward, fully exposed.

"You gasp when he drops to his knees and buries his face against your bare flesh.

"His hot mouth moves from one breast to the other, sending a tingle through your entire body.

"His hands find your skirt and push it up and out of the way.

"Down come your panties.

"He grasps your hips and pulls you forward.

"You moan when he guides you straight to his hot, wet tongue.

"Wave after wave of nothing but pure pleasure explodes through your body.

"You tangle your fingers in his shaggy hair, lost completely in a state of forbidden ecstasy.

"Finally, you cry out.

"You fall back against the mirror, fully satisfied and thoroughly spent.

"Gently, he pulls up your panties.

"Carefully, he pulls down your skirt.

"He stands up.

"He smiles.

"And . . ."

Tish pointed to Zada.

Zada said, "He stands up. Smiles. And says, 'See you at home later.'"

Tish said, "No! This is where the *stranger* should blow a farewell kiss!"

Zada said, "Too bad. I'm not into sex with strangers."

Zada started over.

"He stands up.

"Smiles.

"And says, 'See you at home later.'

"You're waiting for him that evening in the kitchen.

"A low whistle escapes his lips when he finds you wearing nothing but a lacy red thong, red high heels, and the long strand of cultured pearls he gave you as a wedding present.

"You turn around slowly on your red stilettos, giving him a full view, and reminding him what an excellent choice he made choosing you to be his wife.

" 'Dinner?' you ask, motioning toward the table.

"He grins his bad-boy grin.

" 'How about dessert first?' he asks.

"Just as you hoped he would.

"He hurries upstairs to the bedroom.

"You follow, knowing what he'll find.

"Candles, flickering to the beat of a sexy CD.

"A new robe for him waiting on the foot of the bed.

"A new game you want to play.

"*Before* you serve the dessert he requested.

"You walk into the room and follow his gaze to the lone chair sitting in the middle of the room.

"He looks over his shoulder, eyebrow raised.

"You smile and point to the robe first.

"He undresses in a hurry, your pulse racing with every piece of clothing he peels away.

"He slips into the robe.

"But you jerk the silk sash from the belt loops.

"Now, you point to the chair.

"Again, he obeys and takes a seat.

"You tie his hands behind him, securing them soundly with the long, silk sash.

"Dessert can wait.

"You've decided to give him a lap dance first.

"You straddle him as he sits in the chair, losing yourself in a hypnotic beat as you sway seductively back and forth to the music.

"You're so close you're almost touching.

"The fact that there's nothing he can do about it, really turns you on.

"You step back and do a snake-like wiggle as you step out of your thong.

"His eyes turn a deeper blue as they travel over your nude body.

"You move closer, straddling him again as you pull the pearls suggestively through your parted lips, purposely sucking on one perfect pearl at a time.

"He squirms in the chair, rock hard and ready.

"You move slowly down the length of his body.

"His eyes turn even darker with desire when you come back up with the can of whipped cream you've placed beneath the chair.

"'And now, dessert,' you tell him.

"He licks his lips expectantly as you spray the frothy mixture over your bare breasts.

"You straddle him again.

"He sticks out his tongue, eager for a taste.

"You lean closer, thrusting your breasts forward.

"He sticks his tongue out farther, trying to reach you.

"You back away, teasing him a little bit longer.

"His eyes are pleading now, begging for mercy.

"You saunter back in his direction.

"And . . ."

Alicia blinked when Zada pointed in her direction.

She'd been caught up in her own fantasy.

So caught up in the moment was she, Alicia didn't even think twice before she said, "His eyes are pleading now, begging for mercy.

"You saunter in his direction, knowing this is one man who deserves no mercy.

"His eyes widen in fear when you walk up to the chair he's sitting on.

"You have his hands tied behind his back, his body secured to the chair.

"How long you've waited for this moment.

"How stupid of him to believe you when you asked him to drop by to sign papers. How stupid to believe threats from his big-shot lawyer had finally forced you into selling the house.

"He screams at you, ordering you to release him.

"You pull the Taser gun out of your pocket again.

"He wisely settles back down.

"You stand there staring at the man who has stolen your dignity, crushed your self-esteem, and destroyed your faith in every man you'll ever meet again.

"Did he honestly think you would sell the house and give him half of the proceeds after the way he's treated you? That you would contribute one dime to a man who married you on false pretenses? Who set out from the day he met you to defraud, defile, and deliberately humiliate you?"

"You lean forward.

"Smile.

"And spit directly in his face.

"His shocked look tells you he gets the message.

"This time, he screwed with the wrong blonde.

"You walk out of the room long enough to retrieve another big surprise for this monster who has betrayed you so badly.

"His face turns ashen when you walk back into the room with your Latino ex-pool boy, and his ex-lover.

"Poor Javier is another victim this man devastated when he showered him with empty promises, then carelessly kicked him aside like a worthless piece of garbage.

"The monster yells ugly obscenities at both of you.

"You ignore him, ready to set your plan into motion.

"Javier seats himself on the monster's lap, and turns the monster's head sideways so his profile is unmistakable.

"The scene through the eye of your camera shows two men sharing a sensual kiss.

"Luckily, a picture has no sound.

"The people who will see this picture on every bulletin board at the hospital, will never hear the esteemed neurosurgeon screaming in anger once the kiss is broken.

"Javier rises to his feet, mission accomplished.

"You link your arm with his and head to the nearest photo shop to make copies.

"You both laugh as you walk through the front door, but you can still hear the monster screaming in the background as you slam the door behind you."

No one said a word.

For two full minutes, no one said a word.

Alicia finally reached for her wineglass, and drank every drop in one easy gulp. "Well!" she said, looking around the table. "You just can't imagine how much better I feel. Thank you so much for letting me share that fantasy tonight."

Jen, Tish, and Zada only stared at her.

Speechless didn't cover the looks on their faces.

Another mission accomplished, Alicia decided.

And I think they got the message loud and clear.
I'm one blonde you DON'T want to screw with!
She pushed her chair back and got up from the table.
But she paused at the kitchen door.
Turning back to face them, Alicia smiled brightly.

"I insist on holding the meeting at my house next week, ladies," Alicia told them sweetly. "And don't forget the sacred rule. What we say at the meeting, stays at the meeting."

Jen's front door slammed shut.

Jen, Tish, and Zada hurried to Jen's kitchen window.

Alicia was headed back across the street. Head held high. Back straight as a board. A don't-screw-with-me stride to her step.

"I can't believe it," Jen said. "Edward? Gay? You could have knocked me over with a feather. The creep. He was constantly flirting with all of us."

Tish said, "Maybe Edward's flexo-sexual. He can go either way."

"Poor Alicia," Zada said. "I hope that fantasy really was therapeutic for her. I can't imagine how I'd react if I'd been betrayed like that. I was ready to strangle Rick over a silly argument."

"A *silly* argument?" Tish shook her head in disbelief. "Isn't it amazing how four hours of foreplay can totally change your perspective on things?"

"I was just making a comparison," Zada grumbled. "And when you compare your husband cheating on you with another *man* to an argument, I doubt anyone will disagree that an argument seems pretty silly."

"Well, I don't care if Alicia's fantasy was therapeutic for her or not," Jen said. "She scared the pure crap out of me."

Tish said, "I agree. That glazed-over look in her eye was pretty freaking scary."

Jen said, "Scary enough that I have no desire to sit through another one of Alicia's fantasies again. Not next Saturday night. Or any other Saturday night."

Jen and Tish both sent Zada accusing looks.

"What?" Zada said.

"You know what," they both said.

"Okay, okay," Zada said. "I got us into this. I'll figure out some way to get us out of spending next Saturday night at Alicia's."

"And if Alicia decides you deserve no mercy and pulls a Taser gun on you?" Tish teased.

Zada said, "I doubt even a Taser gun could stun me any worse than Alicia did tonight."

"Amen to that," Jen said.

"Scary," Tish repeated and shivered.

"Enough about Alicia," Zada said. She looked over at Tish. "Could I persuade you to wait thirty minutes after I leave before you go home?"

Tish asked, "And that would be because?"

Zada said, "Because the minute you go home, Rick will know our meeting is over. I need a head start."

"A head start for what?" Jen quizzed.

Zada didn't answer. She walked across Jen's kitchen and paused at the kitchen door. She took one last look back over her shoulder and blew Jen and Tish a farewell kiss.

"Oh, yeah," Tish said, laughing. "There's definitely a lap dance in Rick Clark's future tonight."

* * *

Alicia would have been embarrassed over telling her neighbors her deepest, darkest secret, had she truly not felt better than she had since the day she'd come home unexpectedly and found Javier in a much more compromising position than the one she'd alluded to in her fantasy.

And it did feel extremely good, finally getting all that off her chest. Finally putting into words everything she should have done to Edward, and didn't.

But Alicia had decided long ago, he wasn't worth it.

Edward was pond scum, pure and simple.

And thanks to the Housewives' Fantasy Club, she'd finally found a way to get her revenge, if only by fantasizing about it.

That's why she would be happy to host the next meeting. She wanted to tell Jen, Tish, and Zada personally how much they really had helped her, simply by listening. Tonight just hadn't been the right time to have that conversation.

The getting-even-with-Edward fantasy had come as a big shock to her, too. Just as she was sure it had been a shock to them. The outburst had hit her totally out of the blue. She hadn't planned to tell them anything about the true reason behind her divorce. And she certainly wouldn't have been prepared to answer questions if any of the three of them had asked for specific details after she finished spilling her secret.

The reality of Edward's betrayal still hurt.

Better to wait until she hosted the next Fantasy Club meeting, before she thanked Jen, Tish, and Zada properly, until she had the right words formed in her mind. Until she'd had time to think about what she was willing to share if they did ask for specific details about her divorce.

Alicia smiled.

Maybe she'd even turn the meeting into a lavish celebration. Hire a staff and have a fully catered buffet. Give each of them a gift of thanks. A pricey bangle bracelet would be perfect, with HOUSEWIVES' FANTASY CLUB engraved right on the bangle.

Alicia almost felt giddy as she entered her house.

Knowing her life in Woodberry Park was going to be so different now, was even more exhilarating than imagining Edward's picture on the hospital bulletin board.

There'd be no more watching from her bedroom window.

No more exile.

No more being left out of the loop.

At last, she could look forward to new beginnings.

All thanks to the Housewives' Fantasy Club.

And thanking Jen, Tish, and Zada properly was exactly what Alicia intended to do.

When Tish yelled down to the basement that she was home, all interest in the poker game ended. Rick and Charlie both bolted from their chairs and headed for the outside basement entrance.

Even if they had yelled good-bye to Joe, he wouldn't have heard them. Joe had already disappeared up the basement stairs looking for Tish.

Rick hurried across the street, the goofy grin back on his face. He hadn't been privy to Zada's fantasy tonight, but something told him he was still going to like it.

That fact was confirmed when he opened the door.

Zada.

Standing at the top of the stairs.

Wearing nothing but a sexy red thong, red high heels, and the long strand of pearls he had given her as a wedding present.

"Well?" she said. "Your bed or mine?"

Rick said, "Technically, your bed *is* mine."

She crooked her finger in his direction, then disappeared down the hallway. Rick and his goofy grin hurried up the stairs, taking his clothes off as he went. By the time he made it to the bedroom, he was completely nude.

He realized he was in trouble when he looked around the room.

Lights off.

Candles glowing.

Al Greene singing something sexy about "Here I am baby, come and take me."

Baby, oh baby!

Zada pointed to the chair she was standing behind.

Rick raised an eyebrow, but he headed for the chair.

He sat down.

Zada jerked his arms behind his back.

"Be careful with those," Rick warned when he realized she was using the pearls to bind his hands. "Those are more expensive than I think you realize."

Zada walked back around to face him.

She smiled.

Seductively.

"Oh, I know exactly how expensive they are," she said.

Rick tensed when she straddled him and the chair.

She stood above him.

Hands on her hips.

Another sexy smile on her lips.

"And because I do know how expensive my pearls are," she said, "I'm counting on your full cooperation. One false move and you could break them. And we wouldn't want that? Now, would we?"

Rick gulped. "No. We wouldn't."

But Rick forgot about the pearls when Zada made a big production of running her hands suggestively over both breasts. His focus turned to the nipples that instantly came to life.

Be strong. Be strong. Be strong.

Rick forgot about being strong, when Zada lifted her long, dark hair and held it on top of her head as she danced provocatively to the music—this time, old Al singing something about "Oh baby, look what you've done to me."

I can tell you what she's doing to me, Al!

She's killing me here.

That's what she's doing to me!

Those magnificent breasts, right in his face, almost close enough to taste. Until Zada purposely leaned back, completely out of his reach.

Rick let out a sigh of relief when Zada stepped back.

Until she slithered right out of her thong!

Oh God. Oh God. Oh God.

He was nude and at full attention.

She was nude and writhing right above his salute!

"Be careful," Rick warned again.

He leaned his head back and closed his eyes.

One more wiggle that close, and he knew he'd lose it.

Zada fisted his hair.

Rick's eyes popped back open.

She pulled his head forward, covering his mouth in a blistering kiss.

Al belted out, "Love can make you do right. Love can make you do wrong."

At that exact moment, love made Rick do wrong.

He jerked his hands free, pearls be damned.

His hands grabbed Zada's waist, and he pulled her on top of him.

They both gasped when he slid deep inside her.

There was no way of stopping what happened next.

His hands, still clasped tightly around Zada's waist.

Her head, thrown back.

Back arched.

Hips moving.

Faster.

And faster.

And faster.

And faster.

They both cried out.

Their simultaneous orgasm shook the earth and took them both straight to paradise.

Rick fell back against the chair, his heart still pounding. Zada collapsed against him, her head on his shoulder. They remained that way, trying to catch their breath.

One second.

Two seconds.

Five full seconds.

"Oops," Zada finally whispered. "What happens now? Do we both lose the game?"

Rick's mind was still too foggy to answer.

But Al sang out loud and clear, "Let's stay together. Whether times are good, or bad. Happy or sad."

I couldn't agree with you more, Al.

Rick slid his arms beneath Zada's hips. He stood up from the chair, picking her up with him. Zada didn't protest when Rick carried her across the bedroom to *their* king-size bed.

Chapter 14

—🍓—

On Sunday morning, Zada got up at 0500 hours, for the first time in her life. At first light, she even went on a run with Rick and Simon—another first in the life of Zada Clark. A run that slowed to a jog after five minutes. Slowed to a walk after ten minutes. And ground to a halt when she couldn't take another step.

"Keep going," Zada yelled, waving Rick on when he looked back over his shoulder.

Can't you see I'm in no shape to exercise?

Evidently not.

Rick and Simon turned around on the path, and headed back in her direction. Bent over at the waist, Zada looked up at them when they reached her.

"I have a great idea," she told Rick between gasps for air. "You run that way. I'll run back to the house."

"We don't have to make the full loop around the golf course this morning," Rick said. "We'll go back with you."

"No," Zada said. "You and Simon finish your run. But if you get back to the house before I do, come looking for me. I'll be passed out somewhere along the way."

Rick laughed. "Will getting up early and exhausting

yourself this Sunday be worth it? If, say, I take next weekend off and leave the training classes to Scrappy? We'll
sleep in. We won't get dressed all day. *And* I'll even leave
the Sunday paper scattered all over the floor."

"Define 'sleep in,'" Zada said.

"Your idea of sleep in," Rick said. "We'll sleep until
noon."

"Can I have that in writing?"

"Yes," Rick said. "You write it. I'll sign it."

He leaned down and kissed her forehead.

Zada waved as he and Simon ran off.

Surprisingly, she did make it back to the house without
passing out. She also carefully chose her selection from
the soy coffee variety pack this time, instead of picking a
packet at random.

Hazelnut Hugs and Kisses.

Perfect for the new game they'd agreed to play: *Extreme Makeover: Marriage Edition.*

Not a full reconciliation, a trial reconciliation.

Just because they'd orgasmed themselves silly, didn't
mean they weren't fully aware that they were far from
being out of the woods, yet.

What they needed was more time, and they both realized
that. Time to see if they could overlook each other's faults,
learn to compromise. And possibly learn to live together.

And speaking of compromise.

Zada took her coffee cup with her into her private office off the kitchen. By the time she finished her project
on the computer and hit "print," Rick and Simon were
back from their run.

Paper in hand, Zada walked into kitchen.

"What's this?" Rick asked when she handed it over.

Rick laughed when he read the words: "IOU one sleep till noon, not get dressed all day, leave the paper scattered on the floor WITHOUT picking it up, Sunday."

Zada handed over a pen.

Rick grinned. "Okay. Where do I sign?"

"Anywhere you like," Zada said. "Just as long as I have your IOU in writing."

Alicia watched Zada make her morning trek across the street, coffee cup in hand. She cursed herself for being so pathetic—always peering out her bedroom window like some sleazy voyeur.

She just couldn't help it.

Watching Jen and Zada go to Tish's every morning was like that car wreck on the interstate; you knew you'd regret it, but you couldn't keep from looking.

She also cursed herself for being annoyed that they hadn't thought to call and ask her to have coffee with them this morning, but she was. If she had a life, she wouldn't have time to stand at her bedroom window, spying on her neighbors. If she had a life, she wouldn't give a crap who was having coffee without her. *If* she had a life . . .

The telephone rang.

Alicia sighed.

Life's little reminder that she *did* have a brother.

"How did the meeting go last night?" were the first words out of Alfie's mouth.

"Well enough, I guess," Alicia said. "I'm having the meeting at my house next Saturday night."

"Wonderful!" Alfie exclaimed.

"Don't get too excited," Alicia said with a sigh. "Things could still backfire."

Alfie said, "There you go being piss-imistic again. I truly wish you'd see my therapist, Alicia, before you turn into a bitter old troll."

"Well, ex-cuse me!" Alicia said right back. "But I've had a lot to be piss-imistic about lately. I'm pissed that I picked a total ass for a husband. I'm pissed that our nutty mother is a hypochondriac, and our delusional father thinks the twenty-something bimbo he's running around with at the moment really loves him. I'm pissed that you let women walk all over you, which is why you're in therapy. I'm pissed that I spilled my guts about Edward to my snotty neighbors last night, which means they'll probably really treat me like poison now. And most of all, I'm pissed that I can't seem to get out of this stupid blue funk I'm in!"

"And that's why you have me," Alfie said. "I'm the best blue funk slayer in the business. I should be, I've fought my way out of enough blue relationship funks in my lifetime."

"Then tell me, Alfie," Alicia said. "By all means, please tell me what to do to slay a blue funk. Tell me before this stupid blue funk ends up slaying me."

Alfie gasped. "Don't talk like that!"

Dammit!

Wrong choice of words.

"I'm serious, Alicia," Alfie warned. "You've been depressed for months now, and you're really starting to scare me. Maybe I should come stay with you for a few days."

Go ahead and shoot me now!

Alicia said, "Alfie. Listen to me very carefully. I do *not* want you staying with me for a few days. I do *not* want you calling me for hourly reports. And I definitely do *not* want to see your nutty therapist. What I want you to do is let me deal with my problems and my neighbors in my own way. Got it?"

"Got it," Alfie said. "But there still has to be something I can do to help you through this."

Alicia groaned. "I'm hanging up now."

"Okay," Alfie said. "I'll call and check on you later."

Jen peeked into Zada's cup.

"Let me guess. More Arouse Me Mocha?"

Zada shook her head. "Today's flavor is Hazelnut Hugs and Kisses."

"Forget today's flavor," Tish said. "I want to hear about last night's flavor."

Zada took a deep breath and said, "Which part? Me carrying out the lap dance fantasy? Or Rick and I having a simultaneous orgasm?"

Jen gasped. "You didn't!"

"I knew it!" Tish yelled.

She gyrated all around the kitchen.

She looked over at Jen. "Pay up, Jen. I told you they'd zip right past foreplay and head straight to consummation last night."

Zada's mouth dropped open.

"You bet money on us?"

"Of course we did," Tish said. "What are friends for?"

"It wasn't much," Jen said, trying to appease Zada.

Tish said, "Too bad about the eighty-something more

days of foreplay, though. I would have milked that puppy for all it was worth."

"Of course *you* would have, Miss S&M," Jen mumbled.

"On the other hand," Tish said, "now, we don't have to wait in suspense any longer. You and Rick are officially back together in every sense of the word."

Zada shook her head. "Not a full reconciliation. Just a trial reconciliation."

Jen said, "Sorry to bring this up, but doesn't sleeping together void your separation agreement?"

"Neither of us is going to run to the judge with the information we slept together, Jen," Zada said. "But if we can't work things out, we have at least reached a property settlement. Rick wants me to keep the house and Simon. And I've agreed to let him see Simon any time he wants."

Jen said, "You mean, like the two mature adults you should have been from the very beginning?"

"Yes," Zada said. "Like two mature adults, Jen. Rick and I really talked things out last night. He admitted he was disappointed because I wasn't more like his mother. And I admitted I was waiting for him to disappoint me, just like my father did. Now, we're going to take things slow and see if we can learn to compromise, accept each other's faults, and live together without killing each other."

Tish walked over and hugged her. "Well, I'm happy for you, Zada."

Jen said, "I'm happy for you, too, Zada. As long as you and Rick are over the game playing. Marriage is serious. I hope you've both figured that out."

"I just thought of something," Tish said. "Now that you and Rick are at least trying to work things out, why don't

Jen and I get babysitters this weekend, and we'll all go out to dinner on Saturday night to celebrate?"

Jen brightened up. "We could even hit a club later, and make the guys take us dancing. Back when we were in college, Charlie and I practically lived on the dance floor."

Zada said, "God, how I envy all of those 'back when we were in college' stories you and Tish tell. You two grew up with Joe and Charlie. Rick and I haven't even known each other two years."

"Trust me," Tish said. "Joe and Charlie 'growing up' is debatable."

Jen laughed and nodded in agreement.

"In fact," Zada said, "I don't even know if Rick *can* dance."

Jen said, "You've never danced with Rick? Not even at your wedding?"

"You mean the quickie wedding we had in Lake Tahoe?" Zada shook her head. "The gondola ride up the mountain took longer than the ceremony."

Zada sipped a few more Hugs and Kisses.

"And now that I think about it," Zada said, "not having a past together was probably one of our biggest problems. We jumped into marriage too soon. Before we really knew each other."

Jen said, "But now you do have a past together, Zada. And you've proved to each other that your love is strong enough to at least want another chance to work things out."

Tish said, "And *if* we can talk the boys out of their poker game Saturday night, that will give us a perfect excuse not to attend Alicia's Fantasy Club meeting."

Jen said, "What we should do is remind the boys why

they call us the Housewives' Fantasy Club. We'll tell them they have no choice. Our fairy godmother granted us a night on the town."

Zada said, "I hope our fairy godmother grants me acceptance for the new idea I want to send my editor."

Jen and Tish both said, "You're writing again?"

Zada nodded. She hadn't written a word since the separation. "I really want to do something with an environmental awareness theme this time."

"Zada, that's wonderful!" Always-environmentally-conscious Jen exclaimed. "About the theme, and the fact that you're writing again. I know how worried you've been over your writer's block since you and Rick separated."

"Amazing how sex clears the mind," Tish teased.

"True," Zada said. "Sex is like air. You don't really miss it until you aren't getting any."

It was after eleven o'clock when Rick drove the Hummer into the garage on Sunday night. Long hours even on weekends were part of the job during the weeks they were holding training sessions at the center.

The recruits lived at the center full-time, giving them the opportunity to bond with the dogs. But the time after the daily classes ended was just as important as time spent in the classroom and on the obstacle course.

After class time gave him and Scrappy the opportunity to bond with the recruits. Sharing real-life experiences with explosive detection was important information a recruit couldn't learn from reading any textbook.

Rick let himself into the house through the garage door

off the kitchen. He wasn't surprised to find Simon waiting to greet him. He squatted down, scratching Simon's ears, and giving him a few sound pats on his back.

He laughed when Simon gave him a thorough sniffing.

"What? Do you smell those dogs I've been working with today? You could have shown them a thing or two in your day, couldn't you old boy?"

As hard as it had been to retire Simon, he'd taken the vet's advice and kept Simon away from the center after the explosion. The vet's concern had been that bringing Simon back to surroundings he associated with explosive detection would be too traumatizing. Especially when the dog had a new challenge ahead of him—learning to survive sightless.

Traumatizing Simon in any way was not an option for Rick. The reason he'd left Simon with Zada when they separated was to keep Simon's life as trauma-free as possible.

Trauma-free.

Rick smiled.

If he and Zada could work things out, his own life had the potential to be trauma-free.

Thinking of Zada sent him through the house and up the stairs, being as quiet as possible. He headed down the hall to the guest bathroom to brush his teeth.

What?

All of his personal things were missing. He took a quick look in the closet. All of his clothes were missing as well.

Rick headed back down the hall, Simon following. He slipped into the bedroom. Zada was buried beneath the covers so far, all he could see was the top of her head.

Poor baby.

I need to let her sleep.

She'd gotten up early with him. Gone on a run with him. Moved his things for him.

God willing, he would spend the rest of his life trying to make her as happy as she was making him.

Rick undressed quickly, and slipped into bed, trying his best not to wake her. She rolled over and snuggled under his arm, her head resting against his chest.

Rick whispered, "Thanks for moving my things, angel. You didn't have to do that. I would have taken care of it myself."

He kissed the top of her head.

She snuggled even closer.

"I know how busy you are during training sessions," she whispered back. "Did your classes go okay today?"

"I had a great day," Rick said. "How did your day go?"

"Good," she said and yawned. "After I moved your things, I worked on a new book proposal."

She titled her chin up for a kiss. Rick didn't disappoint her. One kiss led to another. Rick was the one to pull away.

"I promised myself I wouldn't do this. I know you're worn out. Try and get some sleep."

"I'm tired," she said, "but I'm never that tired."

Her hand slipped beneath the covers and moved down his stomach.

Lower.

Lower.

Rick moaned and closed his eyes.

"How would you feel about dancing with me?"

His eyes snapped back open.

"Now?"

She giggled. "No, silly. Tish and Jen want us to go out Saturday night. Dinner first, a club later. It made me realize I didn't even know if you liked to dance."

"Dancing isn't really my forte," Rick said. "But if you want to go dancing, I'll take you dancing."

"And what if I want to do this?"

Her whole body disappeared under the covers this time.

The tongue thing!

Oh, baby!

You be the master.

I'll be the slave!

Chapter 15

Monday's choice from the soy coffee variety pack was Cuddle Me Cappuccino. On Tuesday, the flavor for the day was Original Roast Romance. Wednesday, Zada had two cups of Kiss Me Kaloah. And Thursday she made a fresh pot of Back to Bed Blueberry. Zada closed the week on Friday, with French Vanilla Flirt.

On Saturday, in honor of Rick taking the weekend off—for the first time ever during training sessions—Zada made a pot of delicious Love Me Tender Tiramisu. She and Rick enjoyed a cup together before Rick's tee-time with Charlie and Joe.

They walked across the street holding hands, with Zada thinking there had never been a more perfect June morning.

Birds were singing.

There wasn't a cloud in the sky.

The kids were playing in the cul-de-sac.

Jen and Tish, sitting on the steps, supervising.

Charlie and Joe, busy loading the golf cart.

Perfect. Perfect. Perfect.

She and Rick paused for a lingering kiss before Rick hurried off to join the guys. Zada sighed happily, then headed for Tish's front porch steps where Tish and Jen were sitting.

"Ain't love grand?" Tish said and winked at her.

They scooted over to make room for Zada on the steps. As the guys drove off, Rick turned around and waved. Zada blew him a kiss and waved back.

Jen said, "Well, I have to admit I like that wave much better than the one you gave Rick the last time the guys played golf together."

Zada said, "I was just sitting here thinking to myself how much has changed since the Saturday Rick moved back home. Somebody reach over and pinch me so I know I'm not dreaming."

Tish said, "I was just sitting here thinking how far behind I am making preparations for the annual neighborhood Fourth of July party. Can you believe it? July is only a few weeks away."

Jen took the hint and said, "Anything we can do to help?"

"I thought you'd never ask," Tish said. "Let me go get my sticky-note pad, and I'll make you both a list."

Jen and Zada both groaned.

Tish jumped up and hurried into the house anyway.

Zada looked over at Jen. "Is everything still a go for tonight?"

Jen nodded. "But I still can't believe Rick took it upon himself to make dinner reservations for all of us."

Zada said, "He still won't tell me where we're going. He keeps insisting it's a surprise."

"Surprise or not, I am so looking forward to a night

out," Jen said. "And thank God for grandparents. My parents are keeping Sonya, and Joe's parents are stopping by after lunch for the twins. We can party all night if we want."

"Thank God for *brave* grandparents where the twins are concerned," Zada said.

"I heard that," Tish said, walking back out on the porch. She wiggled in between Jen and Zada again. "And I agree completely. Joe's parents are saints. My mother has to have electroshock therapy after a sleepover with the twins."

Affirmative action was Alicia's modus operandi on Saturday morning when she looked out her bedroom window and saw Jen, Tish, and Zada sitting on Tish's front porch steps.

She'd waited all week for one of them to call her. For someone to at least confirm they were having the Fantasy Club meeting at her house on Saturday.

No one, of course, had bothered to call.

Nor had she broken down and called any of them.

She'd chosen to believe the matter was settled.

But now, Alicia was having serious doubts. She was afraid all of her elaborate plans would be wasted. Afraid there would be no one to eat the catered buffet. No one to receive the expensive engraved bracelets. No one to thank for listening to her Edward outburst.

Oh, God.

What if they really are intending to stand me up?

Alicia decided there was no time like the present to find out.

But if they did back out of this meeting . . .

If they dared to snub her again.

If they really were going to be that rude?

She was going to . . .?

She was going to . . .?

Dammit, I don't know what I'm going to do.

But it will be something radical!

"Uh-oh," Tish said. "Look who's headed our way."

Jen and Zada both turned their heads to look.

Zada looked back at Tish. "I forgot to ask you. What did Alicia say when you told her we couldn't make the meeting tonight?"

Tish paled. "Me? I thought you were going to call and tell her."

Zada wailed, "Me?"

"You're the one who said you would get us out of going to Alicia's," Tish hissed, lowering her voice as Alicia grew closer.

Zada whispered back, "But you were the one who came up with the reason why we couldn't make the meeting. That's why I thought *you* were going to call her."

Jen gasped. "Oh. My. God. You mean neither of you called to tell her we weren't coming?" Jen shook her head. "I swear. You two never cease to amaze me."

Zada and Tish both looked at her.

"You tell her, Jen," Tish urged, Alicia almost on top of them now. "Alicia has always liked you best, anyway. She'll take it better coming from you."

"Are you insane?" Jen whispered back. "Alicia probably has that Taser gun in her pocket right now!"

"Oh, shut up! Both of you," Zada grumbled. "I'll tell her myself."

"The way you were *supposed* to do all along," Tish said, sending Zada a mean look.

"Whatever," Zada said and frowned. "But trust me. Alicia is *not* going to take the news well coming from me."

Alicia gave Jen, Tish, and Zada her best smile when she walked up to the porch. "Ready for our meeting tonight, ladies?"

Their expressions answered for them.

Alicia's stomach rolled over. She would have thrown up had a cold calm not settled over her.

Zada spoke up and said, "Alicia, I can't tell you how sorry we are. I thought Tish had called you. And Tish thought I had called you. But we aren't going to be able to make the meeting tonight. The guys are taking us out to dinner."

"Dinner?" Alicia snapped.

I can't believe this!

"Yes," Zada snipped right back at her. "Dinner."

Alicia tossed her hair and said, "Sorry, but I'm a bit confused, Zada. I thought you were trying to get rid of Rick. I'd think about changing my strategy if I were you."

Zada's eyes narrowed.

So did Alicia's.

"I hate to disappoint you, Alicia," Zada said, with a toss of her own hair. "But Rick and I have decided to try and work things out."

Then Rick has my deepest sympathies.

But Alicia forced herself to say, "Congratulations."

"Thank you," Zada said, her nose in the air.

Jen was the only one decent enough to look guilty.

She sent Alicia an apologetic look and said, "You're more than welcome to come to dinner with us tonight, Alicia."

Alicia almost laughed in Jen's face.

Are you freaking kidding me?

Me—and three married couples?

You know I wouldn't accept that invitation!

Which is exactly why you asked.

Alicia didn't even dignify the invitation with a reply.

Before they saw the tears in her eyes, she wheeled around and walked back across the yard. With both fists clenched, Alicia made a silent vow.

Things were about to change in Woodberry Park.

Big time!

Rick was glad Zada had made him sign her IOU.

He couldn't have gotten out of bed before noon on Sunday if his life had depended on it.

He'd surprised all of them when the limo arrived the night before—his solution to someone having to be the designated driver on Saturday night. And yes, it was out of character for him to splurge like that. But during the last few weeks he'd had to face the fact that being out of character wasn't necessarily a bad thing where he was concerned.

He'd made reservations at a great Italian restaurant— Zada's favorite cuisine—in downtown Chicago, close to the nightlife. They'd hit as many clubs as possible before closing time. They didn't even get back to Woodberry Park until around 4:00 AM on Sunday morning.

He usually didn't drink that much.

He hadn't danced since his high school prom.

And he couldn't remember ever just letting go and having one hell of a good time.

But there was always a price to pay *after* the party.

The reason Zada was walking toward him now, at 4:00 *PM* on Sunday afternoon, a glass of water and two aspirins in her hand.

She stepped over the Sunday paper cluttering the floor in the den off the kitchen. "Here, sweetie," she said, handing him the glass.

Rick took the glass, tossed the aspirin into his mouth, and washed the medicine down with water. He handed the glass back to Zada, too hungover to care that she placed it on the end table by the sofa without using a coaster. But he wasn't too hungover to be affected when Zada stretched out on the sofa beside him, and pressed every inch of her incredible body fully against his.

"Talk about the marvels of modern medicine," Zada teased when his erection became obvious.

"Please don't make me laugh," Rick begged. "My hair even hurts."

"Probably from those wild eighties head-banger moves you were doing on the dance floor last night," Zada said.

Rick moaned. "Now you're making fun of me."

"I am so!" Zada exclaimed and grinned. It was her way of agreeing, but still with an argumentative tone.

"Let's compromise," Rick said. "If you'll stop rubbing

your hot little body against me like that, we can both take a nice, long nap."

"I have a better idea," Zada said.

She got up from the sofa and covered him with a throw.

"You take a nap. I'll go work on my proposal."

"I don't get it," Rick grumbled. "You drank as much as I did. Why aren't you hungover?"

"Because I am truly an evil woman," Zada said.

She winked at him and headed out of the room.

Rick rolled over and promptly went to sleep.

The ringing in Rick's dream was the bell, signaling it was time to change classes. He was walking down the hall in his old high school. He had on his black and gold leather high school jacket with BULLDOGS written on the back, and with patches on the front where he'd lettered in football, basketball, and baseball. The girl he had taken to his senior prom was standing by her locker.

She smiled at him and said, "Aren't you going to answer the phone?"

Rick jerked upright on the sofa.

"Zada," he called out. "Are you going to get that?"

The phone rang again.

Damn!

Rick pulled himself up and headed for the nearest phone in the kitchen, fingers to his temples, a groan on his lips.

"Hello."

Silence.

"Hello," Rick said again.

The caller hung up.

Rick clicked the phone off and laid it on the kitchen

counter. When he walked to the sink for a glass of water, he saw Zada through the kitchen window—in the backyard with Simon, tossing him the sensor ball. He had just taken a glass from the cabinet when the phone rang again.

"Hello," Rick said.

Silence.

"This is the Clark residence," Rick said. "Who are you calling?"

Again, the caller hung up.

Rick hit *69.

The message came up "private caller."

A sick feeling, worse than any hangover, instantly hit the pit of his stomach. He was still staring at the phone when Zada and Simon came through the kitchen door.

Zada said, "Hey, sleepyhead. You're up. But the question is, are you feeling any better?"

Rick didn't answer.

He kept staring at the phone, a stricken look on his face.

Possibilities instantly raced through Zada's mind, none of them good. His family? Her family? One of their friends?

"Rick, what's wrong?"

Rick held up the phone. "I've just had two hang-up phone calls, back to back. Maybe you should inform your boyfriend we're back together."

Zada drew a blank. "What boyfriend?"

Rick's blue eyes were turning darker by the second.

He said, "The guy you said you were dating. You were just going to hang out at his place? Remember?"

Zada laughed.

It was the wrong thing to do.

Rick slammed the phone down on the counter. He walked out of the kitchen and into the adjoining den, kicked the Sunday paper out of his way, and flopped down on the sofa.

Zada hurried after him.

He looked up when she stopped in front of the sofa.

"Rick," she said. "I laughed because I made that up. There is no guy. I swear it."

Rick didn't seem convinced.

He said, "Get serious, Zada. Why would you lie about dating some guy?"

Zada said, "To make you jealous, okay?"

"And how sick is that?"

"You're right," Zada said. "It was a sick thing to do. But we were at a sick place in our relationship, Rick. It was the first time I'd seen you in six months. All I could think about was hurting you, the way you hurt me when you walked out."

Rick ran a hand through his hair, the way he always did when he was deep in thought. He looked up at her and said, "You want to hear something else sick? I really couldn't blame you if you were seeing someone else. You didn't have many fond memories of the time you spent with me."

"Don't say that," Zada told him.

She sat down on the sofa beside him.

Zada said, "Don't you realize how much I love you? I knew I had to have you the minute I saw you."

Rick leaned over and kissed her.

"Same here," he said. "We just didn't know what to do when we got each other, did we?"

Zada leaned over and kissed him.

"No," Zada said, "we didn't know what to do with each other before. But I think we're both finally beginning to figure that out."

Rick looked straight at her. "Anything else you want to confess?"

You just had to ask.

Zada knew exactly how Rick felt about lying.

She'd always made excuses for the lies she told—telling herself little white lies were just a fact of life. But if she and Rick were really going to start a new life together, she need to stop making excuses and tell Rick the truth.

About everything.

Zada took a deep breath and said, "I lied about us agreeing that the bedrooms were off limits."

Rick said, "I *knew* it! I knew I didn't remember you saying the bedrooms were off limits."

"And . . ." Zada said, but she didn't finish.

Rick said, "Why do I get the impression this is going to be a big confession?"

Tell him!

Zada said, "That first Saturday you moved home? Tish gave Joe the monitor for a reason while you guys were playing poker that night. Tish knew Joe wouldn't be able to resist listening in on our conversation. We were counting on Joe to manipulate you and Charlie into going along with him. And, of course, he did."

Rick stared at her, absorbing the information.

"Are you angry that we tricked you?"

"Are you angry that we listened?"

"No," Zada said.

"As far as I'm concerned," Rick said, "we got what we deserved."

Zada said, "Just one question. What did Joe do to make you and Charlie go along with him? That's so unlike both of you."

"I'm embarrassed to tell you," Rick said. "Joe called us both wimps. We couldn't let him get away with that."

Zada laughed.

"My turn to ask a question," Rick said. "Are you saying everything about your Zorro fantasy was a lie?"

"No," Zada said. "Just the twist at the end about me being the master and you being the slave. I knew it would make you angry. And I knew if I didn't find a way to get you to back off, I'd never survive another kiss like the one you gave me before we left for Tish and Joe's that night."

"So?" Rick said, raising an eyebrow. "You really have fantasized about me in that Zorro costume?"

"Oh, yeah," Zada said. "Talk about hot! You looked hot!"

Rick looked pleased.

Until the telephone rang.

Rick frowned and said, "You answer it this time."

Zada walked across the room, Rick right behind her.

She picked up the phone from the kitchen counter.

When she said, "Hello?" Rick hit speaker phone.

"Are you alone?" a muffled voice said.

Rick grabbed the phone away from her.

"Who is this?" he demanded.

The speaker phone hissed the dial tone back at him.

Rick handed the phone back to Zada.

The look on his face said he wanted to believe her.

Still, Zada panicked.

Who would be doing this?

She punched *69, hoping to find out. No such luck. The caller had blocked the number.

"I tried *69 already," Rick said. "People who dial wrong numbers do it accidentally, Zada. They don't make it a point to block caller ID before they make a call."

"Meaning what?" Zada asked, irritated at his tone.

"You tell me," Rick said.

He walked out of the kitchen and down the hallway.

Lord, give me patience.

Now!

By the time Zada made it upstairs and walked into the bedroom, Rick was already climbing into bed.

"You're going to bed now?" Zada couldn't believe it. "It's only six o'clock."

Rick turned his back to her and said, "In case you've forgotten, I happen to feel like crap."

"I don't feel so good right now, myself," Zada said. "You basically just called me a liar."

Rick rolled over and sat up. "What do you want me to say, Zada?"

"I know that look, Rick," Zada said. "It's your I'm-pissed-and-I'm-not-talking-about-it look. In the past, I would have stomped back downstairs and let you stay up here and sulk. I'm done with that. I love you, and I'm going to fight for *our* survival. I'm not interested in being the sole survivor anymore."

Rick stared at her for a long time.

He finally held his hand out. "Come here."

Zada walked over and sat down on the bed beside him.

"In the past," he said, "I wouldn't have admitted that I'm a stupid jerk for being jealous, but I am. I'm sorry, Zada. The thought of you dating someone else turns me inside out."

Zada leaned over and kissed him.

"There is no guy, Rick. I can't explain the phone calls. But there is no guy."

"I believe you," he said.

He pulled her to him for another kiss.

He'd said the right words.

But the hurt in his eyes told a different story.

Zada didn't get up with Rick at 0500 hours on their second Monday morning of their trial reconciliation. When the alarm went off, Rick told her to stay in bed.

"It's raining," he'd said. "I'm skipping my run and going straight to the center."

Ten minutes later, he was dressed and ready to leave.

"I'll see you tonight," she heard him say.

Zada sat up.

Too late; Rick was already gone.

She flopped back on the bed, listening to the sounds.

The rain hitting against the window.

The garage door opening.

The Hummer backing out.

The garage door closing.

The Hummer driving away.

Simon's toenails clicking down the hallway.

"No run for you this morning, huh, buddy?" Zada said when Simon jumped up on the bed and licked her face.

No good-bye kiss for me, either.

Nor had there been any lovemaking the night before.

She reminded herself that Rick had been hungover. And that he had at least put his arm around her, pulling her close, when she'd finally come up to bed several hours later.

Still, those hang-up phone calls had been there.

Lying between them.

Eating away at his trust in her.

Driving her crazy wondering who would do such a thing.

It was still raining when Zada got up at seven. Still raining as she watched the hands of the clock *tick, tick, tick* off the time until she could have coffee with Jen and Tish, and ask her best friends what they made of the situation. By the time nine o'clock finally rolled around, Zada had worked herself into a full blown snit.

She was angry at the caller.

Angry that Rick doubted her.

And mad as hell that life just couldn't stand for her to be happy!

Zada stomped up on Tish's porch at 9:15 AM, propped her umbrella against the porch railing, and stormed into Tish's kitchen with a frown on her face.

Tish was the only one there.

"And today's flavor is?" Tish asked like some game-show host waiting for a winning answer.

"Dark Roast Diva," Zada said through clenched teeth.

Tish raised an eyebrow. "How appropriate for your obviously shitty mood."

Zada told her everything at once, even her confession

about tricking the guys. By the time Jen and her daughter showed up fifteen minutes later, Zada was pacing back and forth in Tish's kitchen like a woman possessed.

Jen took one look at her and sent Sonya to find the twins. She looked over at Tish. "What's wrong with Zada?"

"All stressed out," Tish said, "no one to choke."

"Oh, no," Jen said. "She and Rick are fighting again?"

Zada frowned at both of them. "Would you please stop talking about me like I'm not in the room!"

She told Jen everything she'd already told Tish.

Jen sat down at the table, shaking her head in disbelief. "But who would do such a thing?"

Tish had an I-can-think-of-someone look on her face.

"Who?" Jen demanded.

Tish said, "I hate to accuse anyone, but you both saw how Alicia reacted over us standing her up Saturday night. She was literally seething behind that fake smile of hers. She practically left divots in my lawn when she stomped back across the yard to her house."

Jen said, "Oh, Tish. Do you really think Alicia would stoop to making hang-up phone calls?"

"Don't think it hasn't crossed my mind," Zada said. "Alicia made a play for Rick the morning he moved back home, didn't she?"

Tish said, "And you did say you couldn't tell if the caller's voice was a man's voice or a woman's."

Jen said, "I'm only playing devil's advocate here, Zada, but maybe you should ask Rick if there's anyone he needs to tell you about. You were separated for six months. Someone might be upset that Rick went back to his wife."

"Believe me," Zada said, "that's crossed my mind, too."

"But that doesn't make any sense, Jen," Tish said. "If some woman was calling Rick, she would have talked to him instead of hanging up on him."

"Not if her motive was to cause problems for him," Jen argued. "So he and his wife would break up again."

Zada stopped pacing and dropped down onto a chair at the table. Head in her hands, she said, "Why did I have to make that stupid remark about dating some guy! That's really the problem. If I'd never made that comment, Rick would have chalked those phone calls off as some weirdo and would have already forgotten about them."

"You can always call the phone company and get a private number," Jen said.

"I almost told Rick that last night," Zada said. "But asking for a private number only makes me look more guilty."

"Then maybe you should confront Alicia," Tish said. "Ask her point-blank if she's the one who made the phone calls."

"That could backfire," Jen pointed out. "If it is Alicia, and Zada tells her she's causing problems, that would give her even more incentive to continue making the calls."

Tish said, "Well, I still think we should keep a close watch on Alicia over the next few days. Maybe we should invite her over for coffee tomorrow morning. See how she reacts having to sit across the table from Zada and look her in the eye."

Zada said, "Let's wait and see what kind of mood Rick's in tonight. Maybe I'm blowing this whole thing out of proportion."

"Zada's right," Jen said. "Rick has all day today to

think things over. I'm sure he'll realize Zada wouldn't lie to him about something so important."

Tish said, "It still doesn't hurt to keep an eye on Alicia."

Tish left the kitchen, heading for her dining room—the room with the window that faced Alicia's house.

Jen walked up behind Tish.

Zada walked up behind Jen.

"This is silly," Jen said. "What are we going to do? Stand here all day waiting to get a glimpse of Alicia with the phone in her hand?"

No one answered.

But neither did anyone move from the window.

For the first time in weeks, Alicia had no interest whatsoever in watching from her bedroom window as her neighbors made their way across the street for morning coffee at Tish's house. She also had no interest in taking her brother's annoying just-checking-on-poor, depressed-you phone call—she let her voice mail do that for her.

By ten o'clock Alicia was dressed fit to kill and feeling better than she'd felt in months. Even the rain that would have terribly depressed her only days earlier, didn't dampen her spirits.

Alicia walked into her garage. She got into her Mercedes, and drove out of Woodberry Park, never looking back.

And what a pity, on this particular morning.

Had Alicia looked back, even briefly, she might have found it quite amusing that the same neighbors she usually watched from her bedroom window were now spying on *her.*

* * *

Zada was mumbling obscenities to her computer that Monday afternoon, trying unsuccessfully to save the first chapter of her new book *Quack, Quack, Recycle That* onto a backup disc. She jumped when the telephone rang.

Zada grabbed the portable phone sitting on her desk and breathed a sigh of relief when she looked at the caller ID. She answered saying, "I just discovered a new oxymoron compliments of Bill Gates. 'Microsoft Works.'"

"Forget Bill Gates," Tish said. "Is everything okay?"

"Yes," Zada said. "Why?"

"Then what's Rick doing home at three in the afternoon?"

"Rick isn't home."

"Yes, he is! He just stopped at the mailbox. He's driving up your driveway now."

Zada hung up without answering.

She ran to the half-bath in the hallway. Jerking the scrunchie from around her ponytail, she tried to shake her hair out in some kind of shape.

Dammit!

She'd planned to be showered and dressed when Rick got home later that evening. Wearing something less obvious than a thong, but better than the wrinkled shorts and the T-shirt she had on at the moment.

The thought did cross her mind, however, that maybe it was a blessing she did look so ratty. One look at her disheveled appearance was sure to convince Rick he had nothing to worry about. No man in his right mind would give her a second look.

Zada heard the kitchen door open and another thought froze her right where she stood. What if Rick had come home so early to tell her he wanted out—that it really wasn't going to work between them after all?

"Zada?" she heard Rick call.

Zada took a deep breath and left the bathroom.

Ready or not, it was time to find out.

He was standing beside Simon.

He held out a collar and said, "I brought Simon a present. This is one of the new collars I had made for the training session. They look great, don't they?"

He bent down and removed Simon's old collar and placed the new collar around Simon's neck. The collar was bright yellow and SDS was stamped in black letters all the way around it.

And yes, it was a nice collar.

But is Rick freaking kidding me?

Here I am, waiting for my whole world to crumble.

And he's talking about a present he brought home for Simon!

But Zada forced herself to say, "Yes. The collar really looks great."

He walked in her direction.

Zada couldn't interpret the look on his face.

Only that it was serious.

"I brought you a present, too," he said.

Rick reached out and took her hand.

Zada gasped when he slipped a ring on her finger.

"We never got around to the ring part," he said. "We got married on a whim. And then after we were married, you kept insisting you didn't like rings. But we both knew why you were stalling. We were having so many problems, you didn't think we were going to make it."

Zada looked up at him, tears in her eyes.

"I hope this ring shows you how much I love you, Zada. And how sorry I am for being such an ass last night. Can you forgive me?"

Zada kept staring at the diamond on her finger.

If the size of the diamond determined how much Rick loved her—he loved her a lot!

Tears were streaming down her face now.

"Angel," he said, pulling her to him. "Don't cry."

"Women always cry," Zada sobbed against his shoulder. "Tears are all tied up in our emotions. We cry when we're happy. We cry when we're sad. Sometimes we cry just because we need to cry."

Rick bent down and kissed the tears away.

"These are happy tears, I hope," he said.

"I can't even tell you how happy," Zada told him.

She held out her hand and looked at her finger again.

"This is the most beautiful ring I've ever seen."

"I really am sorry about last night," Rick said.

Zada reached up and put her fingers to his lips.

"Forgotten," she told him.

"I agree," Rick said. "But I want you to call the phone company tomorrow and request a private number."

"I'm so glad you said that," Zada told him. "I wanted to suggest it last night, but I was afraid I'd sound guilty."

"I'm not suggesting we get a private number because I think you're guilty, Zada," Rick said. "I just refuse to let the joker making the phone calls get his kicks at our expense."

He pulled her to him and hugged her close.

She was tempted to tell Rick she and the girls suspected Alicia, but decided against it. They had weathered this storm together. She wasn't about to tip the lifeboat now.

"I didn't expect you home so early," Zada said. "Can I get you anything?"

Rick moved his eyebrows up and down.

"How about another lap dance?"

Zada was still laughing as he carried her out of the kitchen, down the hallway, and straight up the staircase.

Chapter 16

---🍎---

Without the threat of another phone call hanging over their heads, Zada and Rick settled into a routine of total peace and harmony. Compromise was becoming a simple fact of life for them.

Days slipped into weeks.

Now, they were approaching what Tish called their one month simultaneous orgasm anniversary.

Zada's road to happiness was no longer under construction. All of the potholes had been filled in. And she found herself sitting on easy street.

Life was good.

Everyone was happy.

Well, maybe not everyone.

Zada thought this as she hooked Simon's leash to his collar and headed out the kitchen door for their morning walk.

Alicia had avoided them like the plague since the Sunday she and Rick received the hang-up phone calls. She'd even turned Tish down flat to come over for coffee one morning.

Tish's ulterior motive, of course, had been to show Alicia

Zada's new ring. Let Alicia see for herself that if she had made the phone calls, her plan to cause trouble between them hadn't worked at all.

Alicia had claimed she was on her way out that morning, which rang a false note. Since her divorce, Alicia rarely went anywhere. And everyone in the neighborhood knew it.

They'd been surprised when Alicia did go out that morning—a fact they'd confirmed a few minutes after Tish hung up the phone. The three of them were again standing at Tish's dining room window, watching as Alicia drove away.

Zada liked to think Alicia had given up, and had accepted the fact she and Rick were back together. But despite protests from her and from Jen, watchdog Tish had continued to monitor Alicia's comings and goings on a daily basis. Tish was fully convinced Alicia had been staying away from home as much as possible, because she was up to more mischief.

"You can't let your guard down where Alicia is concerned, Zada," Tish kept insisting. "Alicia's still fuming over us standing her up, and don't think she isn't. I don't trust that witch. And you shouldn't, either. Not even for one minute."

Zada kept insisting Tish should drop it.

Alicia simply wasn't worth the worry.

Besides, Zada had other things to worry about.

Like the snag she'd run into with her new book.

Zada led Simon toward the walking path, aware that one of the main reasons she was having trouble with the book was because Miss Neighborhood Organizer Tish kept interrupting her writing time obsessing over the annual neighborhood Fourth of July party. They were having the party this weekend on Saturday, though the Fourth fell on the following Monday this year.

The closer it got to the party, the more frantic Tish became.

And since it was Wednesday—only three days away from the party—Zada had decided to do the unthinkable and skip morning coffee with Tishzilla and Jen.

Being assigned yet another new errand was not on her list of things to do today. Taking a long walk with Simon so she could sort out the problem with her book was Zada's Wednesday morning mission.

She walked along with Simon, deep in thought.

Her big dilemma?

How to correctly portray that pollution kills innocent wildlife without angry parents suing her later when their scarred-for-life children ended up in therapy.

Simon's low growl jerked her out of the book.

And right back to reality.

A guy was walking in their direction, less than fifty feet away. He was no one Zada knew, but he was nicely dressed, tall, dark and handsome—the kind of guy she would have been attracted to in her pre-Rick days.

Simon growled again, causing her to put her own guard up.

Zada glanced to her left.

When she saw a party of four on the golf course, she breathed a little easier. The men were on the putting green, in full view. Which also meant if she could see them, they could see her and the stranger who was almost on top of her now.

"Good morning," the guy said when he reached her.

Zada nodded and stopped walking.

The second she stopped, Simon sat down obediently. He didn't growl this time—sensing she wasn't afraid.

"Nice dog," the guy said, looking down at Simon.

"Thanks," Zada told him.

"My wife and I have been looking at a house over on Woodberry Way," he said. "I'm checking out the golf course this morning. You know us guys, first things first."

Zada laughed. "You just described my husband to a 'T,'" Zada said. "No pun intended."

The guy laughed. "Have you and your husband been happy here in Woodberry Park?"

"Yes," Zada said. "We love it here."

He leaned toward her suddenly, touching her hair.

Startled, Zada jumped back.

Simon growled low and mean and lunged for him.

"Whoa!" the guy said, jumping back out of Simon's reach. He held up a caterpillar. "Hey, sorry. I didn't mean to scare you. You just had a hitchhiker in your hair."

Embarrassed, Zada apologized.

He shrugged, waved, and headed down the path.

As an afterthought, Zada called out, "Hey, we're having our annual Woodberry Park Fourth of July party at the clubhouse on Saturday. You and your wife should come."

"Thanks," he yelled back. "We'll do that."

Sheesh, Zada thought as the poor guy disappeared up the path. The whole situation with the phone calls, and with Tish playing super-sleuth day and night, was making her some kind of paranoid.

Still, Zada reached down and gave Simon a proud pat on the head. "Good boy," she told him.

She'd said it before, and she'd say it again: If there was anyone she could depend on, it was Simon.

"Thank God it's Friday," Rick said when Scrappy walked up beside him.

"Amen to that," Scrappy agreed.

They were standing on the sidelines, watching their soon-to-be-graduated recruits lead their dogs around the obstacle course for the last time that day.

"I still think you should come help me out at the Fourth of July party tomorrow," Rick told him.

"And you're entitled to your *wrong* opinion," Scrappy said. "But while you're trying to keep a bunch of screaming kids from putting each other's eyes out with those sparklers you bought, I'll be kicked back with a brewski in one hand and the remote in the other, watching the tube and enjoying the peace and quiet."

"Wiseass," Rick said.

Scrappy grinned. "I am a wiseass. That's why I'm not stupid enough to go to some neighborhood party."

"Did you pick up the mail?"

"Just got back," Scrappy said. "I had to sign for one of the envelopes. Probably those contracts you've been waiting on from Bill Harris. Thought I'd come and wrap things up while you go over the mail."

"Thanks," Rick told him.

Scrappy said, "I'll take the recruits back to the classroom after we finish here. Thought you might want to thank them for a job well done this week, before you send them off for the long Fourth of July weekend."

"You can say that again," Rick said.

"What?"

"'Long Fourth of July weekend,'" Rick said. "I'm really looking forward to three days off."

"You're getting slack on me, Rick," Scrappy grumbled. "There was a day when you would have been at the center even on the Fourth of July."

"Those days are gone," Rick said. "I finally realized how much I wanted a life with my wife."

"Better you than me," Scrappy told him.

Rick laughed and started for his office.

"I put the mail on your desk," Scrappy called after him.

Rick threw up his hand and started up the stairs.

A few minutes later, Rick flopped down onto the chair behind his desk, and began sifting through the mail. He came to the large envelope on the bottom of the stack and put everything else aside. He was reaching for the letter opener when the telephone rang. Rick picked up the receiver, held it between his shoulder and his chin, and punched the blinking light.

"Security Detection Services. Rick Clark speaking."

Rick sliced through the top of the envelope.

"Hey, Bill. Talk about perfect timing. I just got my first chance to look at the mail today. And I think I'm getting ready to open the envelope with your contracts."

Rick reached into the envelope.

"Really?" Rick said. "Okay. Then I'll look for the contracts the first of next week, Bill. Thanks for calling to let me know you're mailing them today."

Rick put the phone back in the cradle, and pulled the contents out of the envelope. Forty-five minutes later, he was still staring at the eight-by-ten glossy color photograph he was holding in his hand.

Scrappy stuck his head around the door.

"The recruits are waiting. Did you get lost or something, Rick?"

"Or something," Rick said.

Scrappy walked into the office.

Rick handed him the photo.

"Son of a bitch!" Scrappy said.

"My thoughts exactly," said Rick.

He'd told Scrappy about the phone calls. Surprisingly, Scrappy had been the one to advise him to get a private telephone number and put the past behind them.

Rick almost laughed.

It was hard to put the past behind you when it was staring you in the face.

"Same as the phone calls, Rick," Scrappy said. "The past is the past. This picture could have been taken before you went back home."

"Great theory," Rick said. "Except for Simon's new SDS collar."

"Son of a bitch!" Scrappy said again.

"Maybe we should count the door prizes again."

"Tish!" Zada said. "We've counted the door prizes twice already. We have more than enough prizes for the games we'll be playing tomorrow."

"Okay, okay," Tish said. "I just don't want anyone to be left out."

Zada looked at Jen.

Jen looked at Zada.

Jen said, "You go through this every year, Tish. We

never run out of anything. And to my knowledge, no one has ever been left out."

"Get a grip on reality, why don't you?" Zada threw in.

"Reality's for people who can't handle drugs," Tish said, already counting the prizes again.

"Then maybe you should up your Prozac," Jen mentioned.

"I agree," Zada said. "Either up your medication, or share your Prozac with me. But do something, Tish. I can't take much more of your hysterics."

Tish glanced out her kitchen window, then back at Zada.

"And I can't take much more of you and Rick."

Zada blinked. "Excuse me?"

Tish pointed to the window. "Rick. Home early again. Probably to bring you another fabulous present."

Zada walked to the window in time to see the Hummer disappear into her garage.

"I agree with Tish," Jen said. "This coming home early and showing up with fancy presents is starting to piss me off. In fact, I might just sucker punch Charlie when he walks through the door tonight."

"I bet he has my pearls back from the jeweler," Zada said happily. "Poor baby. He felt so bad after he broke them. I ask, is my husband a sweetheart? Or is my husband a sweetheart?"

"You're seriously making me gag here," Tish grumbled.

Zada smiled an eat-your-heart-out smile.

She bowed dramatically to Jen and Tish.

"As you can see, ladies," she said. "I'm bowing out now."

Jen looked at Tish.

Tish looked at Jen.

They both looked back at Zada.

Tish said, "If it's a diamond tennis bracelet instead of your pearls, I don't want to know about it."

Jen said, "I don't want to know about it even if it's just a dang candy bar and a pack of peanuts. Charlie never buys me anything."

Zada made a mad dash across the street.

She ran around the side of the house, and hurried up the back steps. She walked into the kitchen. Rick was standing in the den off the kitchen, his back to her.

"Hey you," Zada said, walking toward him. "Tish and Jen are green with envy. They're convinced you came home early to bring me another present. Please tell me it's my pearls back from the jeweler."

Rick turned around.

Zada stopped walking.

He didn't have to say something was seriously wrong; his ice-cold blue eyes said it for him.

"I'm the one who got a present today," Rick said.

He handed her a photograph.

Nothing could have prepared Zada for the shock.

She looked at the photo, taking it all in at once.

Her.

The guy on the walking path.

Him, appearing to caress her face.

Her chin tilted sideways, appearing to let him.

She looked back at Rick. It broke her heart to see the tears in his eyes. "Oh, God. Rick."

"Zada, don't," he said. "Don't say a word. I don't want to hear it."

He walked over and sat down on the sofa. He wouldn't even look at her.

"I know what this looks like," Zada said, her voice quivering. "But, please, Rick. Let me explain."

He shook his head disgustedly. He still wouldn't look at her.

"I don't even know this guy," she began.

Rick exploded. "Christ, Zada!" He spit the words out at her. "He's caressing your face, dammit. Give me a fucking break!"

"He is not caressing my face!"

Zada sat down on the sofa beside him.

Rick jumped up from the sofa when she did.

He stood above her, hands at his waist. He was more angry than she'd ever seen him.

Zada felt like throwing up.

"I swear to you," Zada said, looking up at him. "I do not know this guy."

Rick started to walk away.

Zada reached out and grabbed his arm. "He was on the walking path the other morning, Rick. He was walking one way, Simon and I were walking the other way. We said hello to each other and he said he and his wife were moving to Woodberry Park. He reached out and pulled a caterpillar out of my hair. That's what he's doing in this photograph. Not caressing my face!"

Rick jerked his arm away from her, and walked into the kitchen. Zada got up from the sofa and marched after him.

"I'm telling you the truth, Rick. I just wish whoever took this picture had waited one second longer. Then you would have seen Simon lunging at the guy. He startled me when he leaned too close and touched my hair. I jumped back and Simon almost nailed him."

Rick yelled, "You really expect me to believe that some guy accosted you on the walking path, Simon almost bit him, and you didn't tell me about it?"

"It didn't seem important at the time," Zada tried to explain. "I totally forgot about it. You know how I am when I get engrossed in the first draft of a new book."

Rick grabbed the photo out of her hand. He held it up in front of her face. "I don't call this being engrossed in your new book!"

Zada grabbed the photo and threw it.

It floated across the room like a butterfly.

How ironic, Zada thought, since a caterpillar had started it all.

"Alicia is behind this," Zada said, more to herself than she did to Rick. "This picture is just like the one she described in her fantasy. A picture that looks like one thing, but is actually another."

"Alicia!" Rick looked at her like she was crazy.

"Yes, Alicia," Zada said. "Jen and Tish and I have suspected her from the beginning of being the one who made those hang-up phone calls."

"Let me guess," Rick said. "You've been too engrossed in your new book to mention you suspected Alicia made those phone calls, too."

"Dammit," Zada said, "you're twisting things around."

"Me?" Rick shouted. "These stories you keep coming up with are so twisted the next thing you're going to tell me is that you forgot to mention you're also a closet contortionist!"

Rick threw his head back and laughed.

A rather twisted kind of laugh, Zada decided.

Zada said, "Would you like for me to call Tish? She'll be happy to confirm we've suspected Alicia all along."

"Now there's a reliable source," Rick said. "Yeah, sure. Call Tish. Tell her to send Joe on over with the monitor."

Zada winced and glanced upward to the ceiling.

Seriously, God.

Is it necessary to hit me with every crappy thing I've ever done all at once?

"Just one question," Rick said. "What possible motive would Alicia have for putting caterpillars in your hair, hiding in the bushes with a camera, and waiting for some guy to come along so she could snap a picture?"

"See?" Zada said. "You're twisting things around again. I didn't say I thought Alicia actually took the photo herself. But I do believe she's behind it."

They stood there in the kitchen.

Her, staring at him.

Him, staring at her.

"Okay," Rick said. He folded his arms across his chest. "Let's go over to Alicia's house right now. I'm dying to hear how she set up that photograph."

Zada blinked.

Several times.

What we say at the meeting, stays at the meeting.

Suspecting Alicia was one thing. Getting up in her face with a photograph—and possibly accusing her falsely—was another.

Zada said, "I said I suspected Alicia, Rick. I don't have any proof. Not yet. But . . ."

Rick stomped back to the den before she could finish.

Zada stomped right along behind him.

"This isn't even about who made the phone calls or who took the photo, Rick," Zada said, fuming herself now. "What this is about is trust. As crazy as everything sounds, I've told you the truth. You either trust me, or you don't."

Rick looked at her for a long time.

Long enough that Zada knew she was *not* getting through to him.

"I need some time, Zada," he said. "Time to sort things out."

"Define 'some time,'" Zada said.

He shrugged. "A few days."

"You're kidding yourself, Rick," Zada told him. "If you don't have complete faith in me right now, a few more days isn't going to change a thing."

Chapter 17

———◆———

When Alicia opened her front door, Zada didn't wait to be invited in. She slapped the photo against Alicia's thirty-eight-inch chest and pushed her backward into her own foyer. Unable to keep her balance, Alicia landed on her curvy thirty-six-inch butt in the middle of her expensive Italian marble floor.

Zada threw the photo in her lap.

She glared down at Alicia, hands on her hips.

"I think that belongs to you."

Alicia picked the photo up and turned it over.

All of the color drained from her face.

"Get up!" Zada ordered. "I want you to be looking me straight in the eye when I say what I have to say to you."

Alicia pulled herself up.

The photo, now shaking in her trembling hand.

"Were you really that stupid, Alicia? Did you really think you wouldn't be the first person I suspected when you made the hang-up phone calls?"

Alicia kept silent, a stricken expression on her face.

Zada laughed.

A true she-devil laugh.

"God, I bet you were livid when I changed my phone number."

Still, Alicia didn't say a word.

"And then you were stupid enough to think I wouldn't make the connection with the photo. Who's the guy, Alicia? It obviously isn't your Latino ex-pool boy Javier. Is this guy one of your ex-lovers? Maybe an actor? Or is he just some guy you picked at random off the street and paid to do your dirty work?"

"Zada," Alicia began.

"Shut up!" Zada yelled. "I'm not through yet."

She took a threatening step toward Alicia.

Alicia backed up, still clutching the photo.

"I want you to look me in the eye, Alicia. I want you to look me in the eye right now and tell me to my face you're responsible for that photograph you're holding in your hand."

Tears rolled down Alicia's cheeks.

"I am so, so, sorry, Zada," she finally said. "Yes. I'm responsible for this photograph."

"Congratulations," Zada said. "Your plan to break up my marriage worked."

Zada turned on her heel.

But she turned back to face Alicia before she left.

"And don't worry," Zada said. "I'll give Rick the house. I couldn't stand the thought of living across the street from you!"

Seconds later Zada was standing on Tish's porch.

When Tish opened her front door, Zada fell against her shocked best friend, sobbing uncontrollably.

* * *

When Alfie opened his front door, Alicia didn't wait to be invited in. She slapped the photo against Alfie's chest and pushed him backward into his apartment.

"What in the hell were you thinking?" Alicia yelled.

"Now, Alicia," Alfie said, backing up as fast as Alicia was walking toward him. "Calm down and let me explain."

"Who the hell is Alicia?"

Alicia glanced at the tall redhead who had jumped up from the sofa. Her brother's current flavor of the week was standing with her hands on her hips, glaring at Alfie.

Alicia looked back at Alfie with a glare of her own.

"What did you and Eddie Salvo do, Alfie? Hide out in the bushes until Zada decided to walk her dog?"

"Who the hell is Zada?" the redhead wanted to know.

"I didn't ask Eddie how he got the photo," Alfie said. "Eddie's a pro. I just paid him to get it."

"What photo?" the redhead yelled.

"For God's sake, Alfie," Alicia said. "You're playing with people's lives here!"

Alfie said, "Just like your neighbors were playing with your life, Alicia!"

"They were *not* playing with my life!" Alicia screamed. "I didn't have a life for them to play with. Don't you understand that?"

"Jesus," the redhead said. "I'm outta here."

She stomped past them and slammed the door behind her.

Alicia walked over and flopped down on the sofa.

Alfie walked over and sat down beside her.

That they were twins, was obvious. Same identical features. Same blond hair. Same blue eyes. If the redhead couldn't see that for herself, Alicia decided, to hell with her.

Alicia said, "Do you know what's so tragic about what you've done?"

Alfie winced. "Everything?"

"My neighbors ignoring me has turned out to be the best thing that's ever happened to me. It made me realize that the reason no one likes me is because I've never liked myself."

"Sis," Alfie said. "Don't say that."

"I'm serious, Alfie," Alicia said. "I didn't like myself when we were children, because I was embarrassed that we had so much more than everyone else. I didn't like myself before I married, because I was afraid every man I dated only wanted me for my looks or my money. And I really didn't like myself after I married Edward, because he played me for such a fool."

"And you've been so depressed since the divorce, you've really had me worried," Alfie said. "Until the week you spent getting ready for the meeting at your house. That was the first time in ages you sounded happy."

"And then stupid me burst into tears when you called me that Sunday morning to find out how the meeting at my house went."

"Not stupid you," Alfie said. "Depressed you. And then, you wouldn't take my calls. And I panicked, okay? I didn't care what I had to do, as long as I could make you happy again. The revenge fantasy you told me about gave me the idea. That's when I called Eddie."

"God, this is such a mess," Alicia said. "The reason I've barely talked to you is because I finally realized my happiness is my own responsibility. Not yours. Not my neighbors'. Not anyone else's responsibility but my own. And that realization finally jerked me out of my blue funk. I realized unless I wanted to be miserable the rest of my life, I was going to have to take control of my own life."

Alfie leaned over and hugged her.

Alicia sighed and said, "I was going to wait and tell you after all of the papers were signed, but now is as good a time as any."

Alfie sat up and looked at her. "Tell me what?"

Alicia smiled and said, "I'm going to put my broker's license to good use again and start my own real estate company. That's what I've been so secretive about. I've been busy making all of the arrangements."

Alfie's mouth dropped open.

"Don't worry," Alicia said, "I'm not interested in commercial property. I won't be in competition with you and Dad. I always hated commercial sales. Every deal was so cold and impersonal. That's why I want to sell residential property. Feel-good property. How can I not feel good about myself, knowing I've made some family happy by helping them find the home of their dreams?"

Alfie groaned. "Did you have to bring up the 'happy family' part? I knew trying to make Zada's husband think she was cheating on him was a despicable thing to do. I kept soothing my own conscience, rationalizing that Zada didn't need Rick if he didn't trust her. And that if Rick did trust her, I really hadn't done any damage."

Alfie let out a long sigh.

Alicia reached over and patted his hand.

"Of course," Alfie said. "You being here obviously means the damage has already been done."

"Not if I can help it," Alicia said.

She leaned over and kissed her twin on the cheek.

She got up from the sofa.

And she headed for the door.

Someone else's life was in need of some damage control.

Alicia was the only person who could provide it.

"And then . . ."

Zada blew her nose and looked at Jen, who was hearing the story for the first time.

"And then, I told Rick if he didn't trust me now, a few more days weren't going to change a thing."

Tish looked over at Jen. "He told Zada he'd be back on Sunday. He's staying at the center."

"And like the dumb ass that I am," Zada said, "I said, 'Duh. Okay. It doesn't matter that you can't decide if I'm a liar and a cheat. I'll be sitting right here waiting for you to come home on Sunday and tell me if we're staying together, or if you've decided to kick my lying, cheating ass to the curb.'"

Tish looked over at Jen. "She really didn't say that."

Jen looked over at Tish. "Duh. I realized that, Tish."

Jen looked back at Zada. "But whether you realize it or not, Zada, you weren't being dumb. And neither was Rick. He asked for the time he needed to sort things out. You gave it to him. In the past, he would have walked out again, and you would have been dialing up the locksmith. You've both come a long way."

"And isn't that special?" Zada mocked. "To come such a long way and still end up getting a divorce."

Zada pulled out more tissues when Tish pushed the

tissue box across the table in her direction. She blew her nose again.

"After Rick packed a bag and left, I couldn't stop thinking about Alicia."

Tish said, "And the longer Zada thought about Alicia, the madder she got."

Zada said, "That's when I took the photo and went to Alicia's house."

"She knocked Alicia flat on her ass," Tish said, looking over at Jen and grinning.

Zada said, "I told you it was an accident."

Tish said, "Accident or not, she deserved it."

"And talk about twisted. How twisted is this?" Zada said. "I actually felt sorry for Alicia. I swear, she almost passed out when she looked at the photo. She kept standing there, staring at me as if she had no idea what I was talking about. And then she was so ashamed of herself, she actually started crying."

"Ha!" Tish said. "Crying because she got caught, maybe. But crying because she was ashamed of what she did? I doubt it."

Jen said, "What did Alicia say?"

"Oh, she admitted she was responsible for the photo," Tish said, looking over at Jen again. "She told Zada that with her own twisted lips."

Jen shook her head. "Poor Alicia. I can't imagine anyone being so desperate, they would do something like that."

"Well, she did," Tish said frowning. "And don't *you* start feeling sorry for her, too. There's a special place in hell for people like her."

Zada blew her nose again.

"That stupid comment I made in court that day about some imaginary guy is the biggest mistake of my life," Zada said. "Rick had already decided I was guilty before he ever came home. I could see it on his face the second I walked through the kitchen door."

Jen said, "It's hard to argue with a photograph, Zada. Try looking at this from Rick's point of view."

"I have tried looking at this from Rick's point of view, Jen," Zada wailed. "I just can't get my head that far up my ass!"

"Well," Jen said. "At least you have proof now that Alicia was responsible. You need to call him, Zada, and tell Rick what you found out."

"No!" Zada said. "If Rick can't come to his own conclusion that I would never cheat on him without me having to prove it, I don't want him back!"

Jen looked at Tish.

Tish looked at Jen.

"I want you to stay here tonight," Tish said. "You don't need to be alone."

Zada said, "No. I don't want to leave Simon alone. All I want to do right now is go home, take a hot bath, and hopefully go to sleep the second my head hits the pillow."

Tish looked over at Jen. "I gave her two of my sleeping pills. If she takes those after her bath, she'll get a good night's sleep."

Zada got up from the table and started out of the room.

She turned back around when she reached the door.

"I'm serious," Zada said. "Stay out of this. Both of you. If anyone is going to tell Rick that Alicia was behind the phone calls and the photo, I deserve that privilege."

Jen said, "Which is another way of saying Rick will never know, because you'll never tell him."

Zada said, "I want both of you to swear to me right now that you will *not* tell Rick about Alicia."

"I swear," Tish said.

Jen said, "So do I."

"Thank you," Zada said, and headed for home.

Rick didn't go to the center after he packed a bag and left the house. In the frame of mind he was in, bunking with Scrappy wasn't an option—for Scrappy's sake, not his. He'd burdened Scrappy with his personal problems too much already.

First, he stopped by the liquor store and bought two fifths of tequila—just in case one bottle wasn't enough to dull the pain. Since he rarely drank, Rick had no way to judge how much tequila it would take to make the photo that kept flashing though his mind go away.

One bottle, or two.

It didn't matter.

Rick knew he was going to drink whatever it took.

Next, he checked into a Days Inn on the outskirts of New Hope. Rick tossed his duffel bag on the bed, and took one of the tequila bottles out of the sack. He flopped down on the chair at the motel room table, unscrewed the top off the bottle, and took a long swig.

Zada and the guy.

Swig.

Him caressing her face.

Swig.

No fucking caterpillar in sight.

Swig.

Swig.

Swig.

He kept trying to fit all of the pieces of the puzzle together in his mind, but they just didn't fit.

Zada saying she was dating someone just to make him
jealous. Zada suspecting Alicia made the phone calls, but
never telling him. Simon almost biting some guy—again,
Zada not telling him.

Like fitting square pegs into round holes.

Swig.

Swig.

Swig.

Am I drunk yet?

Rick got up from the table to test himself. He closed
his eyes and held his arms out straight. Right finger to the
nose.

No problem.

Left finger to the nose.

No problem.

Rick sat back down and picked up the bottle again.

Alicia making the phone calls?

No motive.

Swig.

Alicia crouched in the bushes with a camera?

Highly doubtful.

Swig.

Swig.

Swig.

He finally felt a slow tingle spread through his body.

Then, his vision got a little blurry. He tried focusing on
the clothes rack across the room.

Are the coat hangers moving back and forth?
Or am I?

Rick put the bottle down and stood up to find out. He held his arms out straight. He put one foot in front of the other.

Step.
Step.
Step.
Turn around.
No problem.
Step.
Step.
Step.
Back to the table.
No problem.

The photo popped into his mind again.

It made him worry he hadn't bought enough tequila.

Rick picked up the bottle and walked over to the credenza housing the television. He picked up the remote and walked back over to the bed. Turning the pillow around for a back cushion, Rick stretched out on the bed with a tortured sigh, remote in one hand, tequila bottle in the other.

He hit the "power" button.

Commercial.
Switch.
Commercial.
Swig. Swig. Swig.
Switch. Switch. Switch.
Catherine Zeta-Jones.
Pause.
Long, dark hair, just like Zada.

Swig.

Piercing dark eyes, just like Zada.

Swig.

Voluptuous curves, just like Zada.

Swig.

Swig.

Swig.

The pretty Catherine turned around. The sound of a male voice had her attention. The camera zoomed in for a close up.

She smiled.

Seductively.

Just like Zada.

Great big swig!

The camera panned to the opposite side of the room.

Hiccup.

Sit up!

Rick couldn't believe his eyes.

Holy shit, Batman.

It's Zorro!

Chapter 18

———◆———

It was after 10:00 PM on Friday night when Alicia pulled her Mercedes into Tish's driveway. She sat behind the wheel for a second, knowing what she had to do, and dreading every minute of it.

Tish was *not* going to be happy to see her.

Not after Tish had slammed the phone in her ear when she'd tried calling earlier.

The fact that Tish had hung up on her had kept her from calling Jen and getting the same treatment. And facing Zada again wasn't even an option as far as Alicia was concerned.

Zada was too upset to be rational about anything—and not without good reason. But the next time she faced Zada, Alicia wanted it to be after she took *full* responsibility for the phone calls and the photo.

She intended to tell Rick what her brother had done. And why Alfie had done such a horrible thing. Forcing Tish to listen to her was her only hope if she was going to find Rick.

She'd tried calling Rick at his business. But the answering machine informed her that SDS was closed in observance of the long Fourth of July holiday, and wouldn't resume normal business hours until Tuesday morning.

Tuesday morning wasn't soon enough.

She'd gone to the center anyway hoping to find Rick, but the security gate had been closed. She'd even blown her horn several times, but the building sat a good distance back from the gate.

Either Rick didn't hear her, or he wasn't there. There was no way to tell. The large garage doors on the front of the building were closed.

Alicia could have easily bent over and made it under the crossing bar of the security gate blocking the drive. She would have done that, and walked up to the building. But the large round sign fastened in the middle of the security gate kept her from it.

A protective-looking German shepherd was painted on the sign. The words written on the sign were enough to deter her: BEWARE—SECURITY DOGS AT LARGE.

Alicia had been too afraid to even get out of her car.

It didn't take a genius to figure out if she could get under the bar, so could the dogs at large.

Even if invisible fencing had been used across the driveway, Alicia wasn't a big fan of invisible fencing. She'd found the golden retriever from two streets over in her yard more times than she could count—his fur thick enough that he didn't mind the little zap when he bolted through the invisible barrier.

Alicia hadn't been brave enough to take a chance. She'd driven away and headed back to Woodberry Park.

Tish was her last resort. Tish would know Rick's cell phone number.

Alicia took a deep breath and got out of her car.

She pushed Tish's doorbell and braced herself.

Tish's eyes narrowed the second she opened the door.

For a second, Alicia thought she was going to hit her.

"I can't believe you have the nerve to even walk up on my porch," Tish said and slammed the door in her face.

Alicia pounded on the door with both fists.

Tish jerked the door back open.

"I'm one second away from calling the police."

"Call the police," Alicia said, and pushed past Tish before she could stop her. "But while we're waiting for them to get here, you're going to listen to what I have to say."

Tish stomped inside after her.

Alicia whirled around to face her.

They stood there, glaring at each other for a minute.

"Okay," Tish finally said. "But go into the kitchen. I have no doubt this is going to get ugly. I don't want to wake Joe and the twins."

Alicia confessed everything: Her deep depression after the divorce. How desperately she'd wanted them for friends. The elaborate plans she'd made for the meeting. How crushed she'd been when they stood her up. Alfie, insane as his plan was, only trying to help.

Alicia also explained that she'd tried to get in touch with Rick and couldn't. And she was too afraid of the dogs to even dare walk to the building.

By the time Alicia finished what she had to say, she was crying. Tish had dropped the attitude and was actually standing beside Alicia's chair, patting her back, tissue box in hand.

"And that's why I came to you," Alicia told Tish when Tish handed her another tissue. "I knew you would have Rick's cell phone number."

Tish said, "I do have Rick's cell phone number. But Zada made me swear I wouldn't tell Rick anything, Alicia. She's already decided if she has to prove to Rick she wasn't lying, she doesn't want him back."

"And how tragic would that be?" Alicia wailed. "Do you really think I could live with myself if Zada and Rick ended their marriage when I could have prevented that from happening, and didn't?"

She kept staring at Tish.

"Could you live with yourself, Tish? Are you really willing to let some promise you made to Zada when she was upset keep you from saving their marriage?"

"When you put it that way," Tish said, "no. I'm not willing to keep quiet and let Rick make an ass of himself again. Zada's taken him back once. I know her well enough to know she won't do it again."

Tish walked over and began plowing through a kitchen drawer. A few seconds later, she finally came up with an address book.

"Tell Rick I need to see him face to face," Alicia said when Tish picked up the phone. "He deserves that much from me."

The vibration in his pocket put a silly grin on Rick's face. Until his more than a little inebriated brain realized what was tickling the side of his thigh.

Rick fumbled around and finally pulled his cell phone out of his pocket. He raised his head up off the pillow and looked at the phone. Focusing on the screen well enough to see who was calling, however, was a different matter.

Rick closed one eye.

"J," he said aloud.

Too blurry.

He opened that eye, and closed the other.

"J-O."

Still too blurry.

Rick held the phone right up to his nose.

"J-O-N-E-S," he slowly spelled out. "Thas Tish," he slurred. "Oh, hell no! Not talkin' to Tish. No way."

He hiccupped.

Twice.

His head fell back against the pillow.

His arm flopped back on the bed.

"All Lisha's fault," he mumbled. "Thas what Tish'll say. Jus like Zada. Thas their story. I'm stickin' to it."

He laughed out loud at his own mistake.

"Not *I'm* stickin to it. *Tish's* stickin' to it. *Zada's* stickin' to it. I'm *not* stickin' to it."

He held the phone up again and raised his head back off the pillow. "Not answerin'," he told his still wiggling cell phone. "Not talkin' to Tish. Not listenin' to more lies."

When Jen opened her front door, Tish grabbed her by the arm and pulled her outside on the porch. Jen sent Alicia a mean look, and glanced back at Tish.

"For God's sake, Tish, it's eleven o'clock," Jen said. She looked back at Alicia. "And what are you doing with *her*?"

Alicia started to say something.

Tish didn't give her a chance.

"I'll explain everything on the way," Tish said.

Jen put her hands on her hips. "On the way where, Tish? You aren't making any sense."

"We need to help Alicia find Rick," Tish said.

"I *repeat*," Jen said. "You are not making any sense."

"Jen, please," Tish begged. "Tell Charlie you're going with me and come on."

"How much Prozac did you take today?" Jen demanded.

"Jen!" Tish said. "Trust me on this. Rick won't answer his cell phone. And SDS isn't exactly in the safest part of town. Alicia wants to tell him about the phone calls and the photo. It isn't safe for her to go alone at this time of night."

"Exactly," Jen said. "Ask Joe to go with her."

"I did that already," Tish said. "Joe said to wait until tomorrow. And I'm sure that will be Charlie's advice, if you ask him."

Jen stuck her nose in the air. "Excellent advice, if you ask me."

"When tomorrow, Jen?" Tish wanted to know. "Does the Fourth of July party ring a bell? Alicia needs to tell Rick tonight. If she does, Zada won't have to wait until Sunday to find out if she still has a marriage. And Rick and Zada will be with us. At the party *together*."

"*We* promised *we'd* stay out of it," Jen reminded her.

"*We* lied," Tish said. "Now go tell Charlie you're running an errand with me and you'll be back in a minute."

Jen still didn't budge.

"Alicia made a good point earlier," Tish said. "She asked me if I could live with myself if Zada and Rick ended their marriage, and I could have prevented it, and didn't. Could you live with yourself, Jen?"

"God, I hate it when you start making sense," Jen said.

She sent a guilty look over at Zada's darkened house. "I just hope Zada isn't watching us right now."

"Are you kidding?" Tish said. "If Zada took those pills like she said she would, we'll be lucky to get her up at all tomorrow, much less help with the party."

Two minutes later the dark side of the Housewives' Fantasy Club—minus one member—was riding out of Woodberry Park in a Mercedes.

Alicia driving, confident she could repair the damage.

Jen listening intently from the front passenger seat.

Tish, leaning forward from the backseat, bringing Jen up to date on why Alicia was no longer considered the enemy.

Alicia brought the Mercedes to a stop directly in front of the SDS security gate, thinking that the later it got, the spookier this placed looked. The headlights gave the German shepherd's eyes on the sign an evil glow.

Alicia shuddered and looked away.

She glanced back at Tish. "And you're sure about the dogs?"

"For the tenth time, yes," Tish said. "Rick Clark treats his dogs better than most children are treated. They're kept in climate controlled kennels out back. The sign does exactly what Rick wants it to do. It makes people think twice before ignoring that the gate is closed."

Jen turned sideways in her seat to look at Tish. "And what people are you referring to, Tish? Obviously, not you and Alicia."

Tish leaned between the seats a little farther.

"Okay," Tish said. "To appease Miss Politically Correct here, try blowing your horn like you did when you were here before, Alicia."

"No!" Jen reached out and grabbed Alicia's hand.

Eyes wide with fear, Jen said, "Didn't you see those skuzzy looking guys we drove by a second ago standing on the corner? The last thing we need to do is draw attention to ourselves."

Alicia said, "Then what about flashing my headlights?"

"Yes, Alicia, try that," Jen said.

Alicia flashed the headlights.

For a good two minutes she flashed her headlights.

No response.

"If Rick's in there," Alicia said, "he's either in the back where he can't see the front of the building. Or he's ignoring us on purpose."

"Oh, he's in there," Tish huffed. "And he's ignoring us on purpose. I've been calling his cell phone constantly since we left. And I know his phone is on. It would have sent me directly to his voice mail if he had his phone turned off."

"I vote we go home now," Jen said.

Tish leaned forward and handed her cell phone to Jen.

"I vote you stay in the car while Alicia and I walk up to the building," Tish said. "Keep your doors locked, and keep calling Rick. I logged his cell phone number into the phone. All you have to do is punch number four. If he answers, tell him we're outside and he needs to let us in."

Alicia looked over at Jen.

Jen was still craning her neck to look behind the car, on skuzzy guy alert.

Alicia looked back at Tish.

Tish rolled her eyes.

Alicia said, "I just want you both to know how much I appreciate you coming with me. I know I've made a mess of things, but I promise you I'll do everything I can to make things right with Rick and Zada again."

"Just hurry," Jen said, motioning them out of the car. "I'm not exactly the bravest person on the planet."

Alicia left the car.

So did Tish.

Click went the locks when Jen pushed the button.

Alicia made it under the security bar first, but she let Tish lead the way. Tish had been to the center before. Alicia hoped she never had to see the place again.

At least the place had a security light in the parking lot, Alicia kept reminding herself. Even if the light did cast eerie shadows on the building.

"There are some steps that lead up to the second floor at the side of the building," Tish said. "If I remember right, that's the most likely place for Rick to be."

Alicia kept scanning the area with every step.

Despite Tish's promise about the dogs, she was certain they were only one step away from being mauled to death by an angry German shepherd with sharp, pointy teeth.

Alicia glanced back at the car again.

Jen's silhouette said she'd moved to the driver's side of the car—just in case. Alicia was thinking about the "just in case" part when Tish grabbed her arm.

"Oh, God, what?"

"I thought I heard something," Tish whispered.

They were huddled so close together they could have been standing in the same shoes.

Alicia quickly assessed the situation. They were closer to the building now than they were to the car. Should they run? And if so, which way?

"Put your hands on top of your head, and walk toward the building," a gruff male voice said, making that decision for them.

Alicia looked back over her shoulder.

She put her arm up to shield her eyes.

The guy had his flashlight pointed straight at her.

"Move it," the man said. "Before I call the cops."

"Don't do it," Tish said. "If I get arrested, Joe is going to kill me!"

Hands on top of their heads, they moved forward.

"Please don't call the police," Tish called back over her shoulder.

"Keep walking," he said.

"If you'll just let us explain," Alicia called out.

"I said keep walking."

They were getting close to the front of the building.

The man said, "Turn around and put your backs against the wall."

They both flattened against the wall like wallpaper.

The flashlight hit Alicia in the face again.

He did the same to Tish.

He lowered the flashlight and walked forward.

He stopped—hands at his waist, legs spread apart.

Alicia could see him clearly now.

He was older. Tall, well built, and dressed in fatigues. The look on his face said he was anything but amused.

Tish said, "You're Scrappy, right?"

"What of it?" he said.

"We're Rick's neighbors," Tish said and let out a nervous little giggle.

He didn't crack a smile.

"And that gives you permission to trespass on private property?" he growled.

Alicia said, "Sir, like I said before. If you'll give us a minute, we can explain."

He held his arm out and tapped his watch.

"Start talking. You have one minute. I'm timing you."

Alicia was over it.

She squared her shoulders and looked him straight in the eye. "And you have one minute to go inside and ask Rick to come out here!"

Intimidated, he wasn't.

In fact, he grinned.

"Not possible," he said. "I haven't seen Rick since he left the center this afternoon."

Alicia heard the sirens first.

Then she saw the red-and-blue flashing lights.

"Oh. My. God." Tish said. "He did call the police!"

Scrappy turned around to see what was going on. He immediately resumed his military stance. When two patrol cars zoomed up to the security gate and stopped, Scrappy looked back over his shoulder.

"Just for the record," he said. "I didn't call them."

Two police officers started walking in their direction. One had a nightstick in his hand. The other had a radio to his mouth.

Jen was running along behind them, wringing her hands.

Alicia looked over at Tish.

Tish looked over at Alicia.

Tish said, "Promise you'll slap me if I ever give Jen my cell phone again."

"Well, what did you expect me to do, Tish!"

Alicia looked in her rearview mirror.

Jen was sitting in the backseat, arms folded across her chest, lips pressed in an extremely thin line.

Jen said, "I saw a man step out of the shadows and walk up behind you and Alicia. There was enough light to see it wasn't Rick. I didn't know that Scrappy person lived at the center full-time. The first thing that ran through my mind was that it was one of those hooligans we passed on the corner."

Tish said, "You mean one of the hooligans that would have had to walk in front of the car you were sitting in, in order to go under the security gate?"

"Hello?" Jen snapped. "I wasn't exactly leaning back in the front seat, leisurely waiting while you and Alicia took a stroll down the yellow brick road! I had a white-knuckle grip on the steering wheel, Tish. Completely terrified that two of my friends were going to be murdered or worse!"

Tish turned sideways in her seat. "And worse than murdered would be?"

Jen yelled, "Dammit, you know what I meant!"

"And it never crossed your mind," Tish said, "that the police might be a little pissed off that you called 911 to have the *trespassers* protected from the security guard?"

Alicia hadn't missed the "two of my friends" part.

In Jen's defense, she looked in the rearview mirror at

Jen and said, "Don't worry about it, Jen. I would have done the same thing."

"Thank you, Alicia," Jen said, glaring over at Tish.

"Liar," Tish whispered.

Alicia said, "Well, at least Scrappy was nice enough not to press charges. I gave him my cell phone number. He said he'd have Rick call me the second he saw him."

Jen said, "I hate to bring this up, but we're really going to feel foolish if Rick is already back home, and that's why he wasn't at the center."

Tish said, "You'll be calling 911 again, Jen. I will personally kill Rick with my bare hands if he's at home when we get there."

Jen said, "Something else we need to decide is what we're going to tell Zada."

Tish laughed. "You mean about us technically breaking into Rick's business? Almost getting arrested? And purposely breaking our promise to stay out of her business? Nothing, Jen! That's what we're going to tell Zada. Absolutely nothing!"

Tish looked over at Alicia. "But I do think you need to tell Zada it was your brother who was responsible for the calls and the photograph, Alicia."

Alicia said, "Let's focus on telling Rick first."

Tish said, "There's no reason why you can't do both. The Fourth of July party doesn't start until noon. I want you at my house at ten. Jen and I will be there with you when you tell Zada everything you told me tonight."

Chapter 19

Zada stood in front of her bathroom mirror on Saturday morning, rehearsing the speech she was going to give Rick when he came home on Sunday to tell her that he did want the divorce.

She cleared her throat.

Several times.

"Rick," she said, looking at herself in the mirror, "if you don't know in your heart that I would never cheat on you, then I agree. We don't belong together."

Not good.

That expression is too stern and condescending.

Zada changed her facial expression to stricken.

Nope, too pitiful.

I need to have a little pride left!

She tried passive.

Way too cold and detached.

How about hopeful, but slightly pleading?

Perfect!

Zada started over again.

"Rick, if you can't . . ."

Zada grabbed the telephone. The telephone she'd slept

with all last night. The telephone she'd kept with her all morning. Just in case Rick called.

Tish said, "Are you up?"

"Already up and dressed," Zada said.

"Were you able to sleep last night?"

"Yes," Zada said. "Thank you for those sleeping pills. I was in bed by nine, and barely remember turning off my bedside light."

"Have you heard from Rick?"

"No," Zada said with a sigh. "Rick said he'd be home on Sunday. I guess Sunday is when I'll see him."

"Coffee's on," Tish said. "Come on over."

Tish hung up before Zada could tell her she'd decided to skip coffee again this morning. Before the Fourth of July party started, she wanted to ride over to a new condominium complex not far from Woodberry Park.

She needed more information: availability, prices, amenities.

She'd thought everything over carefully. If they were going through with the divorce, Zada had decided she was going to give Rick Simon and the house. She also wasn't going to waste any time making their divorce final.

Better for her.

Better for Rick.

She hadn't been kidding when she'd told Alicia she couldn't stand the thought of living across the street from her. But that wasn't the only reason she would give Rick the house.

It was the right thing to do.

She'd been living in a tiny apartment when she met Rick. Barely able to pay her rent from the money she made writing freelance articles for various magazines, and doing occasional secretarial work for a temp agency.

She hadn't had a penny in savings, nor had she contributed a dime to the purchase of the house. The success of her children's books had come later. Thanks to Simon.

And now, thanks to Simon, she was in better financial shape than she had been before.

Simon.

My sweet, beloved Simon.

The thought of leaving him behind broke her heart, almost as much as losing Rick would break her heart.

Zada picked up the phone to call Tish back. She then thought better of it. Maybe Jen and Tish would ride to the complex with her. She knew Jen and Tish would support her, regardless. That's what friends were for; to stand beside you in time of need. Take your side in bad situations. Put you back together when you fell apart.

As much as I love Rick, I am NOT going to fall apart.

Zada made herself that promise and then headed across the street.

When Zada bounced into Tish's kitchen, sleep-deprived Jen looked over at Tish and said, "I thought you said after taking those sleeping pills, we wouldn't be able to even get Zada out of bed this morning."

Tish shrugged and yawned herself.

Zada looked from one to the other.

"What happened to the two of you? You both look like you need to go back to bed."

Tish pulled the chair out she was standing behind.

"Sit right here," she said. "Jen will fix you a cup of coffee. I'll be right back."

"Whatever," Zada said, frowning at both of them.

She walked over and sat down at the table.

Jen hurried to the coffeepot, avoiding her gaze.

"Okay," Zada said, looking over at Jen who had turned her back to Zada conveniently. "I'm not stupid, Jen. Something's up. Tell me what it is."

The something that was up walked into the kitchen.

Zada took one look at Alicia and jumped up from her chair.

Tish pointed a stern finger at her. "Zada, sit back down and don't say a word. Alicia has something to tell you. You're going to listen to her, even if Jen and I have to use force to keep your butt in that chair."

"I can't tell you how sorry I am, Zada," Alicia said after she finished telling her everything she'd told Tish the night before. "Can you ever forgive me?"

Zada finally said, "Yes."

"Thank you," Alicia said.

Zada got up from the table and walked across the room, her hand held out to Alicia.

"Truce?" Zada asked.

Alicia nodded and shook her hand. "Truce."

Zada said, "But that doesn't mean I don't feel like thrashing your brother from head to toe."

Alicia said, "And I'd hold him down while you hit him, if I weren't afraid Alfie would enjoy it. My brother is into women who cause him nothing but pain and suffering."

"Too bad Tish is already married," Jen said, sending Tish a that's-for-making-fun-of-me-last-night smile.

Tish laughed. "Why, Jen. I was just thinking the same thing!"

Jen lost the smile.

She looked back at Zada and said, "I know Tish doesn't agree, but we have something else to tell you, Zada. You're going to hear about it eventually, anyway. And I'd rather you hear it from us."

Zada put her hands on her hips. "Should I sit back down for this, too?"

Jen looked at Tish.

Tish looked at Alicia.

Alicia looked at Zada.

Alicia said, "Sitting back down might not be a bad idea."

By the time they finished telling Zada about their fiasco of a visit to SDS—from Tish's always humorous perspective—Zada was laughing so hard, she was holding her sides.

Alicia, Tish, and even Jen, were laughing right along with her until Zada suddenly stopped laughing.

Zada stood up and put her hands on her hips again. "If Rick isn't at the center," Zada said, "then where in the hell is he?"

Where in the hell Rick was, was standing under a hot shower in his Days Inn motel room on the outskirts of New Hope. He turned off the water, got out of the shower, and toweled himself off. He found no comfort whatsoever in the fact that he now knew it took exactly one and a half fifths of tequila to get him so officially shit-faced drunk that the photo disappeared from his memory.

That is, the photo disappeared from his memory until he woke up lying on the motel room floor earlier.

Rick also found no comfort in the fact that he now had thirty-seven missed calls on his cell phone. As far as Rick was concerned, their nosy neighbors needed to butt out of their business.

That's why he had no intention whatsoever of showing up at the Fourth of July party. He didn't need Tish or Jen pulling him aside, trying to influence his decision.

His mind was made up.

And he already knew what he had to do.

For his sake.

And for Zada's.

But would it be difficult for him?

God, yes.

Rick grimaced, just thinking about it.

He only hoped Zada would realize how difficult what he had to do would truly be for him.

Rick let out a long sigh.

He'd never be able to show his face in Woodberry Park again.

Zada looked for Rick's face in the crowd all day.

She'd looked for Rick during the sack race, her leg tied to Jen's as they hobbled toward the finish line. They'd won the race, and got the first door prize of the day.

She'd looked for Rick during the annual men versus women Fourth of July volley ball tournament. The women had won the championship for the first time ever. Charlie and Joe had both conveniently blamed Rick's absence as the reason they lost the tournament.

She'd looked for Rick during the kids' relay races that were held at the clubhouse pool. Tish had been so excited Mark was ahead that she accidentally fell into the pool. Joe had been more embarrassed than Tish when he'd pulled her out.

Sopping wet, Tish had still looked like a fashion model.

Zada had heart-achingly searched the crowd for Rick during the annual Fourth of July picnic—probably her lowest point in the day. Happy families sitting all around her, everyone laughing and enjoying each other, only reminded her even more of Rick's absence.

Of all people, Alicia had been the one to come over to sit with her. They'd never said a word to each other. They just sat there, pretending to enjoy the picnic.

But Zada didn't miss the irony that the person responsible for Rick not being there was the one person who had come to her rescue so she wouldn't have to sit alone.

She'd looked for Rick again later that night, as she handed out sparklers to all of the neighborhood kids before the big fireworks show started. Sparklers Rick had bought for the occasion. Sparklers Zada wished Rick had been there handing out himself, instead of her.

That's the last time she'd let herself look for Rick, right before the fireworks. It was her favorite part of the party.

That's when she'd finally accepted Rick wasn't coming.

Not for the fireworks.

And not to walk her home.

As soon as the fireworks ended, Alicia started looking around for Zada. She finally found her, already heading down the path from the clubhouse—alone.

Alicia hurried to catch up.

Zada didn't say a word when she did.

And that was okay.

As bad as Alicia felt for causing trouble between Zada and Rick, she knew Zada felt worse.

Alicia knew that kind of pain. Being alone. Everyone else all paired up and happy.

She was responsible for the problem and she'd see Zada through it. If it meant nothing more than walking her home.

Zada finally looked over at her.

They had just reached Owls Roost Road.

Zada said, "Just because we called a truce, Alicia, doesn't mean we'll ever be great friends. I think you know that as well as I do. So, you didn't have to walk with me. I'm not some suburban charity case."

"Don't flatter yourself," Alicia said right back. "I'm not walking with you. You're walking with me."

Alicia's gut instinct had been right: The last thing Zada wanted was sympathy. And she didn't intend to give her any.

In fact, she and Zada were actually a lot alike. That was the main reason they were always butting heads.

Zada said, "Are you always this annoying?"

"Always," Alicia said. "Just like you are."

Zada snorted.

But she didn't disagree.

They were starting up the incline to Owls Roost Road, again in silence.

Until Zada looked over at her and said, "Not that it's any of your business, but I'm giving Rick the house."

"You mentioned that already," Alicia said. "You can't

stand the thought of living across the street from me. Remember?"

Zada stopped when they reached the top of the hill.

Alicia stopped and turned to face her.

"Okay," Zada said, hands on her hips. "I'm tired of dancing around the issue, so let's get to the heart of the matter. I want something cleared up once and for all."

Alicia said, "And that would be?"

Zada's eyes narrowed. "You know exactly what that would be. Rick! I want the truth, Alicia. Are you interested in Rick? Or aren't you?"

Alicia couldn't help herself.

She burst out laughing.

It was the *wrong* thing to do.

Zada lunged forward.

Alicia jumped back. Just not far enough.

Zada managed to grab Alicia's arm as she fell. Alicia landed right on top of her. Had they not been standing at the top of the hill, they both would have popped back up like two jacks-in-the-box.

The hill made sure they didn't.

Alicia and Zada rolled down the hill in a human ball of flailing arms and legs, landing in a ditch at the side of the road. A muddy ditch to be exact, compliments of the summer thunderstorm the day before.

Alicia reached up and wiped the mud out of her eyes.

Zada did the same.

They looked like two raccoons glaring at each other.

"How dare you laugh at me!" Zada yelled.

"I couldn't help it," Alicia yelled back. "You are such an idiot if you can't see that Rick Clark is hopelessly in love with you. He has that dreamy can't-live-without-her expression on his face every time he looks at you! It's enough to make a person sick."

Zada's mouth dropped open and closed again. "Dreamy?" Zada asked. She smiled. "Really?"

Alicia groaned.

She pulled herself up and brushed herself off. "I take it back," Alicia said, looking down at Zada. "Rick isn't hopeless. *You're* the one who's hopeless!"

Alicia stomped back up the hill.

Zada stomped up the hill right behind her.

She finally caught up.

"So?" Zada said. "You really *aren't* interested in Rick?"

"You figure it out," Alicia said.

She turned her back on Zada and marched up her driveway. She was almost to the door when Zada yelled her name.

Alicia turned back around, hands on her hips.

"Thanks for walking me home," Zada called out and waved.

Imagine that, Alicia thought with a smile as she turned and opened her front door. There still might be hope that she and Zada could eventually become friends.

Chapter 20

———●———

Simon jumping off the bed awoke Zada from a restless sleep. She sat up, pulling the bedsheet with her, and looked across the room. She always left her bedroom door open in case Simon needed to go out during the night.

Zada tensed. Her bedroom door was closed. Her eyes adjusted slowly to the darkened bedroom.

There!

In the shadows.

A man's silhouette.

He moved toward the bed.

He was dressed all in black.

Black hat.

Black shirt.

Black cape.

Sinister black mask, hiding his face.

Zada wanted to cry out, but she didn't.

Her excitement quickly overrode her fear.

He stopped by the side of the bed.

Dark blue eyes peered out at her through the mask.

The look in his eyes told her what he had in mind.

He reached out and pulled the sheet from her hand.

Slowly.

Methodically.

Inch after inch, he exposed her body.

"Why are you here?" she whispered.

His answer was to pull a sword from its sheath.

The glint of a blade flashed in the darkness.

A small excited cry escaped her lips.

His eyes never left her face.

But he used the tip of the blade to toy with her.

Lightly.

Seductively.

Purposely.

He ran the tip of the cold steel across her bare foot.

Zada shivered.

The sensation, incredible.

The danger, more of a turn-on than she ever imagined.

Upward the blade moved.

Threatening.

Tantalizing.

Taunting her tender flesh.

Upward.

Along the inside of her right thigh.

Zada moaned.

Across her abdomen.

Zada moaned louder.

Right up to the valley between her breasts.

"Take the top off," he ordered. "Slowly. There's no need to hurry. I hope we have the rest of our lives."

Tears filled Zada's eyes.

Her fingers fumbled with the buttons of her silky top.

They couldn't work fast enough to suit her.

Zada ripped the top off and threw it aside.

His gaze traveled downward to her lacy thong.

He ran the tip of the sword lightly across the fabric.

The sensation took her breath away.

"Off," he commanded.

"And if I don't take it off?" Zada asked.

"I'll take it off for you," he answered.

Slowly, she removed the thong.

She was exposed now.

Completely.

In more ways than one.

Her heart, full of an undying love for him.

Her body, naked and waiting for anything he wanted.

He lowered the sword, and placed it on the bed.

Those dark blue eyes, still holding her captive.

Zada smiled.

Seductively.

Rick wasn't prepared when Zada slipped off the bed. She picked up the sword before he could stop her. Rick laughed when she pointed it at him—nervous-like.

"This wasn't part of your fantasy," Rick reminded her.

"My fantasy," Zada said. "My prerogative to change it until it suits me."

Rick didn't like the tone in her voice or the gleam in her eye. He walked over and turned on the bedside light. When he turned back around, Zada placed the tip of the sword lightly against the waistband of his pants.

"Be careful with that thing now, Zada," Rick told her, and he meant it. "It isn't a toy."

"Have you talked to anyone?"

What?

Rick said what he was thinking. "What did you say?"

"Have you talked to anyone?"

"No," Rick said. "Why?"

"No one?"

"No," Rick said. "The last person I've talked to is you."

She moved the blade up the front of his shirt.

Rick gulped.

The blade moved up to his neck.

Rick was afraid to gulp.

Lightly.

Slowly.

Thankfully, the blade moved up to his chin.

Rick held his breath.

The blade moved lightly across his lips.

Up to his nose.

Their eyes met.

Zada smiled.

And knocked the hat right off his head.

"Jesus, Zada!"

Rick frowned at her.

"Take the cape off," she ordered.

"Put. The. Sword. Down," Rick pleaded.

"Do you want me to take it off for you?" she asked.

"Okay, okay!" Rick said and frowned at her again. "Cape coming off here, master. Cape coming off."

He jerked the cape off and threw it on the floor.

"Now, the shirt."

Rick pulled the hem of his black Zorro shirt out of the waistband of his black tight-fitting Zorro costume pants, pulled it over his head, and threw it across the room.

"And *this*," Rick said, hands at his waist now, "is exactly why no self-respecting man should ever dress up in a flipping Zorro costume trying to fulfill his wife's fantasy."

"No talking," she ordered.

She pointed at his pants with the tip of the sword.

"Now, the pants."

Rick laughed nervously. "No way," he said, shaking his head. "Not until you put down that sword."

"Shall I slice them off for you?"

Rick jumped back when Zada made the sign of Zorro—zip, zip, zip—through the air.

"Okay, Zada, I get the picture," Rick said, his fingers fumbling with the buttons on the pants as fast as possible. "I know this is payback for me being such an ass. And if it makes you feel any better, I know I deserve it."

"*Keep* talking," Zada said this time.

Rick slipped off his loafers. He pulled the pants down, and stepped out of them. After he stood up, he kicked the pants aside.

He reached up to take off the mask.

"Leave the mask on," she ordered.

Rick dropped his hands and wisely covered his privates.

"I said keep talking," she said. "Go back to that 'I know I deserve it' part."

It was all Zada could do to keep a straight face.

Too bad she was holding a sword, instead of a camera.

Rick? Wearing nothing but a black mask? His hands over his privates?

A Kodak moment if I've ever seen one!

"Well?" Zada said, practicing the Zorro sign again.

Zip. Zip. Zip.

Dark blue eyes peered out at her through the mask.

But the look in his eyes left no doubt he was sincere.

"I still haven't figured everything out, Zada," Rick said. "You have to admit yourself, from my point of view, none of it makes any sense. But I know just as well as I know that I'm standing here right now, buck naked and with a sharp sword pointed at my privates, that you're telling me the truth. As crazy as it all sounds, I trust you. And I know you wouldn't cheat on me."

"Where were you last night?" Zada demanded.

"I stayed in a motel," Rick said. "Why?"

"And you're sure no one told you that Alicia's brother was responsible for the phone calls and the photograph?"

"Alicia's brother?" Rick look surprised. "I didn't even know Alicia had a brother."

"Right answer," Zada told him.

She walked over to the armoire on the other side of their bedroom, opened the door, and placed the sword safely inside the cabinet. When she turned back around, Zada smiled.

"Turn the light off," she told Rick.

Rick reached over and switched off the light.

She walked up and pushed him backward onto the bed. Rick grabbed her hand and pulled her on top of him.

"I really do like the mask," Zada whispered.

"Want me to leave it on?" Rick whispered back.

Zada's answer was a long, delicious I'll-love-you-forever kiss.

Chapter 21

Six months later.

Zada's soy coffee flavor on Monday morning—exactly two weeks before Christmas—was Sugar & Spice and Everything Nice. She'd chosen that particular flavor for a special reason: that's what little girls are made of.

Besides, Zada doubted any coffee company—soy or not—would name a flavor Nails & Snails and Puppy Dog Tails.

But boy or girl, it didn't matter to Zada.

She knew it didn't matter to Rick, either.

She smiled, running her hand over her flat stomach, and wondering what it was going to feel like in a few more months when she started showing.

She smiled again, thinking how nervous Rick had been the night before—pacing back and forth in the den—both of them waiting the torturous time it took for a plus or a minus to appear in the test circle.

They'd both been so excited, they'd jumped around the den screaming like children themselves, poor Simon barking his disapproval at their rowdiness. Another smile crossed her lips, thinking about Rick's last words when he'd left for the center only a few hours earlier.

He'd said with a proud grin, "Go ahead and tell the girls the good news, Mommy. You tell each other everything else. No reason to keep something this important from them."

She'd hugged him.

And kissed him.

And thanked Rick for understanding.

They'd called their families as soon as they found out. His parents, both ecstatic over a first grandchild. Her mother, already praying for a granddaughter. Sally, promising to go through her baby clothes.

When she thought about it, getting pregnant really couldn't have come at a better time. Her book *Quack, Quack, Recycle That!* was finished. Her editor loved it. Her publicist was even working on a guest appearance for her and Simon on the Animal Planet network, during the week after Christmas when they would begin their tour of children's hospitals.

By the time it was close to the baby arriving, all of her commitments would be completed. Then she would do what a mother was supposed to do—focus on nothing but her newborn baby.

Baby.

Jen, Tish, and Alicia were going to freak!

Zada walked to the laundry room, and pulled on her jacket. She stepped into her snow boots, and went back to the kitchen for her cup of Sugar & Spice and Everything Nice.

It had snowed over the weekend. And with the weather they'd been having so far this winter, it looked as if a white Christmas would be a good possibility.

Zada smiled at that thought, too.

She headed out her front door, and started across the street. But she stopped midway, surprised to see the large moving van sitting in the middle of street, two doors down.

Alicia had sold the house a few weeks back, but all of the details had been handled by an attorney, not the buyers themselves. Alicia had been a little worried because everything had been completely hush-hush throughout the entire sale.

Not knowing who their new neighbors were going to be had driven Tish crazy. She'd come up with every scenario possible from victims in a witness protection program to a Chicago mobster hoping to hide his family out in the 'burbs. She and Jen would never admit it to Tish, but the fact that everything had been kept under wraps had worried them, too.

Zada glanced at the moving van again.

Mobster or whoever, what person in their right mind would move this close to Christmas? Especially if they had kids?

Kids.

Zada smiled and hurried on across the street.

She walked up Tish's porch and stomped the snow off her boots. Once she stepped inside, she left her wet boots by the front door, and padded down the hallway in her stocking feet.

"Hey, have you guys seen the moving van? I guess our mystery neighbors have finally arrived." Zada said this as she walked into Tish's kitchen. She was talking to an empty room.

"We're in here," Tish yelled out.

Zada walked into Tish's dining room.

Tish, Jen, and Alicia were all standing at Tish's dining room window, sipping from their coffee cups, staring out the window. Zada didn't have to ask what had drawn them to the window.

Zada walked up behind them. Everyone shifted over to make room. They all stood at the window, sipping coffee, staring.

"Who in their right mind would move two weeks before Christmas?" Zada asked, saying exactly what she'd been thinking as she walked across the street.

Alicia said, "I'm sure Jake Sims is asking himself that same question right now."

Zada's mouth fell open. "Get out!" she said. "You mean as in retired Chicago Cubs first baseman, Jake Sims?"

Tish said, "I prefer to think of him as he who looks damn good in those underwear commercials, Jake Sims."

"You would," Jen snorted. "How about always making the headlines for his wild parties, Jake Sims? Or, dated every bimbo starlet from coast-to-coast, Jake Sims? And especially not exactly the kind of neighbor we need in Woodberry Park, Jake Sims?"

Alicia said, "Who, as of six weeks ago, became a single dad with custody of his twelve-year-old daughter who hasn't lived with him since she was an infant, Jake Sims."

Tish said, "I don't care what Jake Sims you want to call him, the twins are going to pee themselves when I tell them a famous Chicago Cubs baseball player is moving right across the street."

"The twins are going to pee themselves?" Zada laughed. "Try Joe, Charlie, and Rick are going to pee themselves."

Zada looked back at Alicia. "Are you sure about this, Alicia?"

Always quick to answer Tish said, "Alicia finally got the scoop last night. Jake's attorney handled the sale so the past owners wouldn't jack up the price because Jake was the buyer. He called Alicia since she was both the Realtor and Jake's new neighbor, and asked Alicia if she would let the movers in this morning."

"It's a sad story, actually," Alicia said. "You may have heard it on the news when Jake's ex-wife was killed in a car accident out in LA. That's where she and the daughter were living. His ex-wife was only thirty-eight years old. Tragic, for her and the daughter."

Daughter.

Zada absently ran her hand over her stomach.

Tish said, "Jake's taking the daughter on a Disney cruise over the holidays. He obviously realizes how hard this first Christmas is going to be for his daughter without her mother. They won't officially move in until after the New Year."

Tish paused, then looked over at Jen. "Tell me, Jen," Tish said. "Does that sound to you like someone we don't want for a neighbor?"

Jen rolled her eyes.

Zada was still thinking about the car accident. The poor daughter, losing her mother so young.

Mother.

I'm going to be someone's mother!

Without warning, Zada burst into tears.

Tish handed Zada a tissue.

Zada blew her nose.

Alicia handed Zada a glass of water.

Zada took a drink.

But when Jen put a hand on her forehead to check her temperature, Zada had had enough.

"Would the three of you stop it, already?"

Jen looked at Tish.

Tish looked at Alicia.

Alicia looked back at Zada.

"Sorry, Zada," Alicia said, "but you scared us half to death. One minute we were standing there talking. The next minute you were sobbing your heart out."

"I'm sorry I scared you," Zada said. She reached for her coffee cup and held it up. "I think my bursting into tears has something to do with the flavor of coffee I'm drinking this morning."

Alicia looked at Tish.

Tish looked at Jen.

Jen tried to take her temperature again.

Zada laughed, and pushed Jen's hand away.

"Let me try this again," Zada said. "I say I think it must be the flavor of coffee I'm drinking this morning. The three of you ask, what flavor is it?"

"What flavor is it?" they asked in unison.

Zada smiled. "Thank you for asking. It's Sugar & Spice and Everything Nice."

Jen looked at Alicia.

Alicia looked at Tish.

Tish looked back at Zada.

"And the flavor is important because?" Tish asked.

Good, Tish is finally catching on.

"Because that's what little girls are made of," Zada said happily.

Evidently not.

Total silence.

No one said a word.

"Oh, forget it," Zada finally said, giving up. "I'm pregnant!"

The screams were so loud, Rick could have heard them ten miles away at the training center.

"Man," Rick said. "I can't believe it. Jake Sims living only two doors down."

"You might want to tone your level of excitement down just a notch," Zada told him. "It's starting to rival the plus sign appearing in the circle last night."

"Come here, you," Rick said and pulled her to him. "You know better than that."

He kissed her.

Zada kissed him back.

Rick had just come home, and they were standing in the middle of the den, arms around each other. He glanced down at the coffee table. He didn't even grimace at the clutter of magazines.

He reached down and picked up the top magazine. When he stood back up, he had a puzzled expression on his face. "Baby names? You really think we need this?"

Zada nodded.

Rick still looked puzzled. "Why? You've already told me there's no room for discussion. Our son will be named Richard Avery Clark, the second, and we'll call him Chip."

Zada said, "Hello? There's a possibility we might need a girl's name."

"We have one," Rick informed her.

That was news to Zada.

"Since when?" Zada wanted to know.

"Since today," Rick said. "I decided if you get to name our son, it's only fair that I get to name our daughter. I want to call her Elizabeth Ann. Elizabeth for your middle name. And Ann for both of our mothers' middle names."

Zada leaned over and kissed him. "Our mothers did make it convenient for us having the same middle name, didn't they?"

"But we'll call her Lizzie," Rick said. "I can already picture her. Dark hair, dark brown eyes, too pretty for her own good, and feisty as hell. Just like her mother."

"Ha-ha," Zada said and pushed him down on the sofa.

She sat down beside him, and snuggled against him. Simon came over, and hopped up on the sofa. He turned around twice, then settled down beside Zada. Zada reached out and rubbed his fur.

"When are we going to break the news to Simon about the baby?" Rick asked, looking over at the dog.

"We had a long talk about the baby this morning," Zada said. "Didn't we, buddy?"

Simon's tail thumped against the sofa in answer.

"Sometimes you two scare me," Rick said. "Sometimes I think you really do talk to each other."

"How dare you imply that we don't," Zada said. "We talk to each other all the time, don't we, buddy?"

Again, Simon thumped his tail.

"Scary," Rick said and shook his head.

Zada reached across him for the remote control lying on the end table by the sofa.

"There's a new reality show coming on I want to see," Zada told him.

Rick didn't groan, but Zada knew he wanted to.

The big screen came to life.

Zada burst out laughing.

It was Jake Sims in his underwear commercial.

"Poor Tish," Zada said. "She'll never survive Jake Sims living right across the street. She's already drooling buckets full."

Rick looked at the screen. Then back at her. "And you? Are you drooling buckets full?"

"Absolutely not," Zada said. "I prefer my men blond and wearing sexy black masks."

"Ha-ha," Rick said, but he leaned over and kissed her.

Zada snuggled against Rick again, put her head on his shoulder, and looked back at the screen.

She had to admit Jake Sims was a handsome devil.

Black wavy hair. Piercing gray eyes. A bad-boy grin that would steal any woman's heart.

Maybe he did have a bit of a bad reputation. But like most bad boys, Zada suspected old Jake just hadn't met his match yet.

"Alicia!" Zada exclaimed and sat up. She looked back at Rick. "I just thought of something," Zada said. "Jake Sims and Alicia would be perfect for each other."

"Now, Zada," Rick began.

"I'm serious," Zada insisted. "Alicia has as much money as he does. And she's as beautiful as he is handsome."

Zada reached over Rick again and grabbed the portable phone from the end table.

Alicia couldn't help but laugh.

Jake Sims?

"Absolutely not," Alicia said into the phone.

"Zada!" Alicia said. "Jake Sims is *not* my type. He's the furthest thing possible from my type. Even if he weren't a hopeless womanizer, a constant partygoer, and not to mention a celebrity who's always in the spotlight, Jake Sims has a daughter.

"Because, Zada, children never like me. Neither do dogs. Your dog hates me. And I hate to say this, but your son or daughter will probably hate me, too.

"I'm not being ridiculous. You're being ridiculous.

"I'm hanging up now, Zada. No, we are *not* going to discuss whether Jake Sims and I are a perfect match at coffee with Jen and Tish in the morning. There's nothing to discuss. I am not interested in Jake Sims in any way, shape, or form.

"No. I will not turn on my television right now so I can actually see his shape and form in his underwear!

"Good night, Zada.

"Zada. I said good night.

"I'm hanging up now."

Click!

Zada handed the phone back to Rick.

Rick placed it back on the end table.

Zada didn't say a word. She snuggled back against him and put her head back on his shoulder.

Two seconds.

Three seconds.

Five full seconds.

Rick gave in and said, "I can already hear your mind spinning, Zada."

"It is so," Zada said.

"And I couldn't help but hear everything Alicia just said. She was practically shouting at the end of your conversation."

"She was so," Zada said.

Rick said, "Then you are going to drop it, right? No trying to play matchmaker between Alicia and Jake Sims. Right?"

Zada got up from the sofa and walked out of the room.

Rick pulled himself up and went after her.

"Right, Zada?" he said from the bottom of the stairs.

She paused at the top of the stairs, turned around, and faced him with a flirty smile. "Right about what, Rick?"

"You know what," Rick said.

Zada said, "All I know is how much I love it when my gorgeous blond husband puts on his sexy black mask."

"What you're trying to do is change the subject," Rick argued.

Zada crooked her finger.

Seductively.

She turned around and disappeared down the hallway.

Rick let out a defeated sigh.

Poor, clueless Jake Sims.

The guy had no idea what he was walking into.

When Zada made her mind up, there was no changing it.

Zada called out his name.

"Coming, master," Rick called back.

He grinned, shook his head, then skirted the stairs two at a time.

About the Author

When Candy Halliday first started sending manu-
scripts out to publishers, the rejection letters all said
the same thing: too humorous for our needs. It didn't
take Candy long to decide that romantic comedy was
where she needed to be. Six years and eight books
later, Candy's romantic comedies have been translated into six different languages and published in
nine different countries around the world. Candy lives
in the Piedmont of North Carolina, loves to hear from
readers, and can be reached via e-mail at her Web
site: www.candyhalliday.com.

Chapter 1

Alicia Greene grabbed her bedside phone on the first ring and said, "I'm running late this morning, Alfie. I'll have to call you later."

"This will only take a minute, sis," her twin insisted. "I have great news."

Alicia sighed. One Alfie minute always equaled *thirty* Alfie minutes. And they both knew it.

"Then I'm putting you on speaker phone," Alicia told him. "You talk. I'll finish getting ready."

Alicia slipped on her blouse and buttoned the buttons while Alfie rambled on about the new woman he'd met at Starbucks earlier that morning. She was stunning. Absolutely the most beautiful woman he'd ever seen.

"And you know I'm a sucker for beautiful women," Alfie said.

"I won't argue with that," Alicia said, and walked across the bedroom toward her closet.

He'd seen her at Starbucks several times before, but he'd never had the courage to approach her. She really *was* that beautiful. *And* she was a redhead.

"And you know I've always been a sucker for redheads," Alfie said.

"Uh-huh," Alicia agreed, and reached into the closet for her skirt.

They had been the only two early birds at Starbucks this morning, so he'd finally found the courage to talk to her. He explained he'd always been an early riser. She explained she was an emergency room nurse, and always stopped for coffee on her way to the hospital.

"And, I hate to keep repeating myself," Alfie said, "but you know I've always been a sucker for nurses."

Alicia wrinkled her nose at any mention of the medical profession; her famous neurosurgeon ex-husband being the reason for her frown.

Edward Carlton had fooled her completely during the entire year they'd dated before he proposed. Not once had Edward given her, or anyone else, any reason to suspect he was marrying her only to preserve his sterling reputation. If she hadn't caught him in a compromising position with their twenty-something Latino pool boy less than a year into the marriage, she still might be trapped in a tragic farce of a marriage.

That thought made Alicia shudder.

But she was past the ugly divorce now. Past her deep depression that followed the divorce. Past letting Edward destroy her self-esteem. Thankfully, past Edward Carlton altogether.

"Her name is Gwen, and I really think she could be the one, sis," Alfie said, but a needy please-let-it-be-so sigh followed his statement.

And how many times had Alfie said that before? *Too many times to count.*

Alicia refrained from pointing that out, however. If she argued, the conversation would quickly escalate into a full Alfie hour. She didn't have an hour to spare this morning. Not when her neighbor, Zada Clark, was determined to play matchmaker. Not when Zada fully expected to set her up with the womanizing playboy who had recently moved into their quiet Woodberry Park subdivision. And especially not when she intended to tell Zada at coffee this morning to back off and forget her matchmaking idea once and for all!

"Good for you, Alfie," was all Alicia said about her twin's *great news.*

"Good for you?" Alfie's disappointed snort blared through the speaker. "I've just told you I think I've met the love of my life this morning, and all you have to say is 'Good for you?'"

"I told you I'm running late," Alicia reminded

him as she slipped her feet into her high heels. "But I'll call you later and we'll talk as long as you like."

Another snort echoed through the speaker.

"Let me guess," Alfie said curtly. "The reason you don't have time to talk to me, is because you're hurrying off to have coffee with the Housewives' Fantasy Club."

Alicia glanced at the speaker.

Her twin's ability to read her mind always amazed her.

And yes, before she headed off to her real estate office, she planned to have coffee with the women in her cul-de-sac who were fondly known as the Housewives' Fantasy Club. Tish Jones, Jen Marshall, and Zada Clark had become her closest friends.

Which certainly hadn't been the case six months ago.

Six months ago, she'd been depressed over the divorce. She'd been out pushed out of the loop. And she'd been downright bitter toward Tish, Jen, and Zada, who were basically treating her like a piranha at the time.

"Those women wouldn't give you the time of day six months ago," Alfie said, again saying out loud exactly what she'd been thinking.

Alicia frowned at the speaker this time.

Scary.

"What was it they said about you behind your

back after your divorce?" Alfie asked, refusing to drop the subject. He mimicked in a high-pitched voice, "Alicia Greene is what you'd get if you put Anna Nicole Smith and Pamela Anderson in a blender. Except with ten times the class, old family money, and an MBA from Harvard. In other words, every wife's nightmare."

Alicia walked over, turned the speaker off, and picked up the phone. "Yes, Alfie. That's exactly what they said about me after my divorce. And in retrospect, I really don't blame them. An attractive, wealthy divorcee doesn't exactly fit in with the suburban married couple's social scene."

"My point exactly," Alfie said. "So why is attractive, wealthy, and divorced you still living in the suburbs with a bunch of jealous housewives?"

"They aren't jealous of me now, and you know it," Alicia said. "We've all become good friends."

"Are you sure about that?" Alfie cautioned. "Jealousy is the only motive I can think of that would make your so-called good friends try to fix you up with the likes of Jake Sims."

Jake Sims.

As in infamous retired Chicago Cubs baseball player, Jake Sims. King of the tabloids, Jake Sims. A new model or starlet on his arm every week, Jake Sims.

Who looks yummy in his underwear commercials, Jake Sims.

Alicia pushed that thought aside. Besides, her new neighbor was also the Jake Sims who had recently become a single dad when his equally famous supermodel ex-wife was tragically killed in a car accident. Jake had custody of his thirteen-year-old daughter now. Thus, the reason Mr. Playboy had been forced to give up his penthouse in downtown Chicago, and was now living in the suburbs.

Having custody of his daughter was yet another reason Alicia wasn't interested in Jake Sims. As if she really needed another reason in addition to his notorious reputation with the ladies. She couldn't explain it, but kids and dogs always hated her on sight.

Alicia sighed and said, "For your information, Jake Sims is the reason I'm in a hurry this morning. Zada is planning a dinner party on Friday night, and guess who happen to be the only two single people on her guest list?"

Alfie gasped. "And what are you going to do about that?"

Alicia said, "I'm telling Zada at coffee this morning to back off, and I mean it. I am *not,* nor will I ever be interested in Jake Sims."

"Thank you," Alfie said, obviously relieved. "There

isn't a brother in his right mind who would want his sister paired up with a known player like Jake the Rake Sims."

"Good morning, Jake," Tish Jones said with a smile when she opened her front door. "Come on in. Zada and Jen are in the kitchen."

Jake followed Tish down the hallway, thinking that having morning coffee with three extremely attractive women used to mean one of his famous parties had lasted all night. But that was before Carla's tragic accident had turned his life upside down. Before decisions had to be made that would change the course of his life forever.

Doing what was best for his daughter hadn't been an easy decision, in fact, far from it. The easiest thing would have been allowing Danielle to remain in LA and live with his ex-mother-in-law, Ranatta Harper, of the famed Harper Modeling Agency in Hollywood. He'd considered that option briefly for Danielle's sake, knowing uprooting her from her home and her friends, and forcing her to live with a father she only saw on her birthday and occasionally at Christmas would only add to the trauma of losing her mother.

But that had been before news broke out in the gossip columns that all-business Ranatta was already lining Danielle up to step into Carla's supermodel shoes. Jake simply couldn't allow that to happen. Carla had been on the cover of every teen magazine available by the time she was thirteen, and where had that gotten her? Caught up in world where image was everything, where the pressure to stay thin and beautiful was constant, and where drugs were simply a way of life. In other words, dead before her time.

News of the high levels of cocaine found in Carla's system had made the headlines for days. To keep the story alive as long as possible, the media had even dragged him and his own free-wheeling bachelor lifestyle into the picture for a little more drama. That's when Jake realized if he truly wanted a better life for his daughter, things in his own life had to change.

Exit Mr. Big Time.

Enter Mr. Housewife.

The women who had invited him to coffee this morning had also taken him under their wing and had given him a crash course in *Domestic Living 101* over the last few weeks. The new house in the suburbs was ready now. Danielle was registered in a good school. He was signed up to car-pool three days a week, and his chicken casserole wasn't half bad, even if he had to say so himself.

A new and improved Jake Sims was ready to step up to the plate now—the challenge ahead of him far more important than any baseball career.

"Alicia should be here in a minute," Zada told him as Tish placed a cup of coffee on the kitchen table in front of him. Zada pushed a plate of fresh blueberry muffins in his direction. "I wanted you to meet the only other single person in our cul-de-sac before my dinner party on Friday night. I think you and Alicia will really hit it off."

"About the dinner party . . . ." Jake began.

Zada pointed a stern finger at him. "You are *not* backing out of my dinner party, Jake Sims. I understand your main focus has to be on your daughter. But Danielle doesn't arrive from LA until Sunday. You can attend one last adult function before you become super-dad."

Jake started to argue, but Zada jumped up from table at the sound of the doorbell. "That's Alicia now," she said and darted out of the kitchen.

The guilty looks Tish and Jen exchanged told Jake something wasn't right. But he never had the opportunity to ask. Raised voices from the hallway gave Jake his answer.

"Don't shush me, Zada! The very idea that you think I would be interested in Jake Sims makes me mad enough to spit. You, Tish, and Jen might be in awe of his baseball fame and glued to the television every time his stupid underwear commercial flashes across the screen, but don't include me in your little fan club."

"Alicia, please!"

"And spare me the reformed bad-boy speech you gave me yesterday. I've never been attracted to bad boys. Especially not bad boys who prance around in their underwear, claiming to be reformed! So don't expect me to be nice at your matchmaking dinner party Friday night. I intend to tell Jake Sims to his face I'm not interested. Got it?"

"Well, I got it loud and clear, didn't you?" Jake asked. He looked over at Tish, then at Jen.

Tish and Jen were both too embarrassed to speak.

Embarrassed also described the look on Alicia Greene's face when she came to a screeching halt in the kitchen doorway. But she was breathtaking. Possibly, the most genuinely beautiful woman Jake had ever seen: long, blond hair, a definite stop-traffic figure, deep blue eyes round with shock at finding him sitting at Tish's kitchen table.

Until their eyes met.

She quickly recovered, the lift of her chin saying she meant every word. She'd never been attracted to bad boys like him. And reformed or otherwise, she never would be.

Jake managed to suppress a bad-boy grin. Maybe he would go to Zada's dinner party on Friday night after all. If for no other reason than to enlighten his feisty neighbor with a few very important facts.

First, bad boys didn't *prance.*

Second, even bad boys could be reformed.

And third, never say *never.*

THE DISH

Where authors give you the inside scoop!

♥ ♥ ♥ ♥ ♥ ♥ ♥ ♥ ♥ ♥ ♥ ♥ ♥ ♥ ♥ ♥ ♥ ♥

From the desk of Amanda Scott

I've always loved Sir Walter Scott's poem "Lochinvar," the tale of a young Scottish hero who rode off with his lady-love from her wedding to another man:

> *"While her mother did fret, and her father did fume,*
> *And her bridegroom stood dangling his bonnet and*
> *   plume;*
> *And the bride-maidens whisper'd, "Twere better by far*
> *To have matched our fair cousin with young*
> *   Lochinvar."*

While constructing the plot for **Lady's Choice** (on sale now), I was hiking in the High Sierras one day when that poem popped into my mind and every writer's favorite phrase began to twitch: What if I were to begin **Lady's Choice** with a fourteenth-century Highland version of that wedding? What if the "Lochinvar" everyone cheers turns out not to be the young gallant, "so daring in love and so dauntless in war," but someone truly dangerous?

To stir more trouble, *what if* my Macleod bride believes at first, just as everyone else does, that the abductor is her Lochinvar? And *what if* her own sister, firmly believing the bride loves someone else, set the whole thing in motion and then has to deal with the consequences when she learns someone has usurped her plan to suit his own evil purpose?

Best of all, *what if* Sir Hugo Robison, the hero meant to benefit from that plan, knows nothing about it because he did not bother to reply to the urgent messages sent him by the bride's loving, caring sister, or to attend the wedding? And *what if* all of the above somehow impacts the fate of the legendary, long-lost Knights Templar treasure found by Lady Isobel Macleod and Sir Michael Sinclair in my previous book, **Prince of Danger**?

To say that **Lady's Choice** was fun to write is an understatement. I hope you enjoy it.

Sincerely yours,

Amanda Scott

http://home.att.net/~amandascott/

♥ ♥ ♥ ♥ ♥ ♥ ♥ ♥ ♥ ♥ ♥ ♥ ♥ ♥

From the desk of Candy Halliday

When my editor mentioned she'd like a switch in my next book from single-in-the-city to married-in-the-suburbs, I jumped at the chance. *Finally*, I thought. Domestic divas are going to get their due. Any wife will tell you that as hard as it is to find Mr. Right, the real quest begins after the wedding. Making the marriage a success—now that's the challenge of a lifetime. Or a hopeless cause, to some desperate housewife.

Like Zada Clark, my *she*ro in **YOUR BED OR MINE?** (on sale now). Poor Zada thought she'd found Mr. Right—until she realized his name was Mr. *Always* Right. Divorce has to be the only solution, but the old-school judge won't grant it unless she and Rick reach a compromise over who's keeping the dog and the house.

What does Rick do? Move back in and challenge Zada to a real-life game of *Survivor*. The first one to outwit, outplay, and outlast the other wins. Never one to back down from a challenge, Zada says, "Game on!" Of course, Rick doesn't know she's got a secret weapon: the three other members of her Housewives' Fantasy Club. Together, they'll help Zada create a fantasy that will *out-tease*, *out-tempt*, *and out-tantalize* Rick into losing the game with four little words: Your bed or mine?

The battle of the sexes has always been fascinating to me, and boy did I have fun forcing Zada and Rick to live together again. The icing on the cake for me, however, was creating a group of women best friends who stick together (yes, I'm a 9 *to* 5, *First Wives Club*, *and Thelma and Louise* junkie) but in YOUR BED OR MINE? I've added a slightly naughty but incredibly delicious twist—these women are sensuously secure enough to get together once a week to share their most secret desires.

Need a little spice to jump-start your sex life? Want to be entertained with thoughts of guilty pleasures you'd

never allow yourself to pursue? Welcome to the Housewives' Fantasy Club series. Viva Domestic Divas, ladies!
Enjoy the fun and start a Housewives' Fantasy Club of
your own.

Cheers!

Candy Halliday

http://www.candyhalliday.com/

Want to know more about romances at
Warner Books and Warner Forever?
Get the scoop online!

WARNER'S ROMANCE HOMEPAGE

Visit us at www.warnerforever.com for all the
latest news, reviews, and chapter excerpts!

NEW AND UPCOMING TITLES

Each month we feature our new titles
and reader favorites.

CONTESTS AND GIVEAWAYS

We give away galleys, autographed copies,
and all kinds of fun stuff.

AUTHOR INFO

You'll find bios, articles, and links to personal
Web sites for all your favorite authors—and
so much more!

THE BUZZ

Sign up for our monthly romance newsletter,
and be the first to read all about it!